THE FLYING BEAVER BROTHERS AND THE HOT-AIR BABOONS

MAXWELL EATON III

ALFRED A. KNOPF
NEW YORK

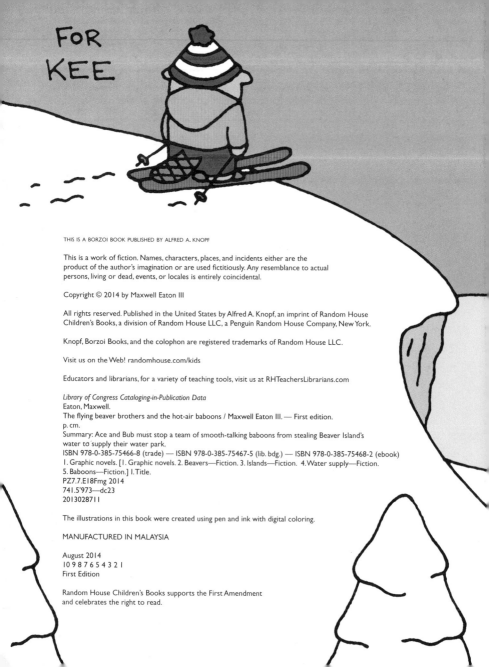

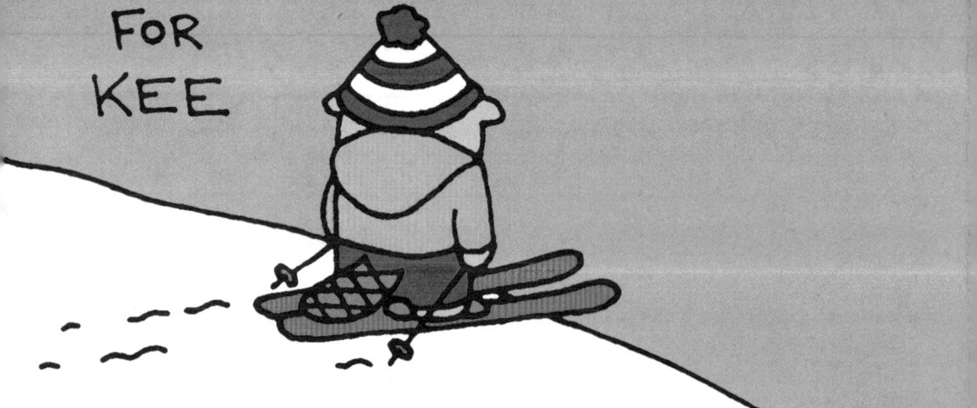
FOR
KEE

THIS IS A BORZOI BOOK PUBLISHED BY ALFRED A. KNOPF

Visit us on the Web! randomhouse.com/kids

Educators and librarians, for a variety of teaching tools, visit us at RHTeachersLibrarians.com

Library of Congress Cataloging-in-Publication Data
Eaton, Maxwell.
The flying beaver brothers and the hot-air baboons / Maxwell Eaton III. — First edition.
p. cm.
Summary: Ace and Bub must stop a team of smooth-talking baboons from stealing Beaver Island's water to supply their water park.
ISBN 978-0-385-75466-8 (trade) — ISBN 978-0-385-75467-5 (lib. bdg.) — ISBN 978-0-385-75468-2 (ebook)
1. Graphic novels. [1. Graphic novels. 2. Beavers—Fiction. 3. Islands—Fiction. 4. Water supply—Fiction. 5. Baboons—Fiction.] I. Title.
PZ7.7.E18Fmg 2014
741.5'973—dc23
2013028711

The illustrations in this book were created using pen and ink with digital coloring.

MANUFACTURED IN MALAYSIA

August 2014
10 9 8 7 6 5 4 3 2 1
First Edition

Random House Children's Books supports the First Amendment
and celebrates the right to read.

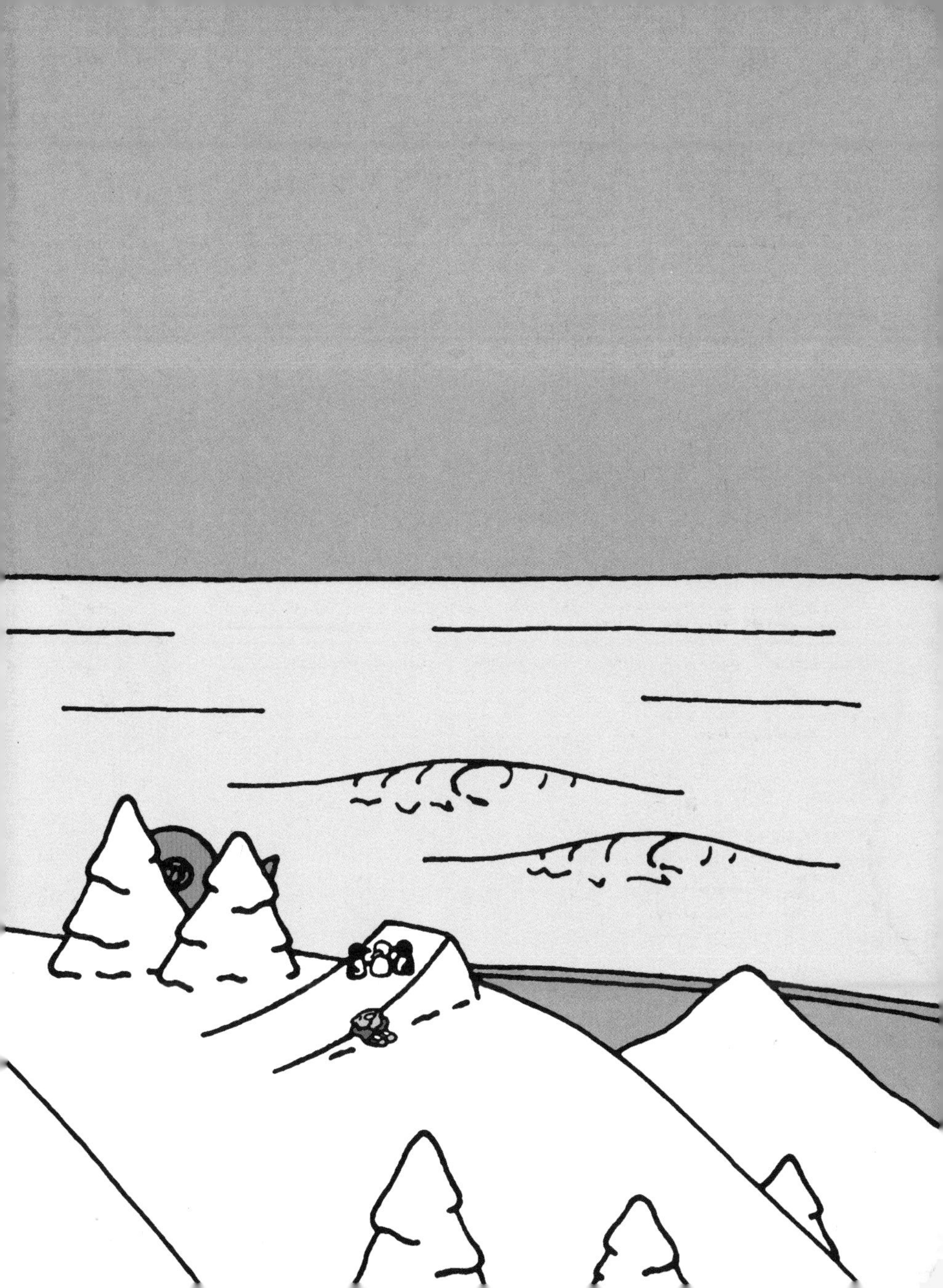

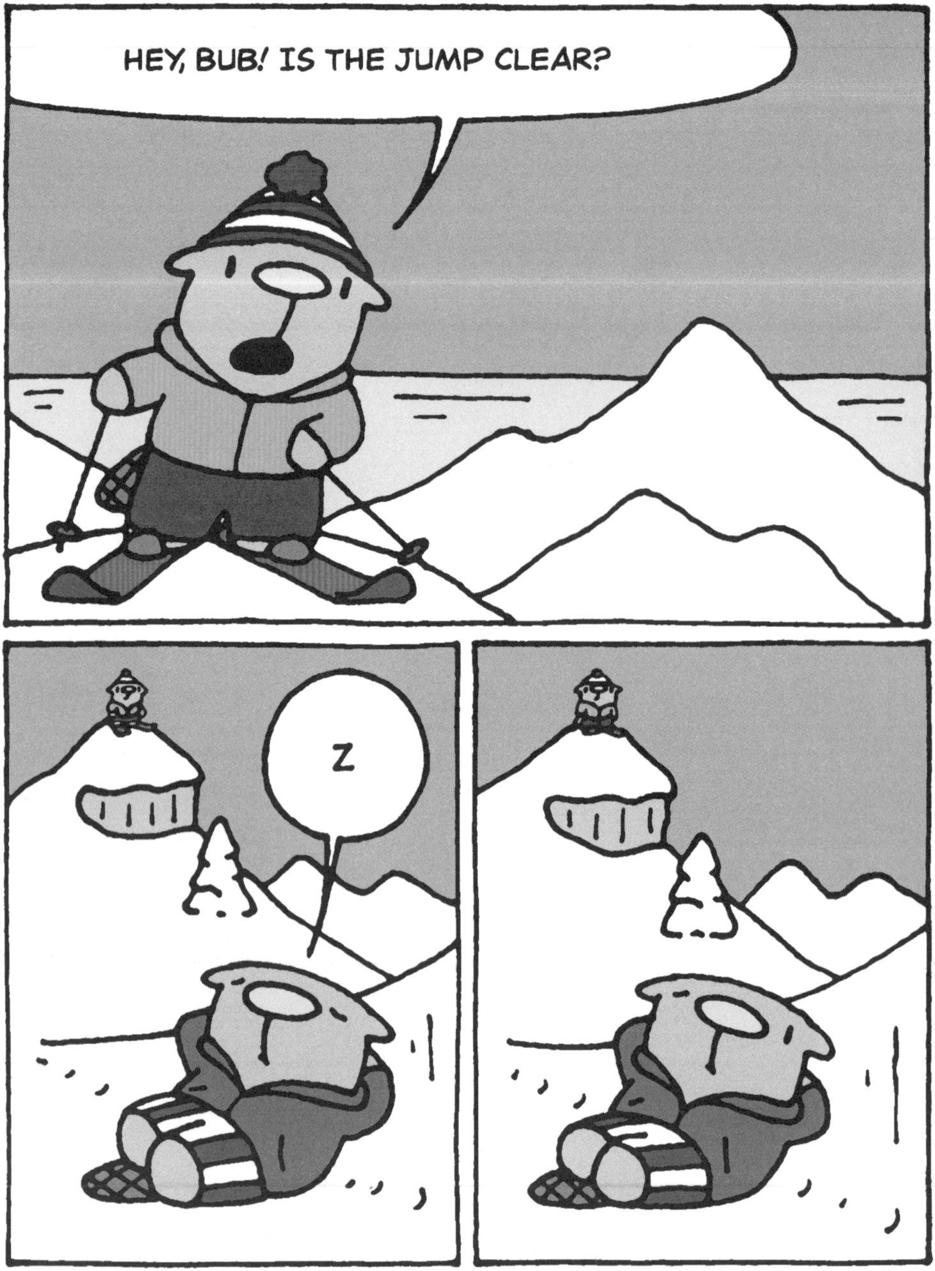
HEY, BUB! IS THE JUMP CLEAR?
Z

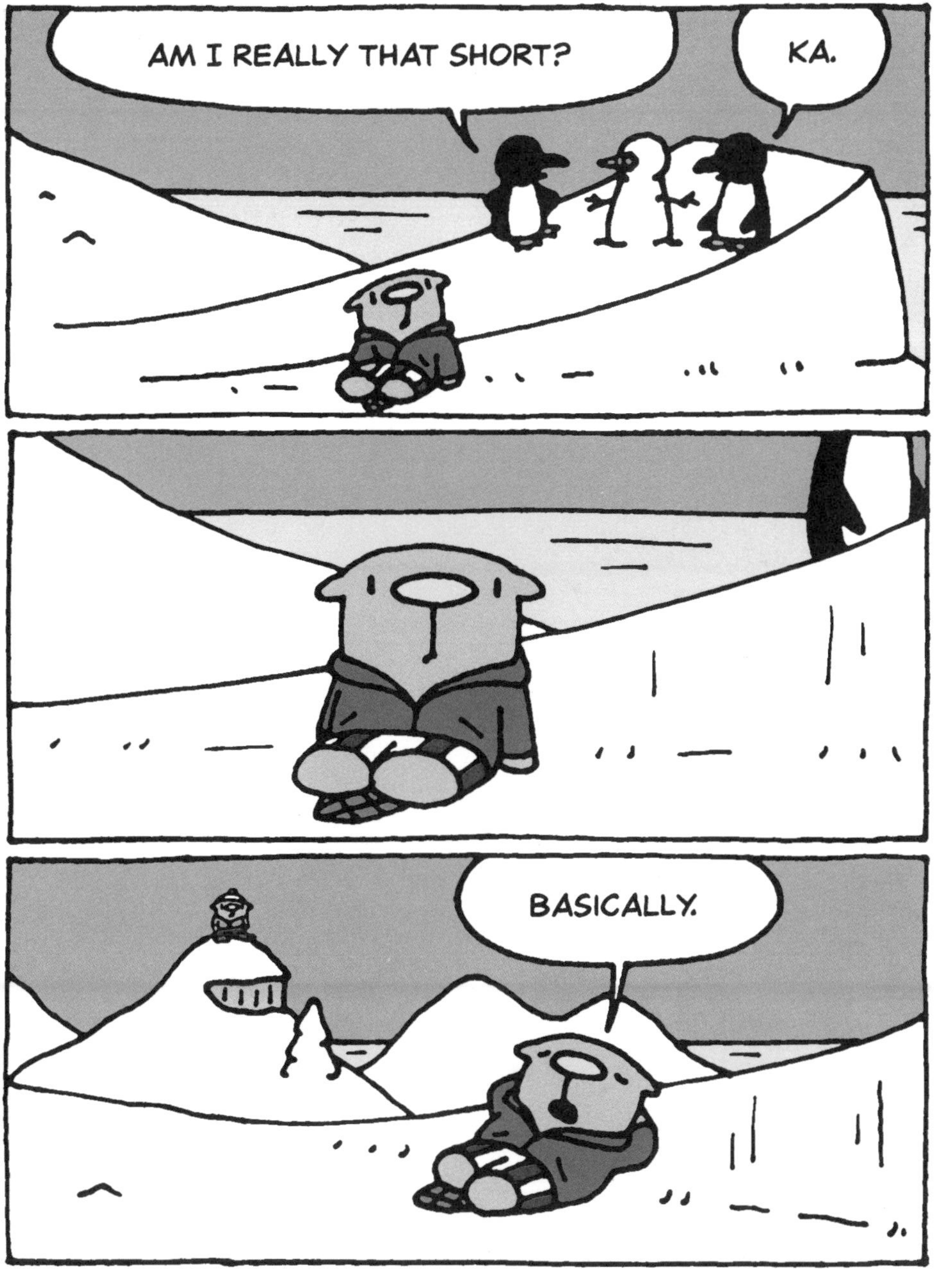
AM I REALLY THAT SHORT?
KA.
BASICALLY.

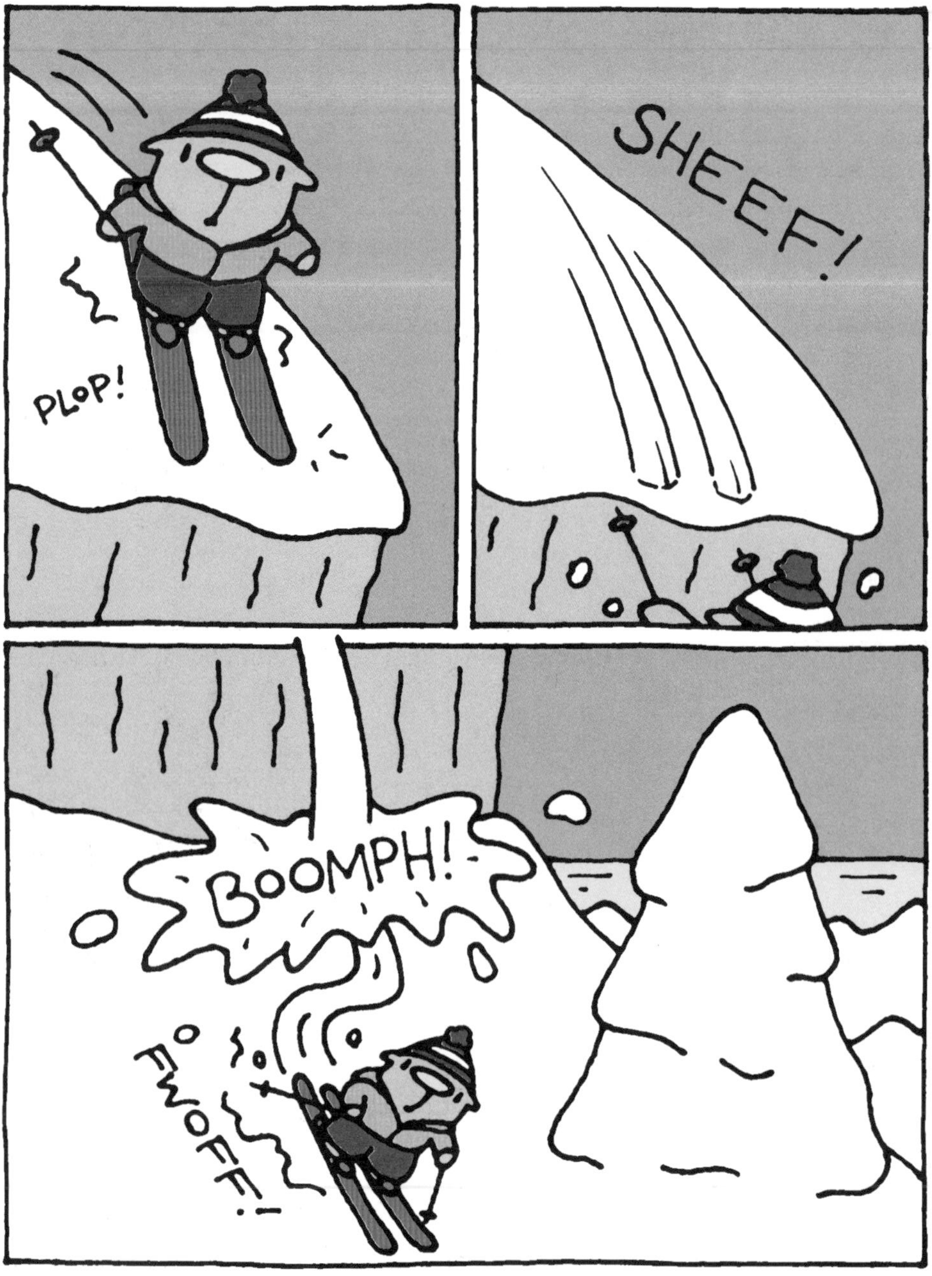
PLOP!
SHEEF!
BOOMPH!
FWOFF!

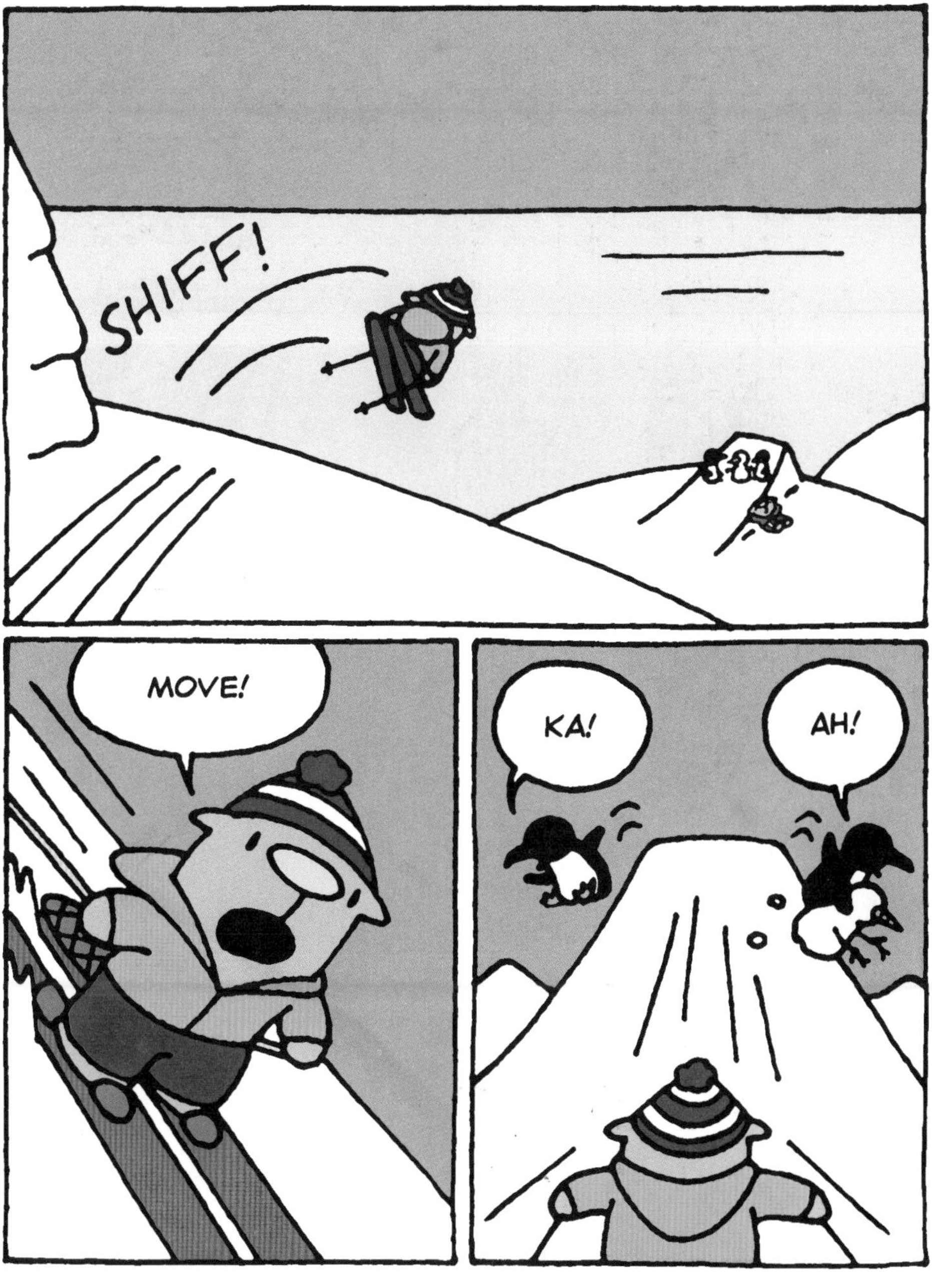
SHIFF!
MOVE!
KA!
AH!

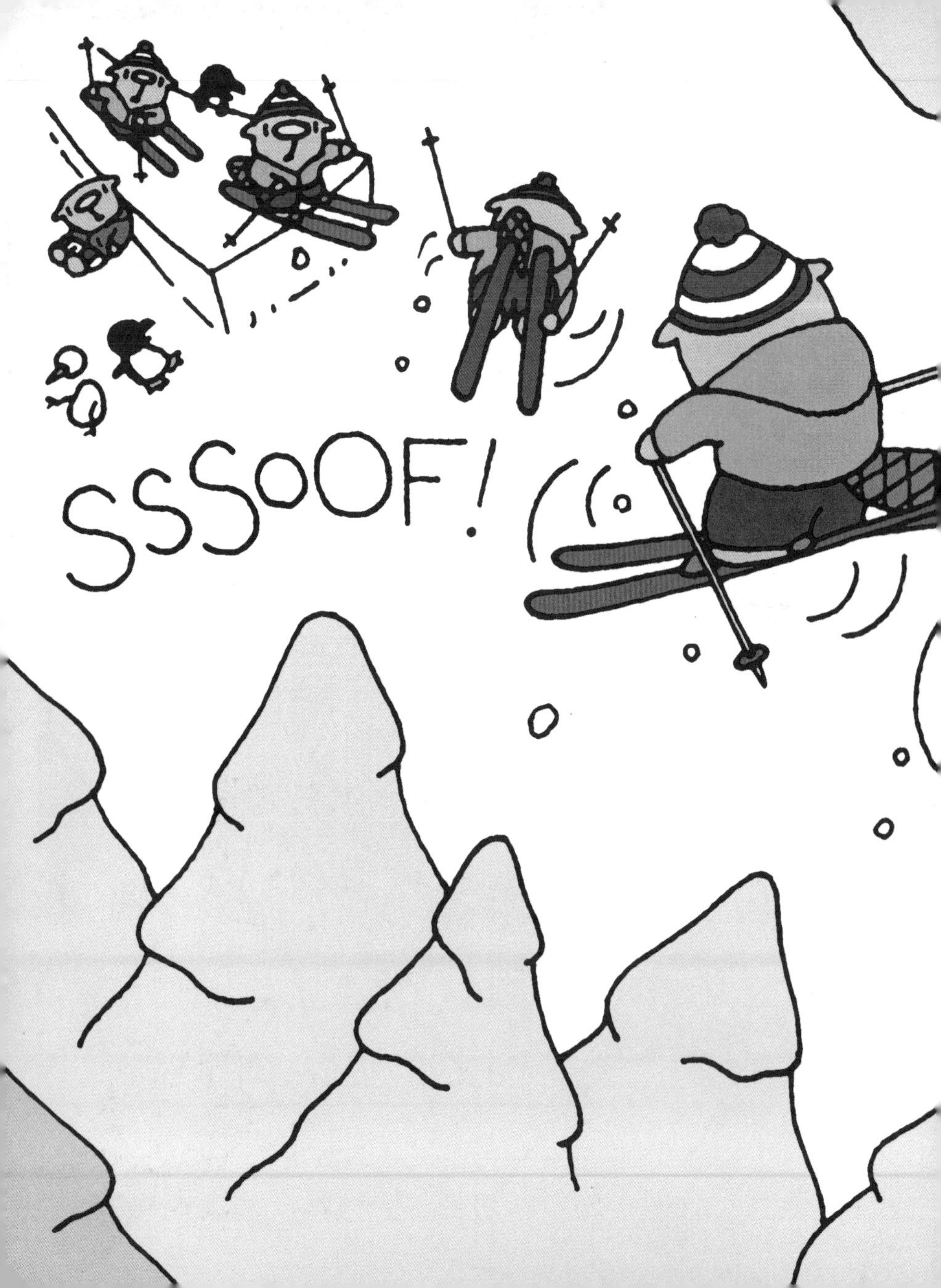
SSSOOF!

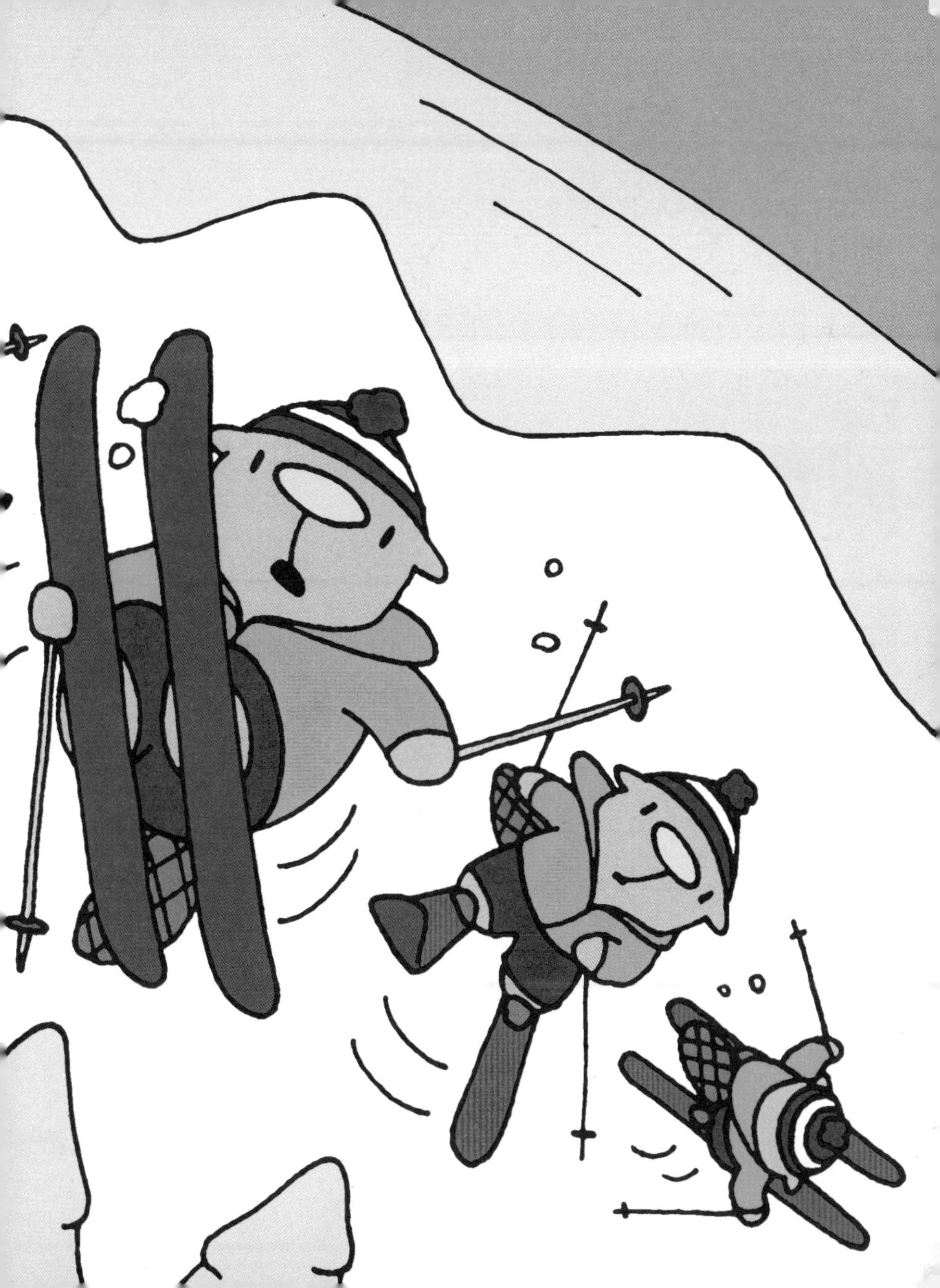

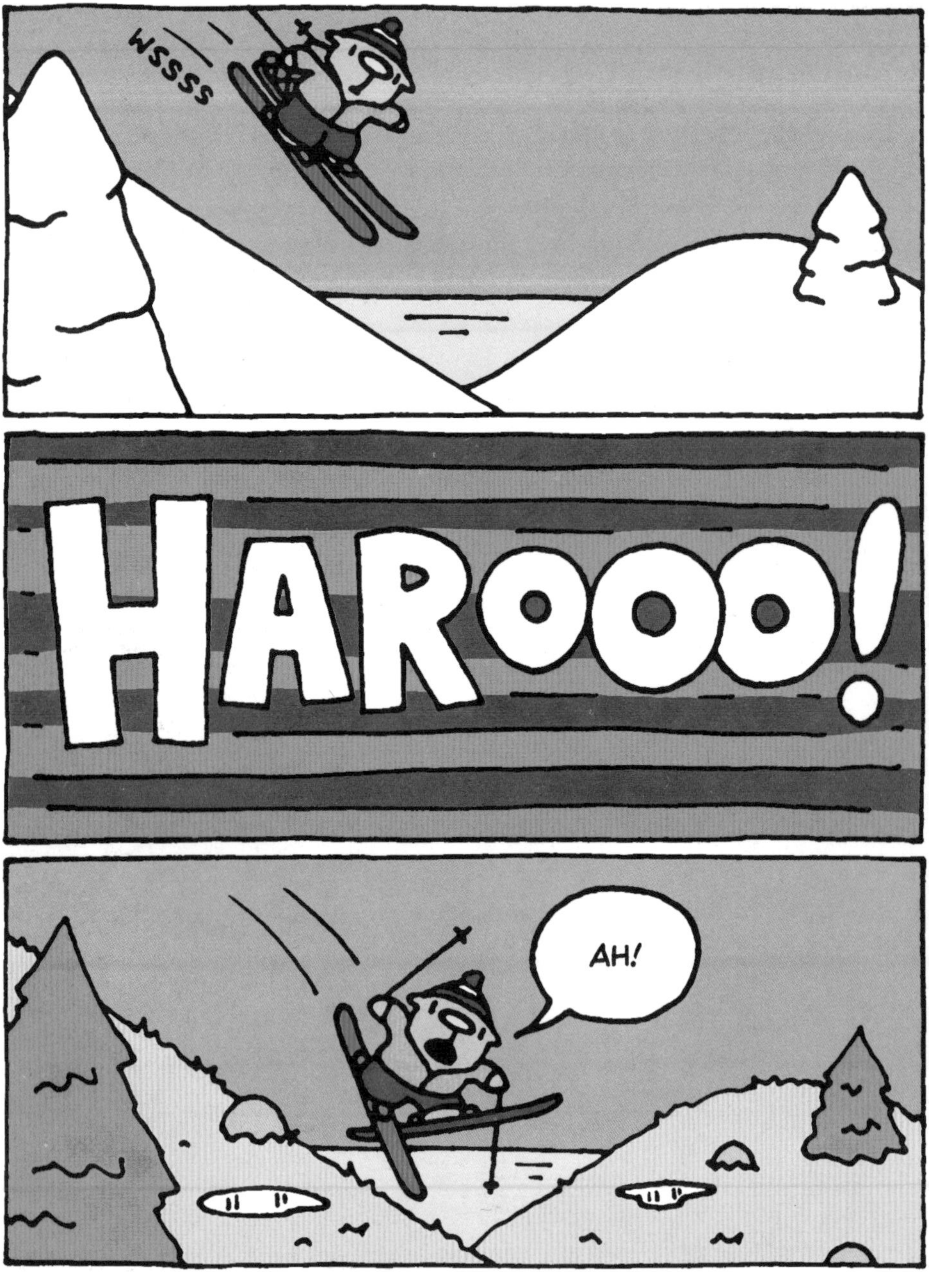
WSSSS
HAROOO!
AH!

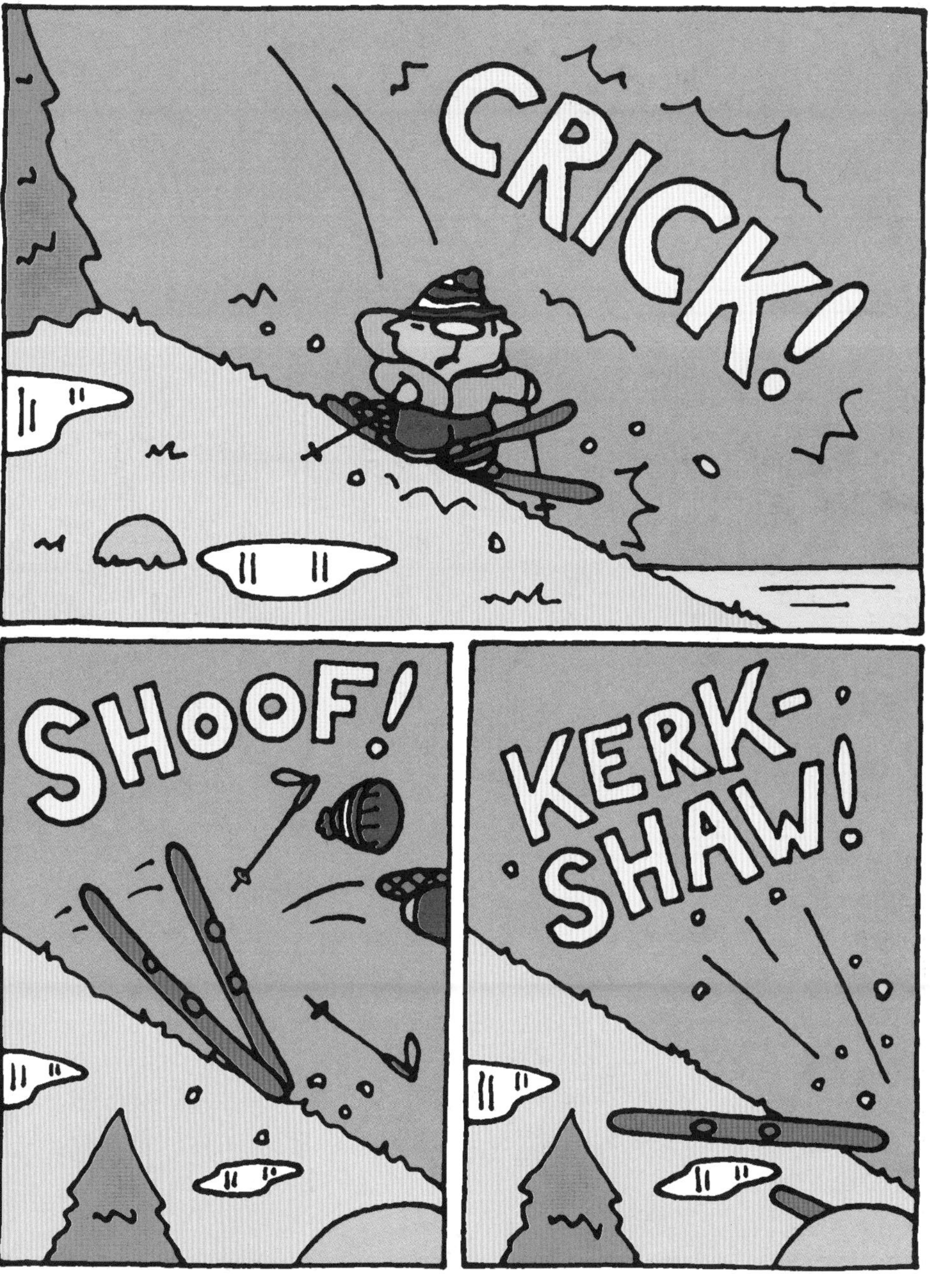
CRICK!
SHOOF!
KERK-
SHAW!

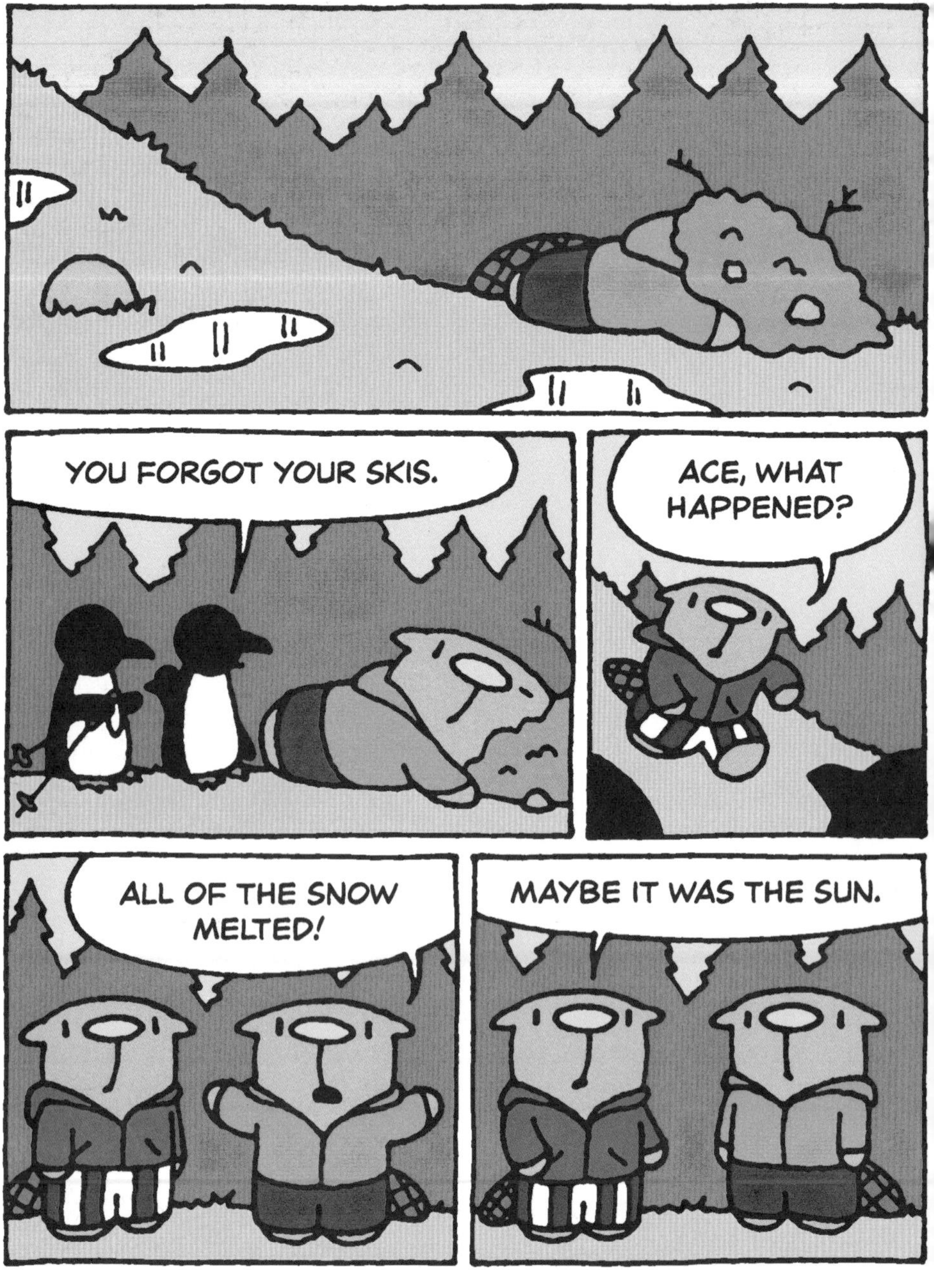
YOU FORGOT YOUR SKIS.
ACE, WHAT HAPPENED?
ALL OF THE SNOW MELTED!
MAYBE IT WAS THE SUN.

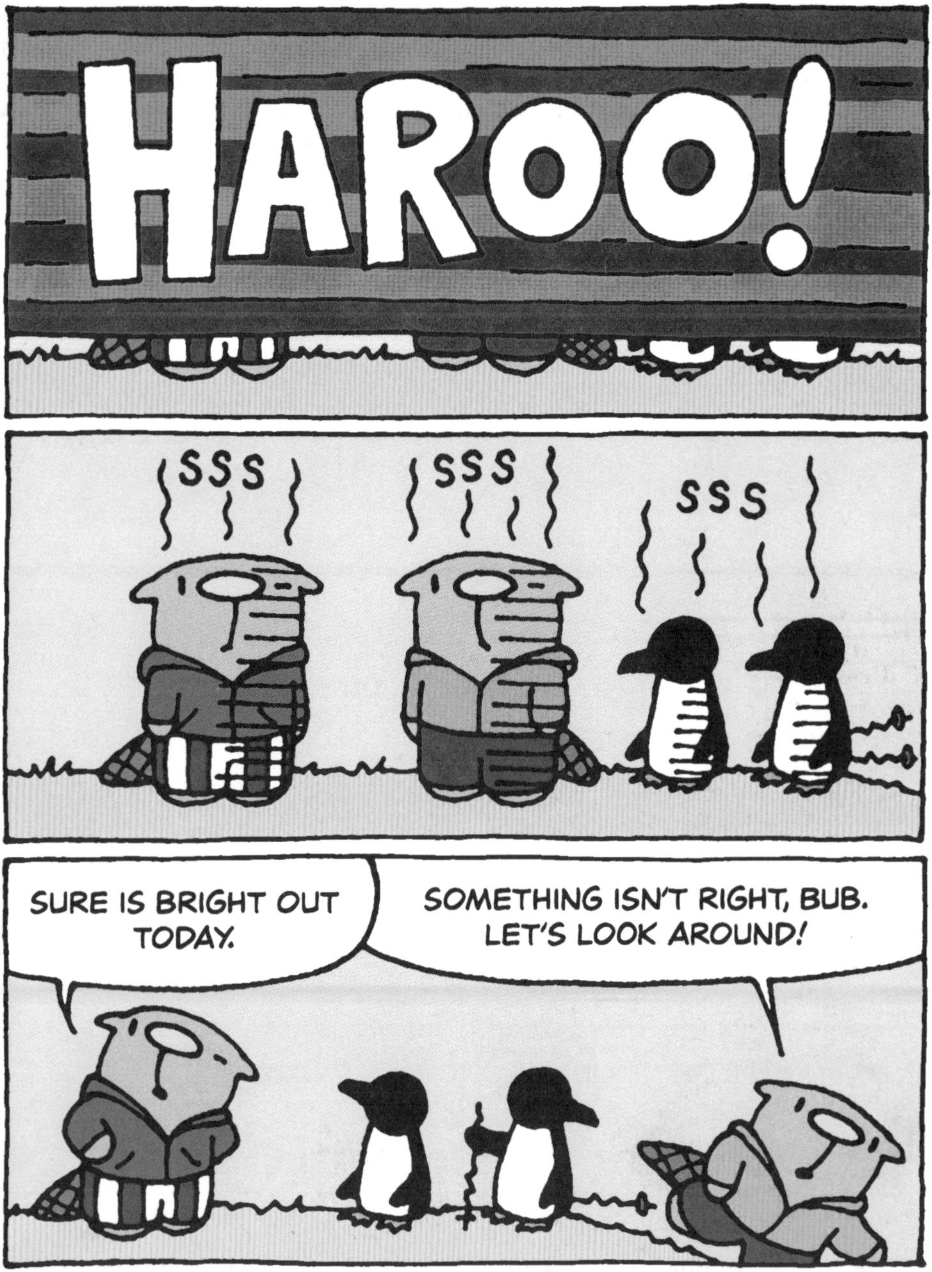
HAROO!
SSS
SSS
SSS
SURE IS BRIGHT OUT TODAY.
SOMETHING ISN'T RIGHT, BUB. LET'S LOOK AROUND!

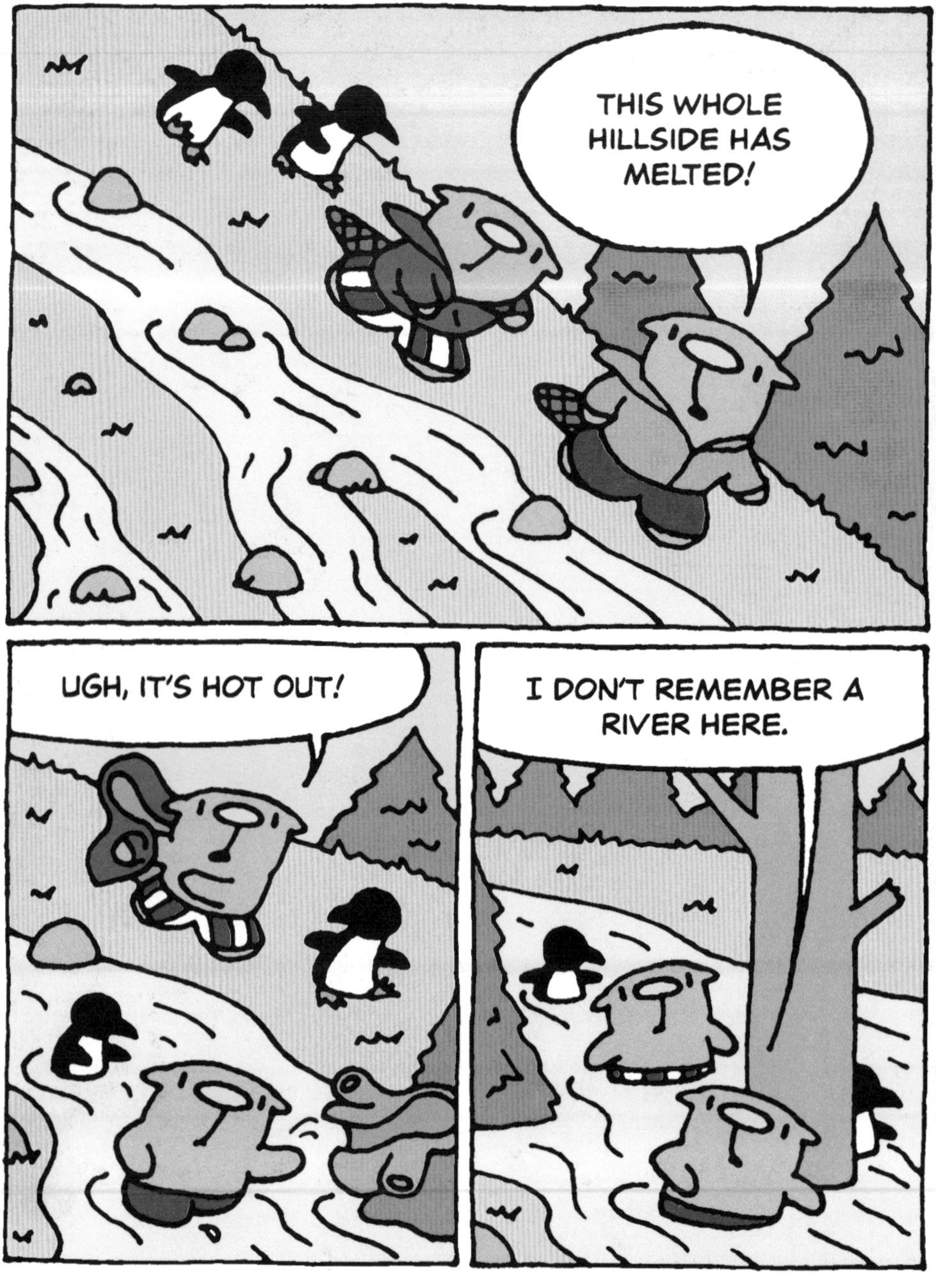
THIS WHOLE HILLSIDE HAS MELTED!
UGH, IT'S HOT OUT!
I DON'T REMEMBER A RIVER HERE.

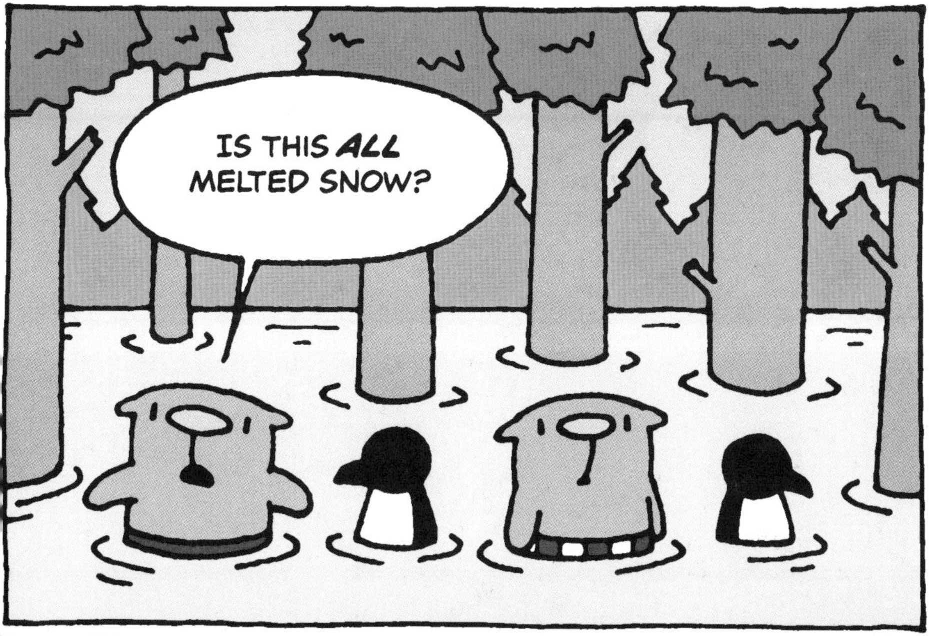
IS THIS ALL MELTED SNOW?

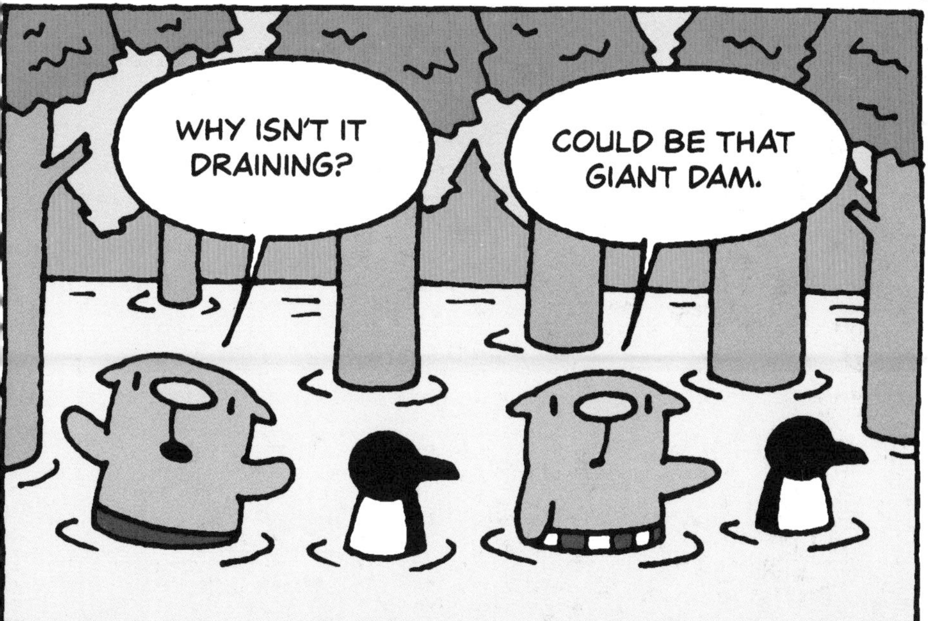
WHY ISN'T IT DRAINING?
COULD BE THAT GIANT DAM.

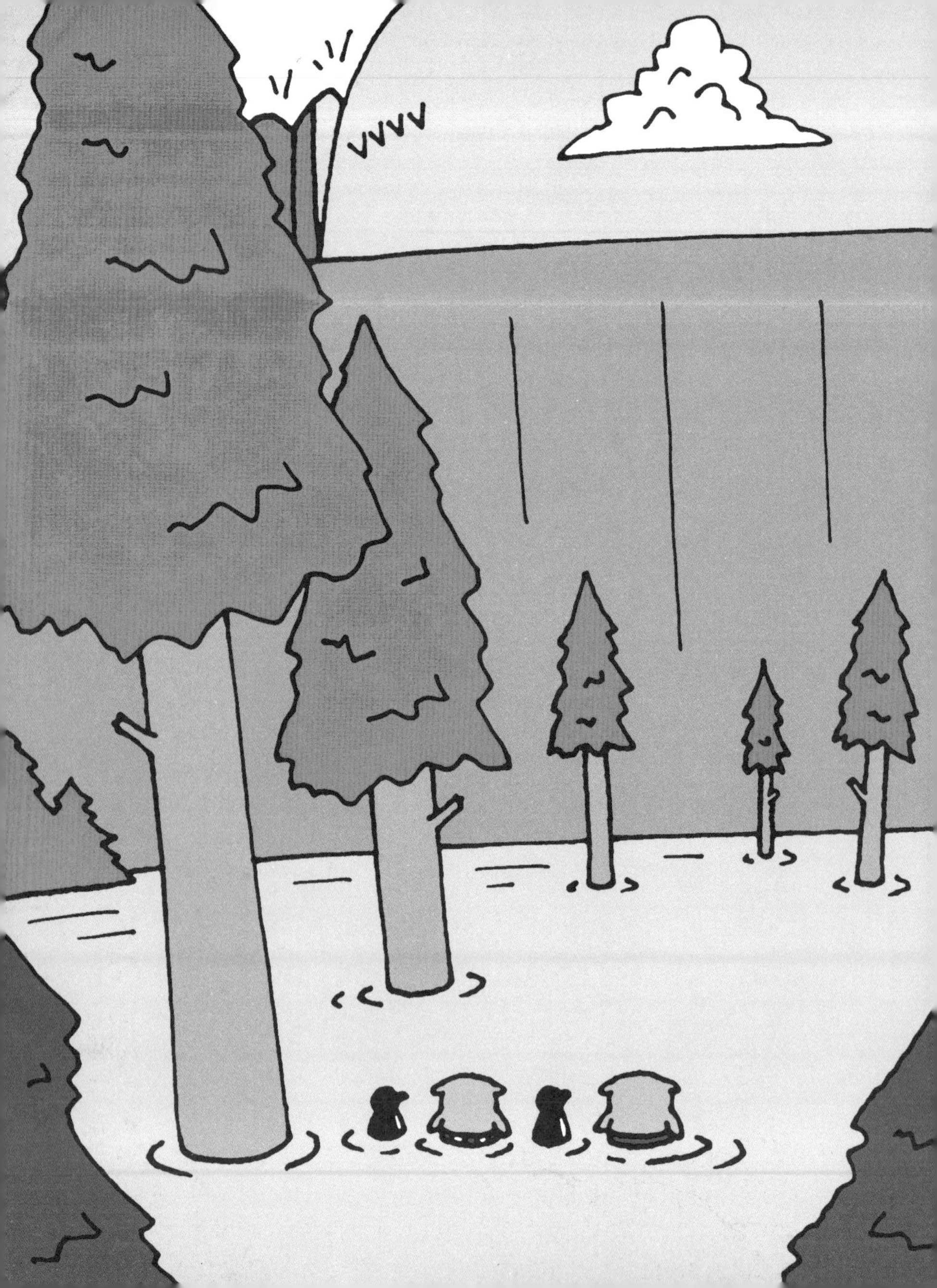

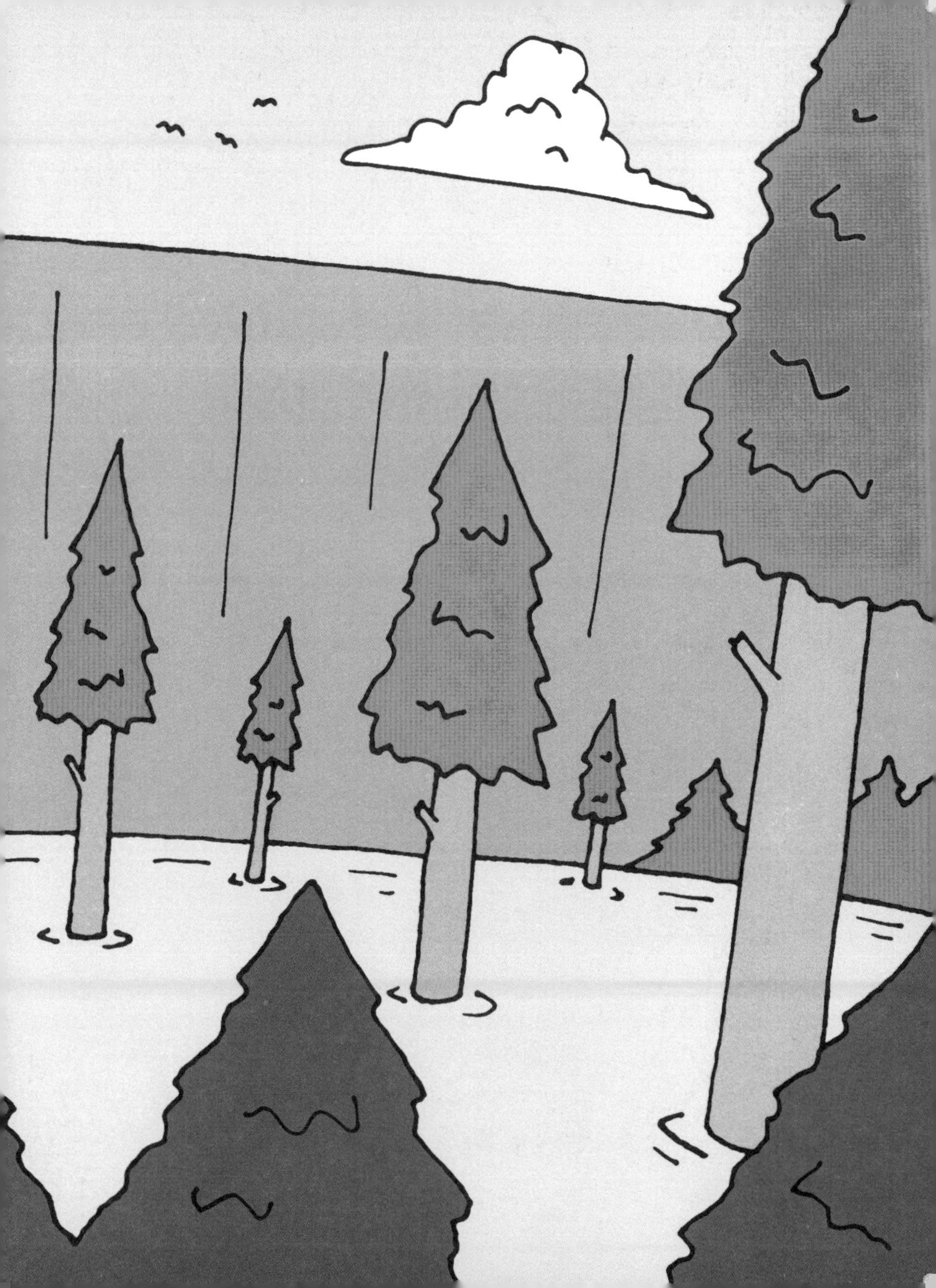

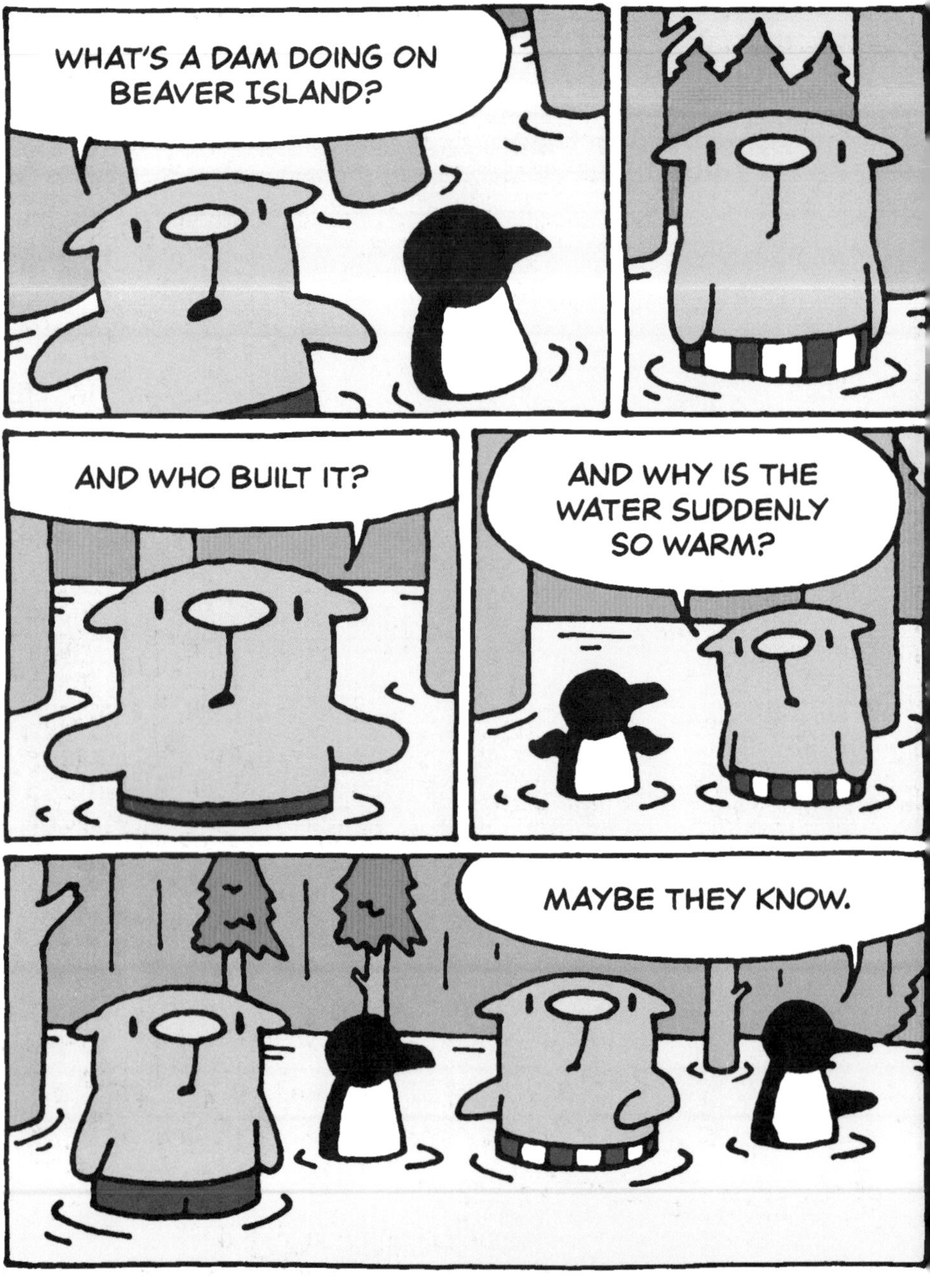
WHAT'S A DAM DOING ON BEAVER ISLAND?
AND WHO BUILT IT?
AND WHY IS THE WATER SUDDENLY SO WARM?
MAYBE THEY KNOW.

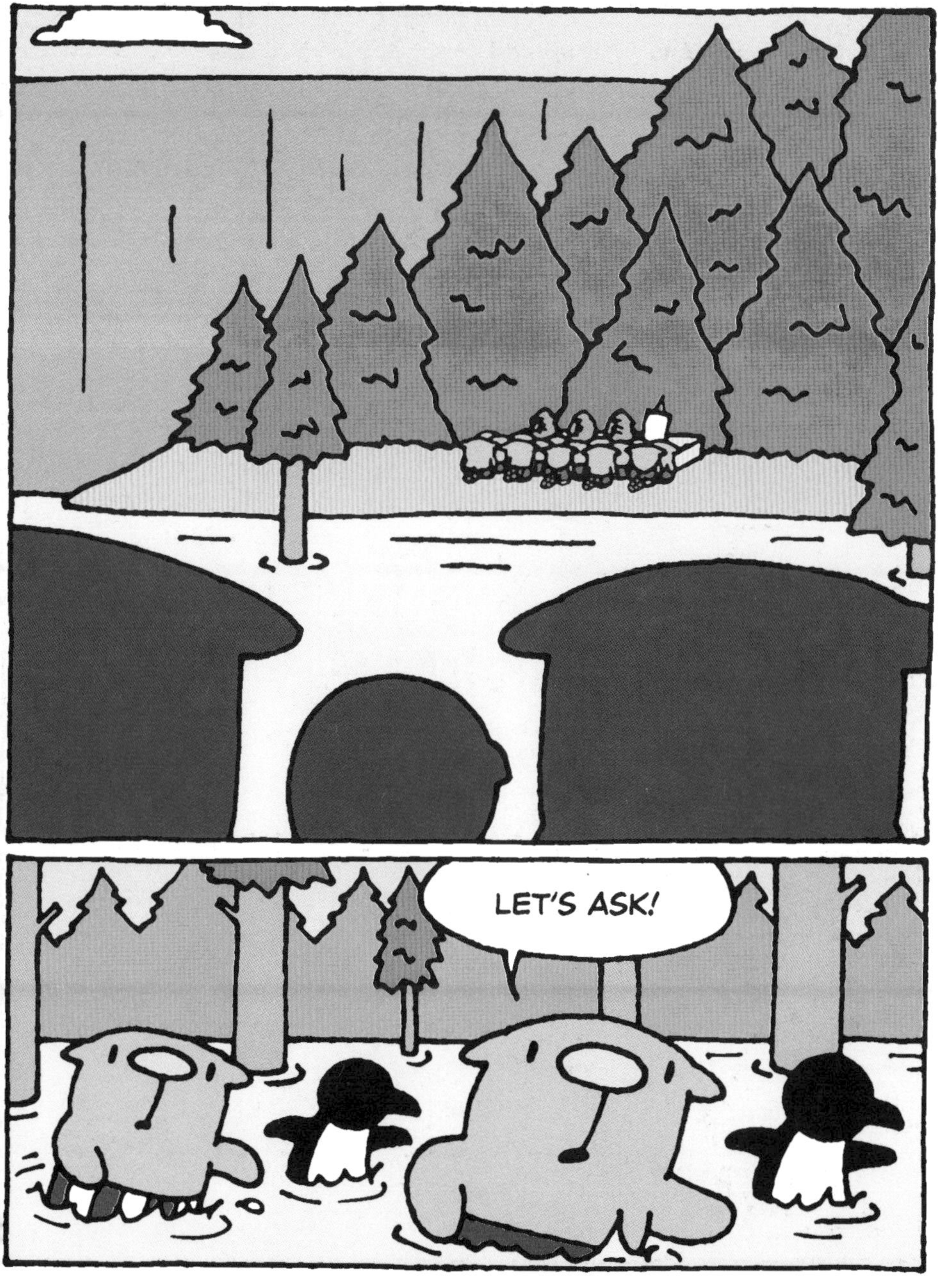
LET'S ASK!

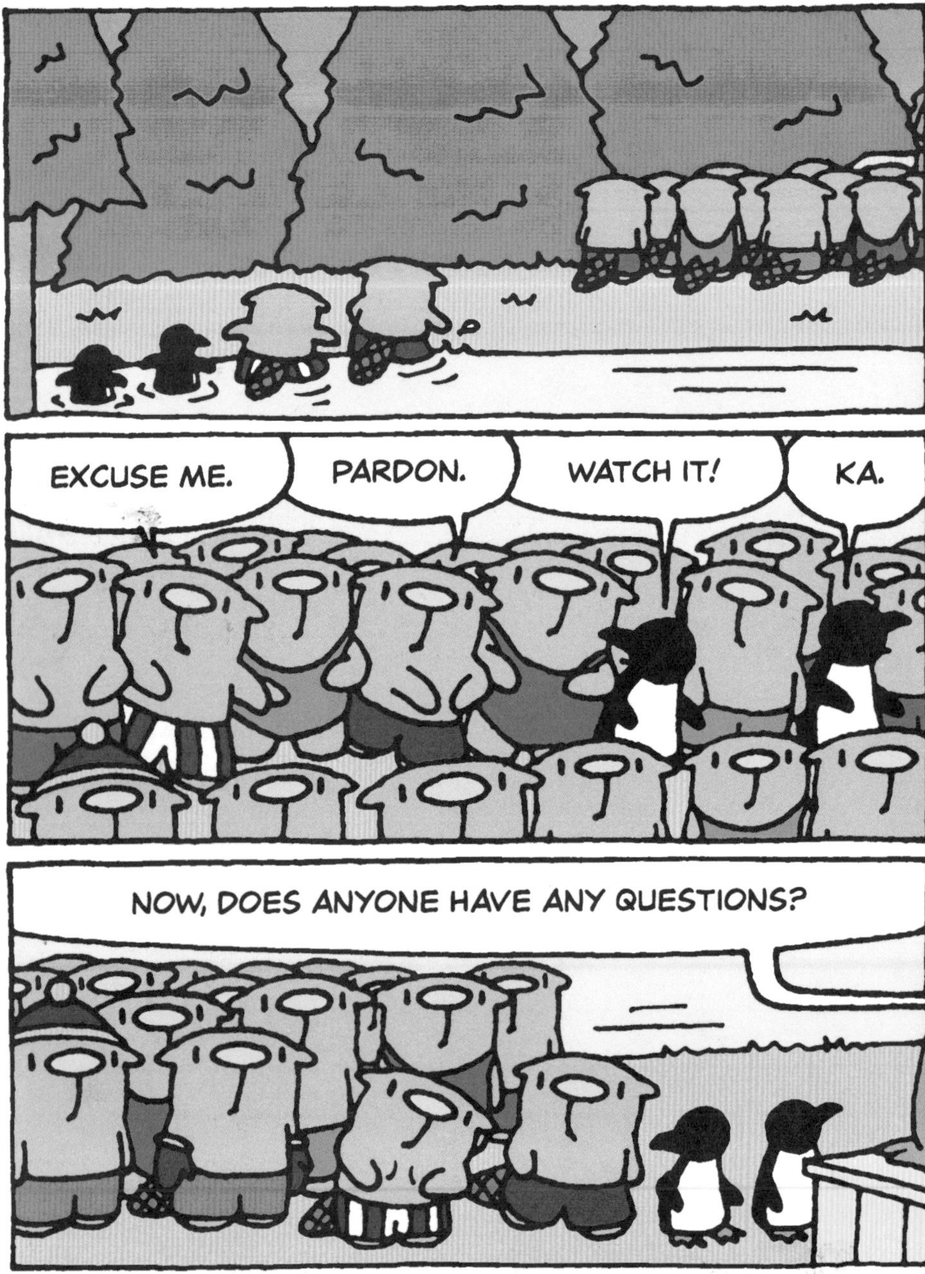
EXCUSE ME.
PARDON.
WATCH IT!
KA.
NOW, DOES ANYONE HAVE ANY QUESTIONS?

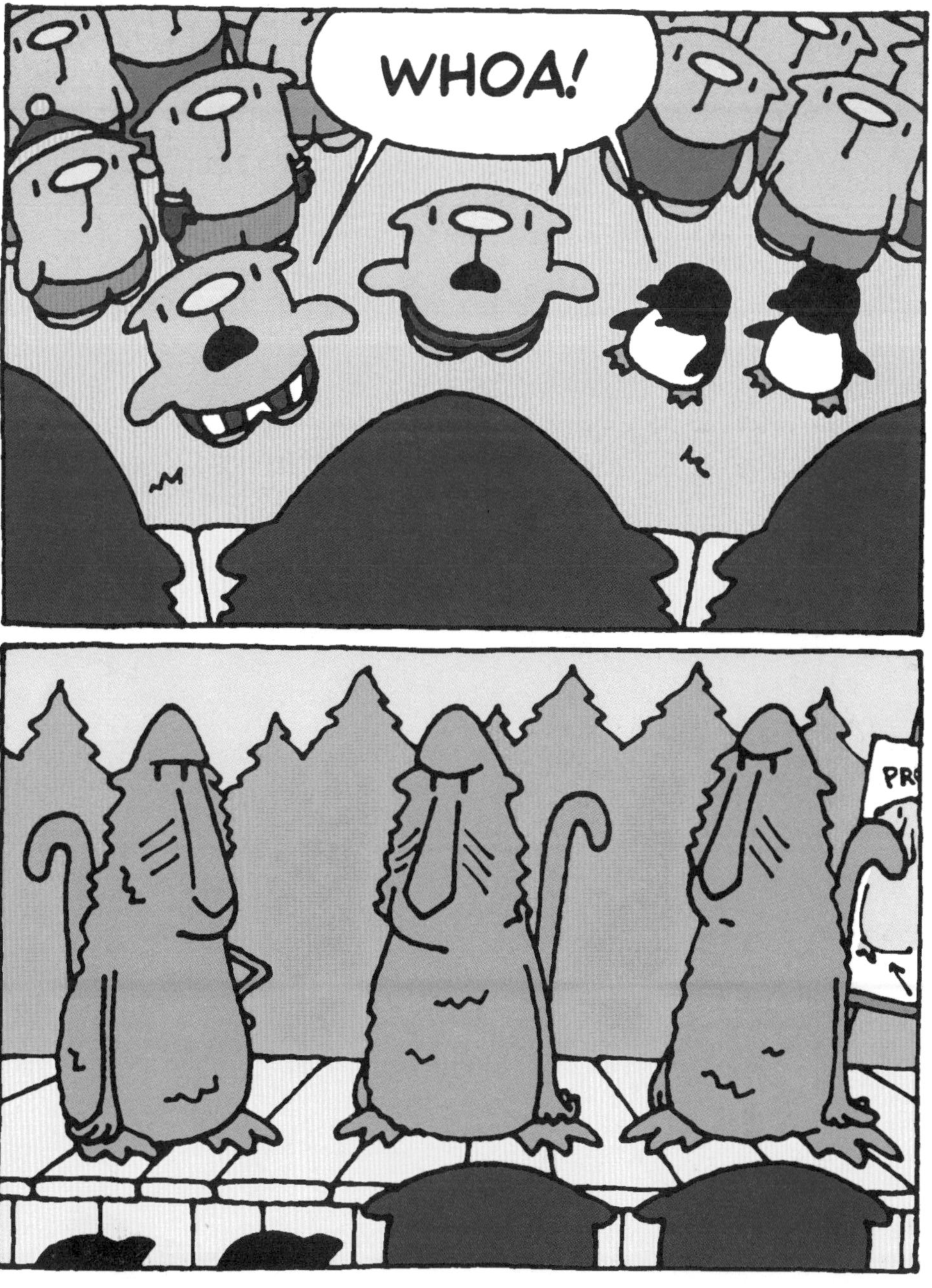
WHOA!

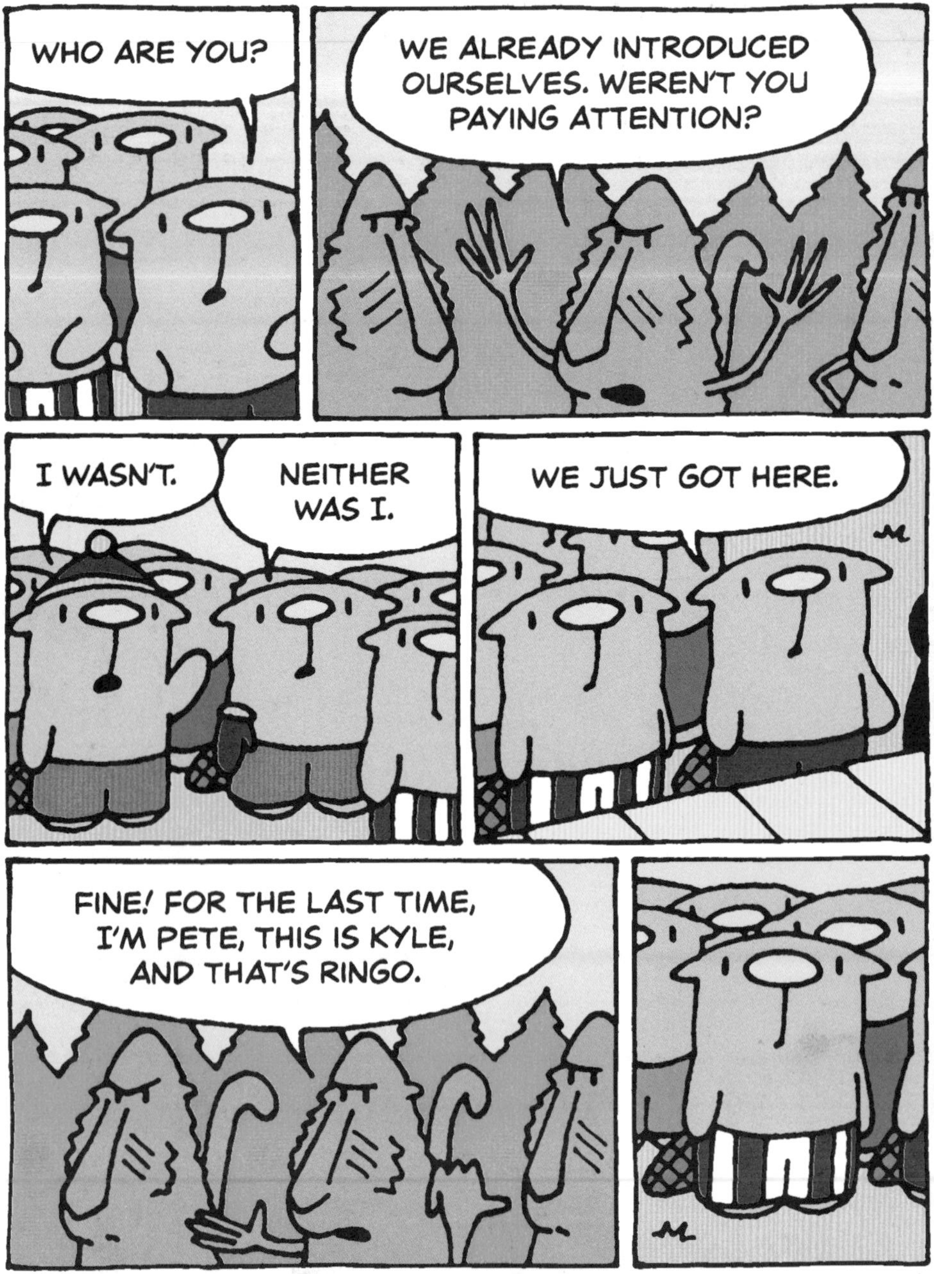
WHO ARE YOU?
WE ALREADY INTRODUCED OURSELVES. WEREN'T YOU PAYING ATTENTION?
I WASN'T.
NEITHER WAS I.
WE JUST GOT HERE.
FINE! FOR THE LAST TIME, I'M PETE, THIS IS KYLE, AND THAT'S RINGO.

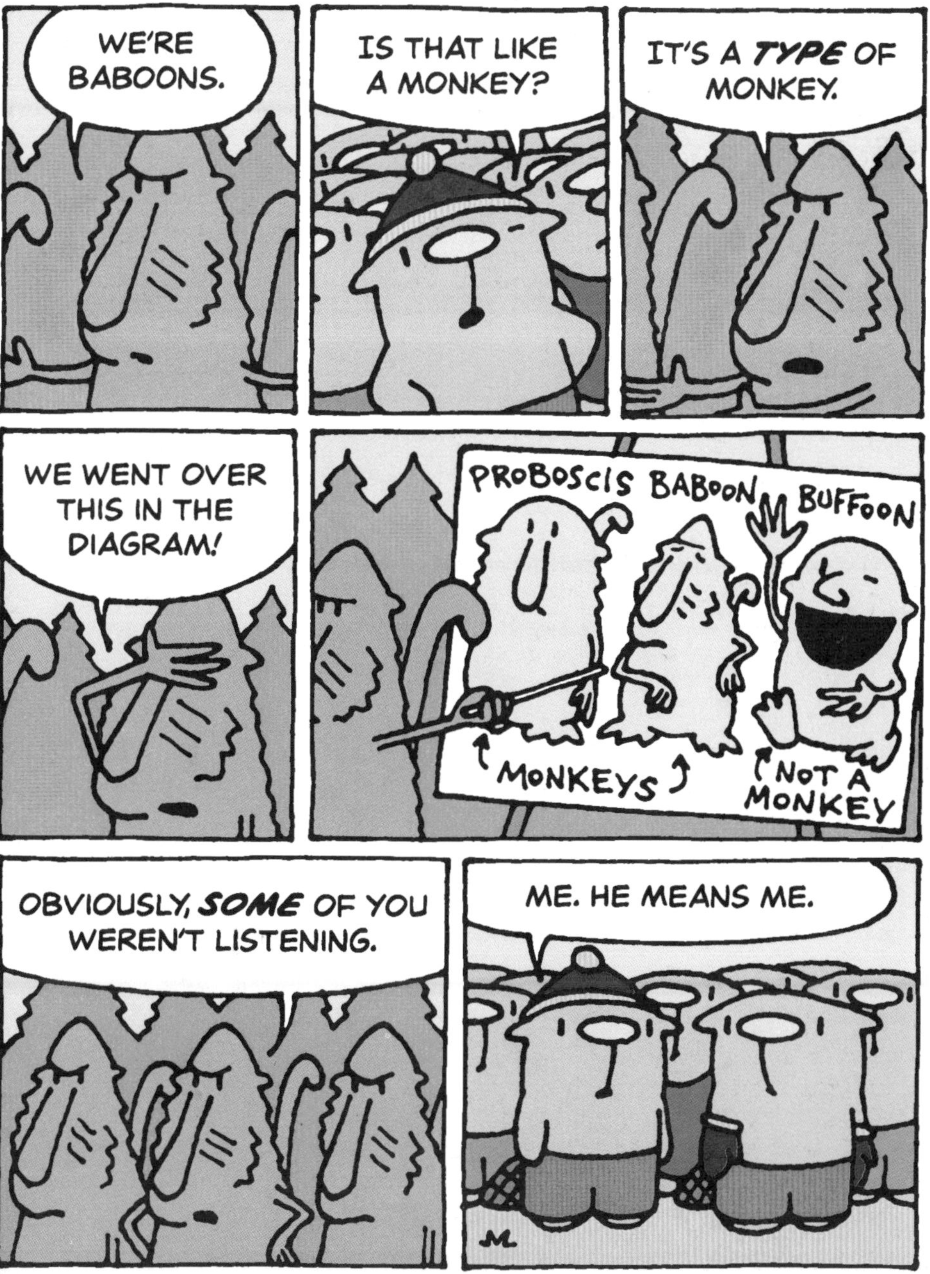
WE'RE BABOONS.
IS THAT LIKE A MONKEY?
IT'S A *TYPE* OF MONKEY.
WE WENT OVER THIS IN THE DIAGRAM!
PROBOSCIS
BABOON
BUFFOON
MONKEYS
NOT A MONKEY
OBVIOUSLY, *SOME* OF YOU WEREN'T LISTENING.
ME. HE MEANS ME.
M.

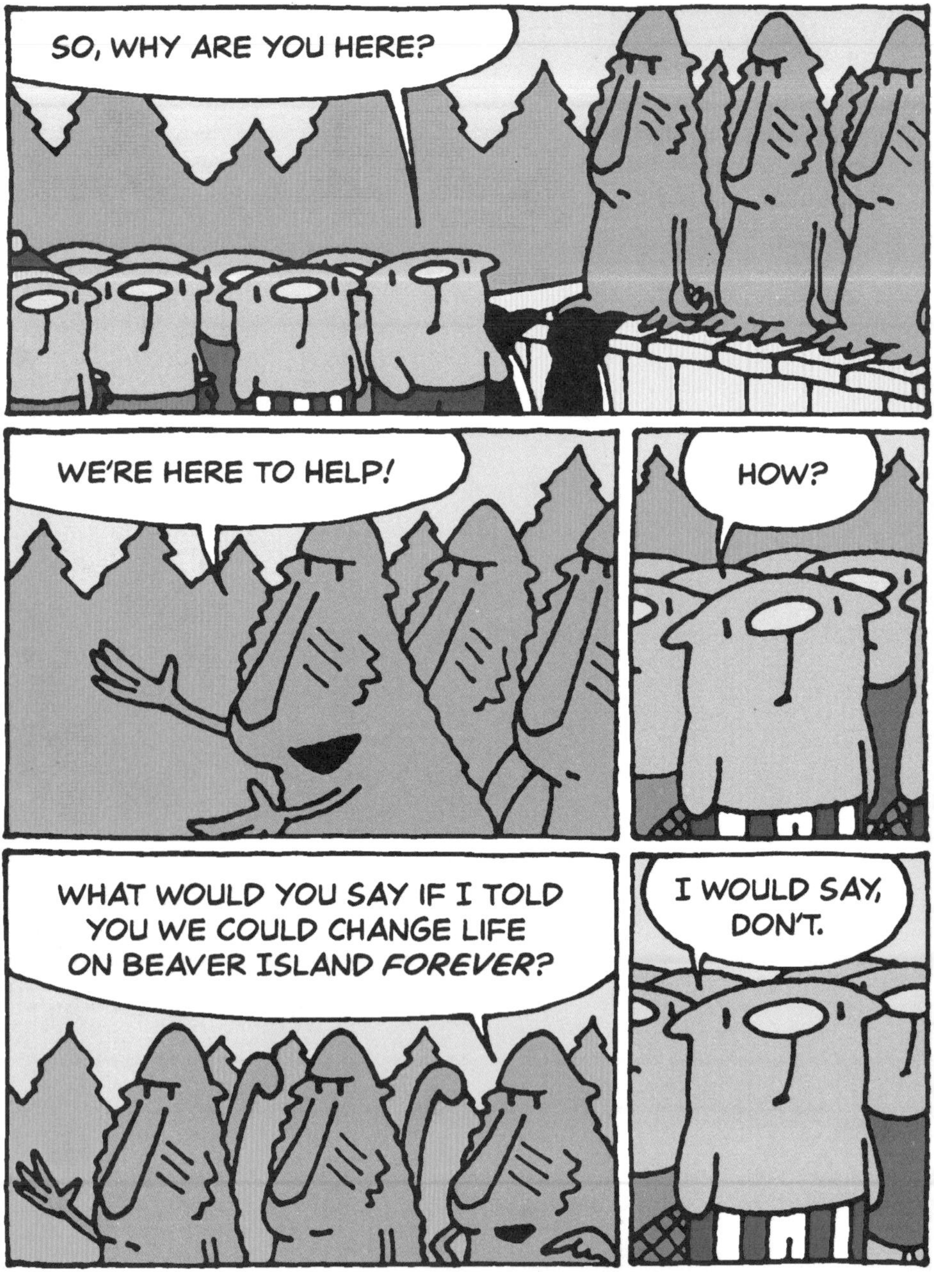
SO, WHY ARE YOU HERE?
WE'RE HERE TO HELP!
HOW?
WHAT WOULD YOU SAY IF I TOLD YOU WE COULD CHANGE LIFE ON BEAVER ISLAND *FOREVER*?
I WOULD SAY, DON'T.

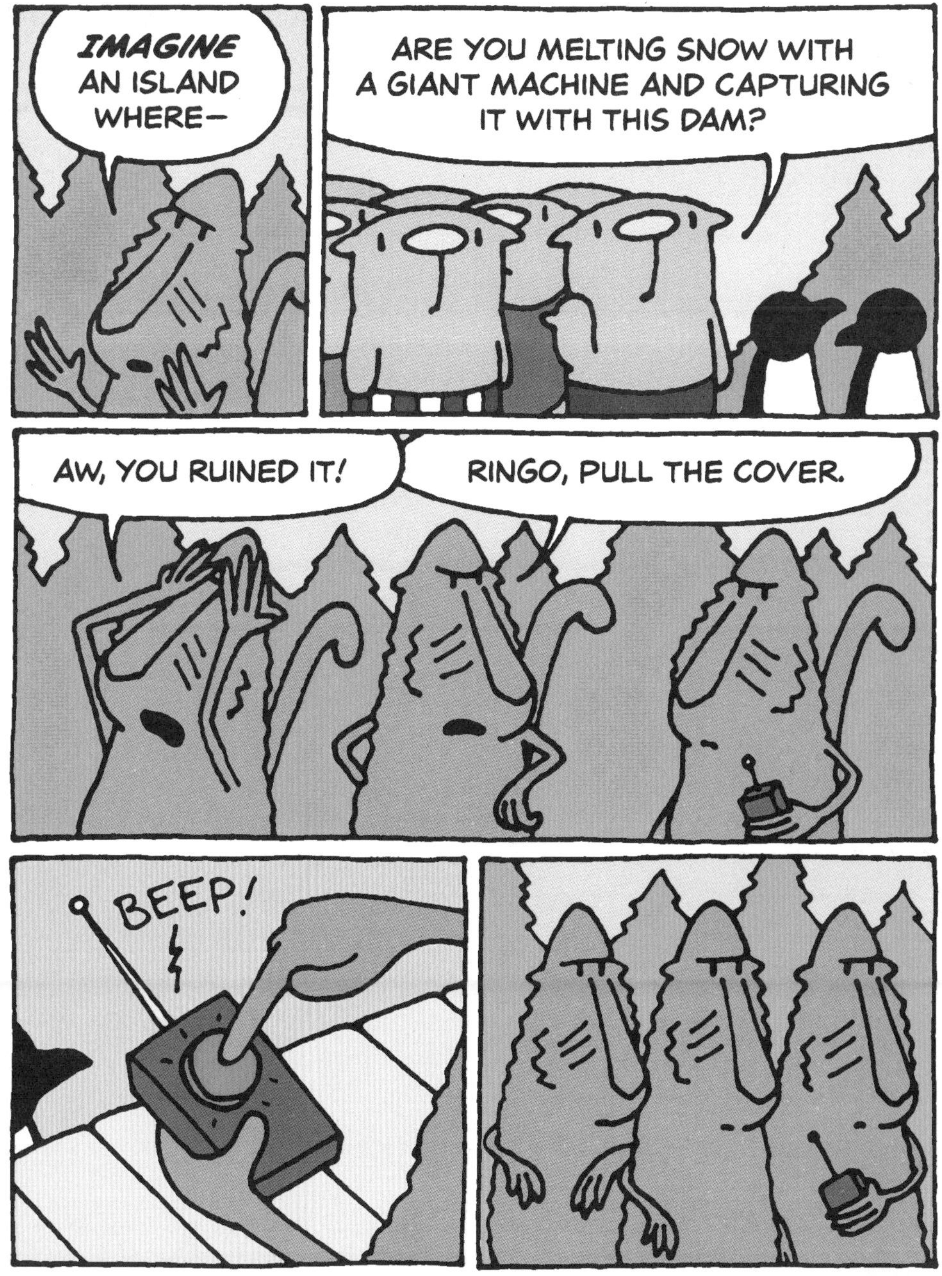
IMAGINE AN ISLAND WHERE–
ARE YOU MELTING SNOW WITH A GIANT MACHINE AND CAPTURING IT WITH THIS DAM?
AW, YOU RUINED IT!
RINGO, PULL THE COVER.
BEEP!

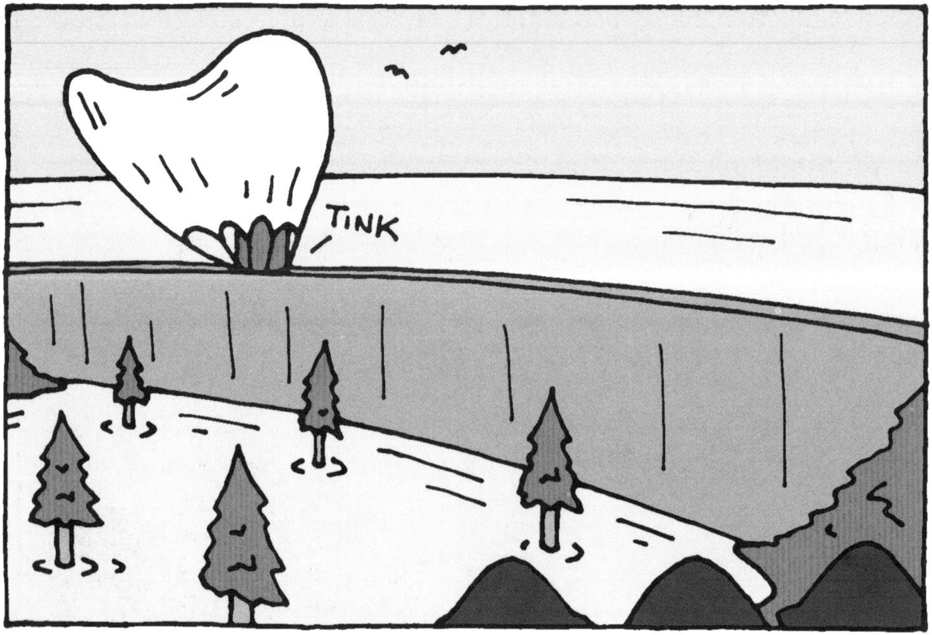
TINK

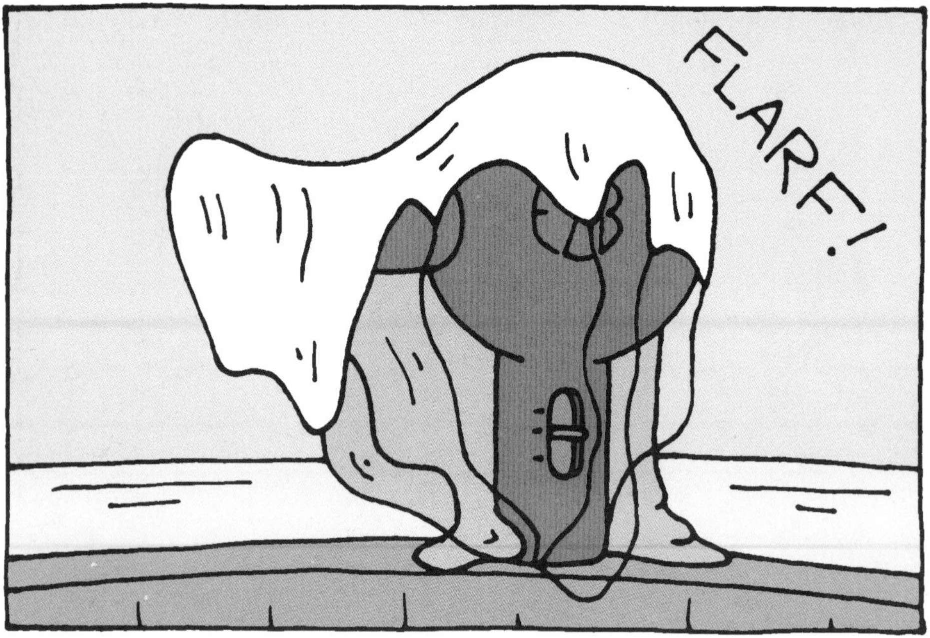
FLARF!

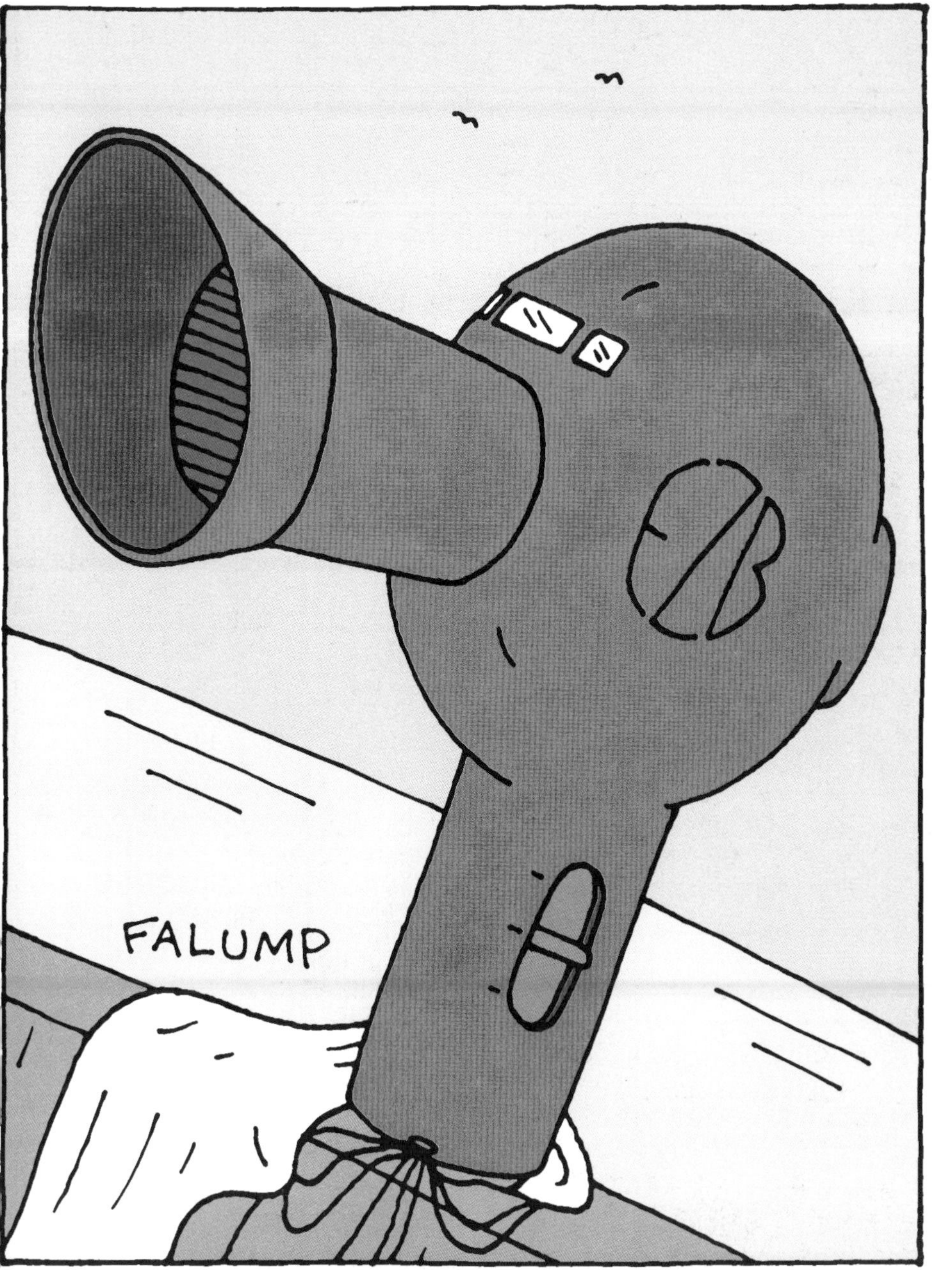
FALUMP

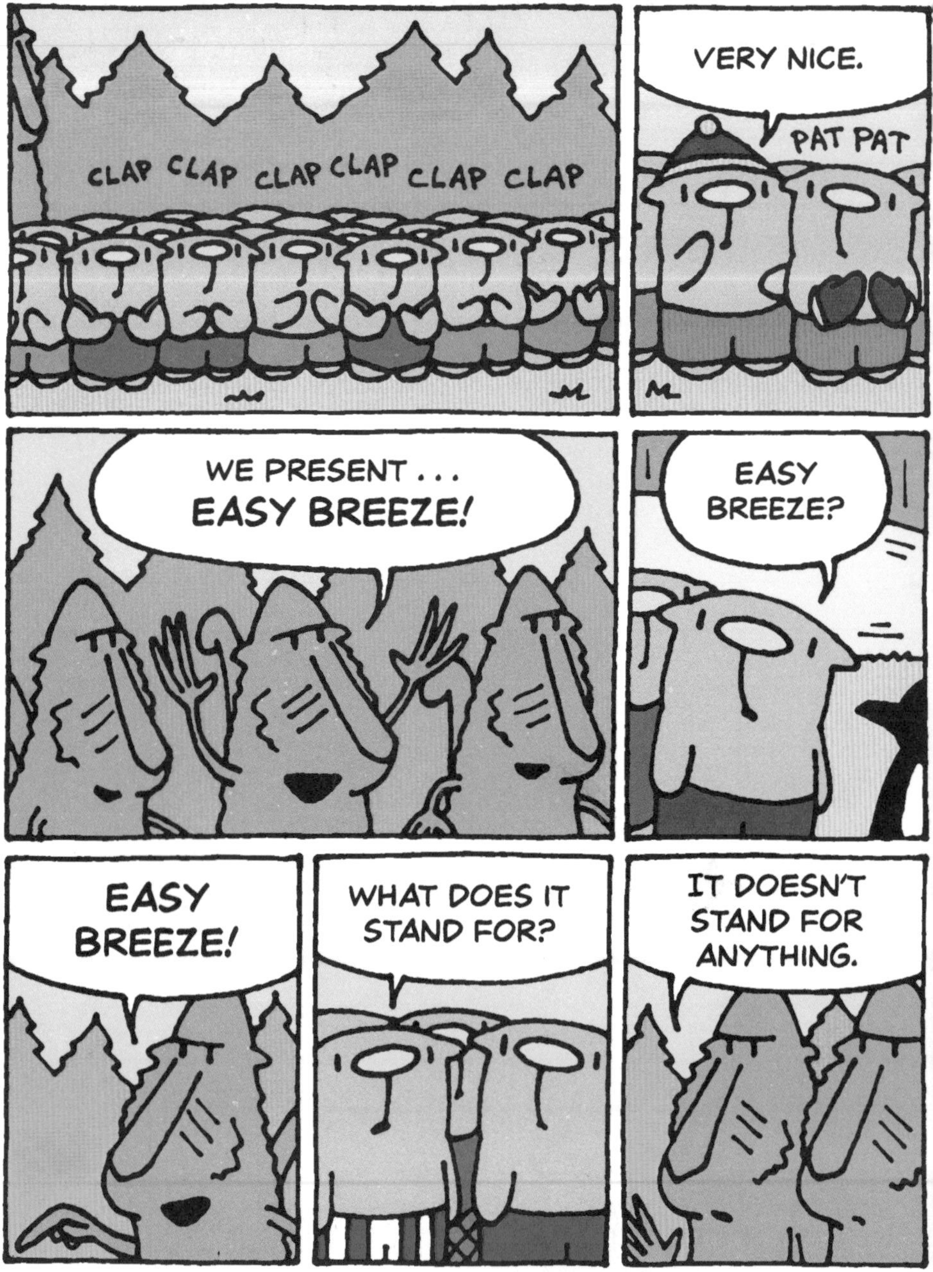
CLAP CLAP CLAP CLAP CLAP CLAP
VERY NICE.
PAT PAT
WE PRESENT . . .
EASY BREEZE!
EASY BREEZE?
EASY BREEZE!
WHAT DOES IT STAND FOR?
IT DOESN'T STAND FOR ANYTHING.

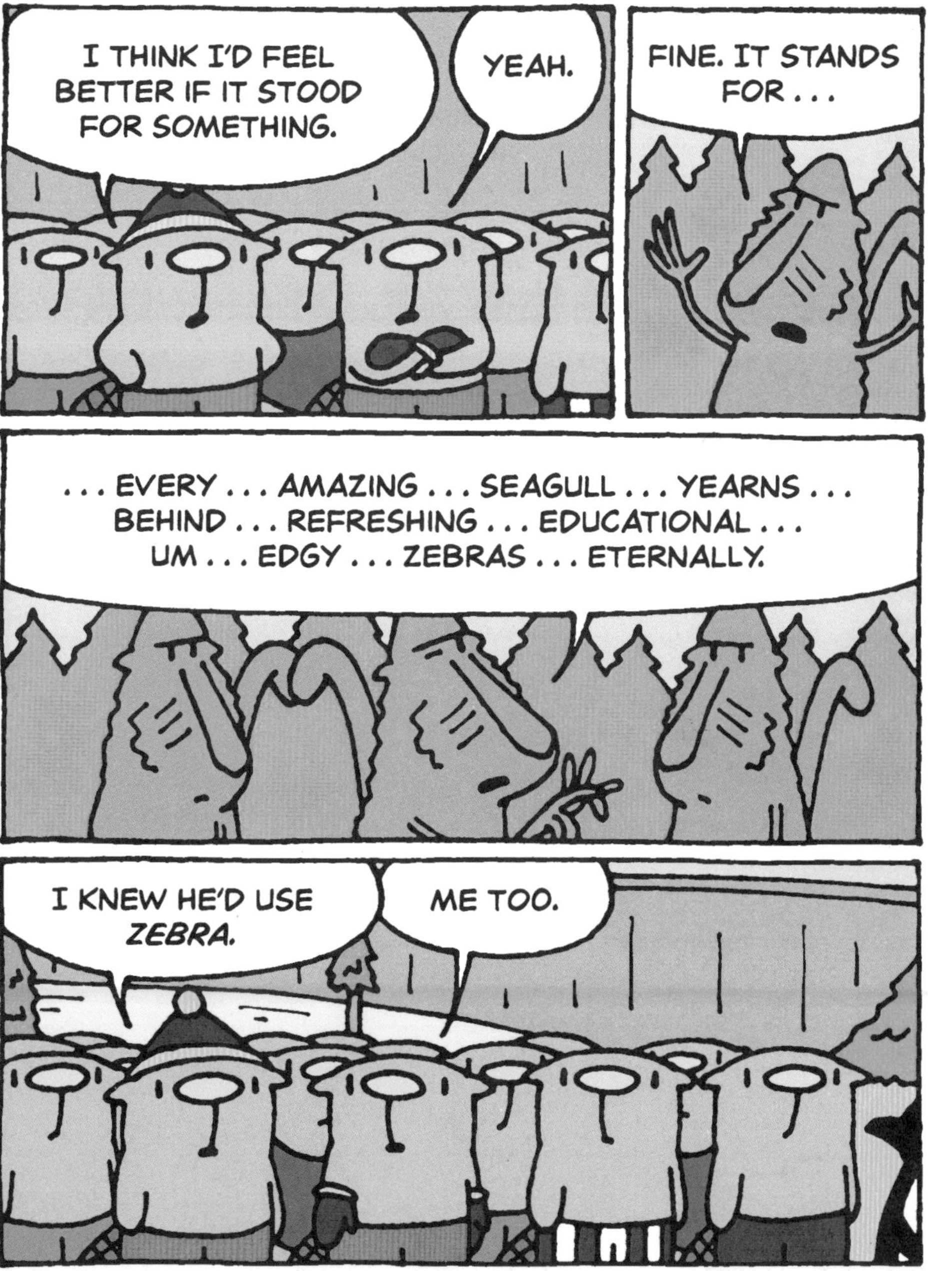
I THINK I'D FEEL BETTER IF IT STOOD FOR SOMETHING.
YEAH.
FINE. IT STANDS FOR . . .
. . . EVERY . . . AMAZING . . . SEAGULL . . . YEARNS . . . BEHIND . . . REFRESHING . . . EDUCATIONAL . . . UM . . . EDGY . . . ZEBRAS . . . ETERNALLY.
I KNEW HE'D USE *ZEBRA*.
ME TOO.

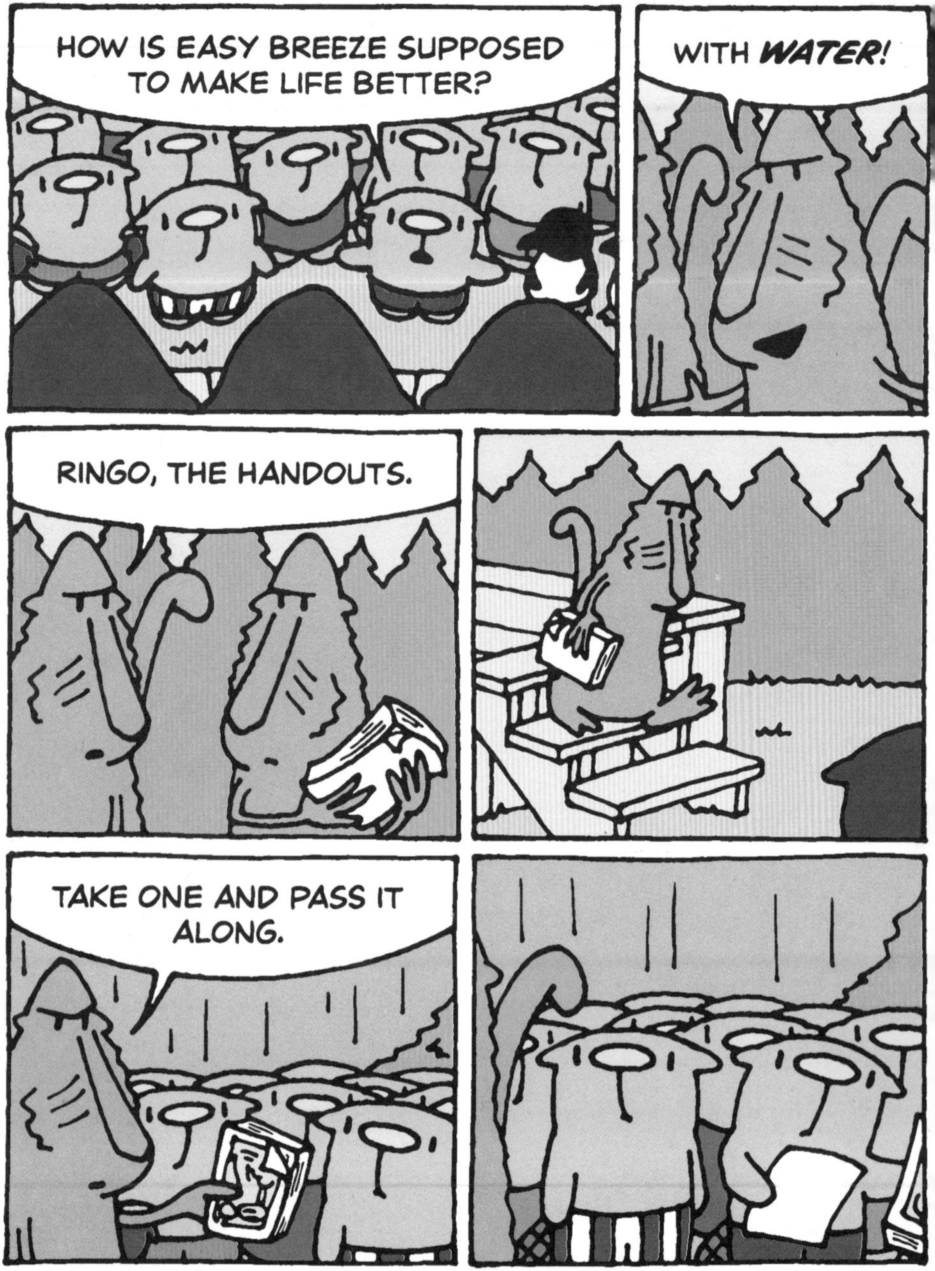
HOW IS EASY BREEZE SUPPOSED TO MAKE LIFE BETTER?
WITH *WATER!*
RINGO, THE HANDOUTS.
TAKE ONE AND PASS IT ALONG.

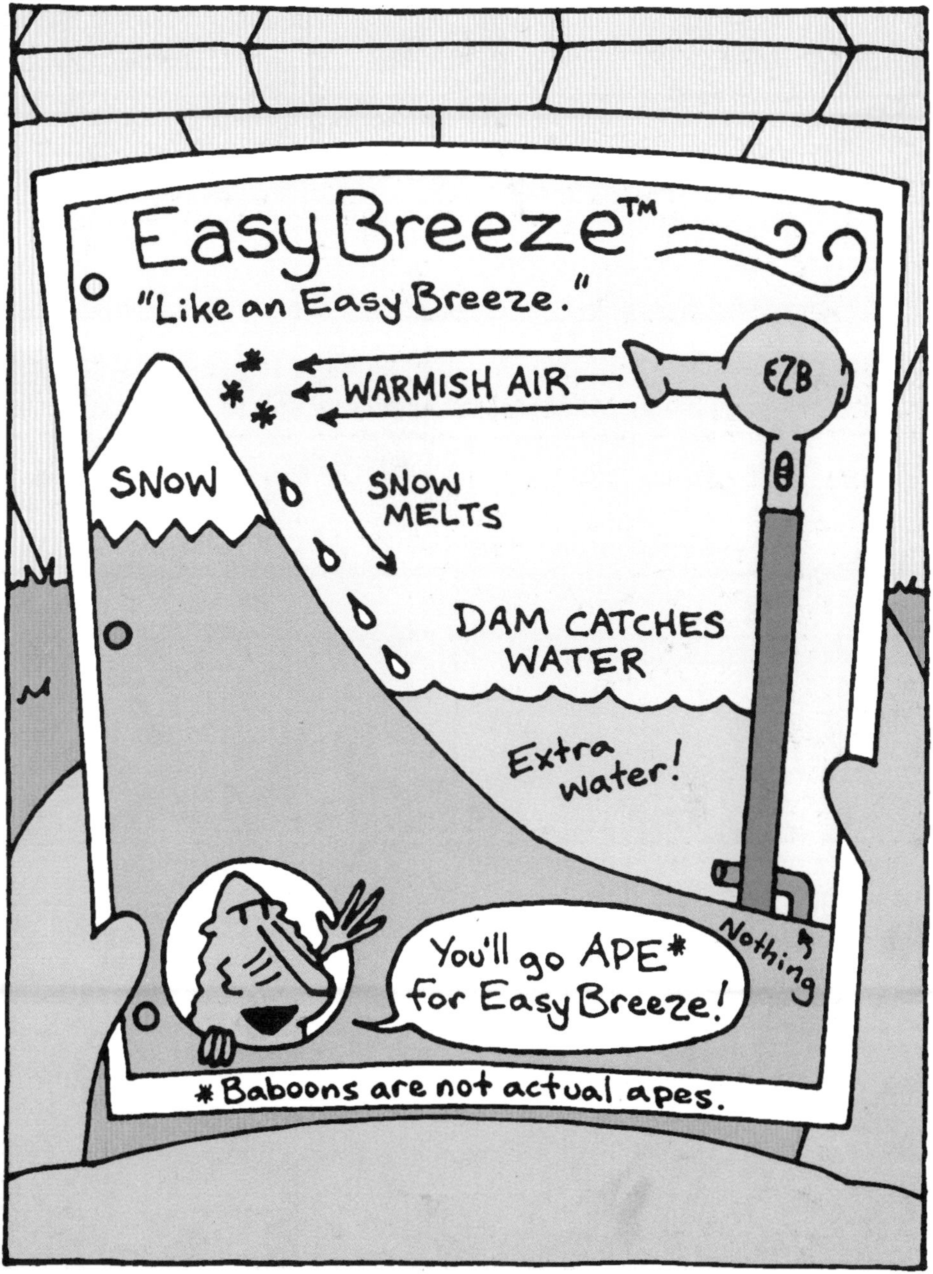

Easy Breeze™
"Like an Easy Breeze."
WARMISH AIR
EZB
SNOW
SNOW MELTS
DAM CATCHES WATER
Extra water!
Nothing
You'll go APE* for Easy Breeze!
* Baboons are not actual apes.

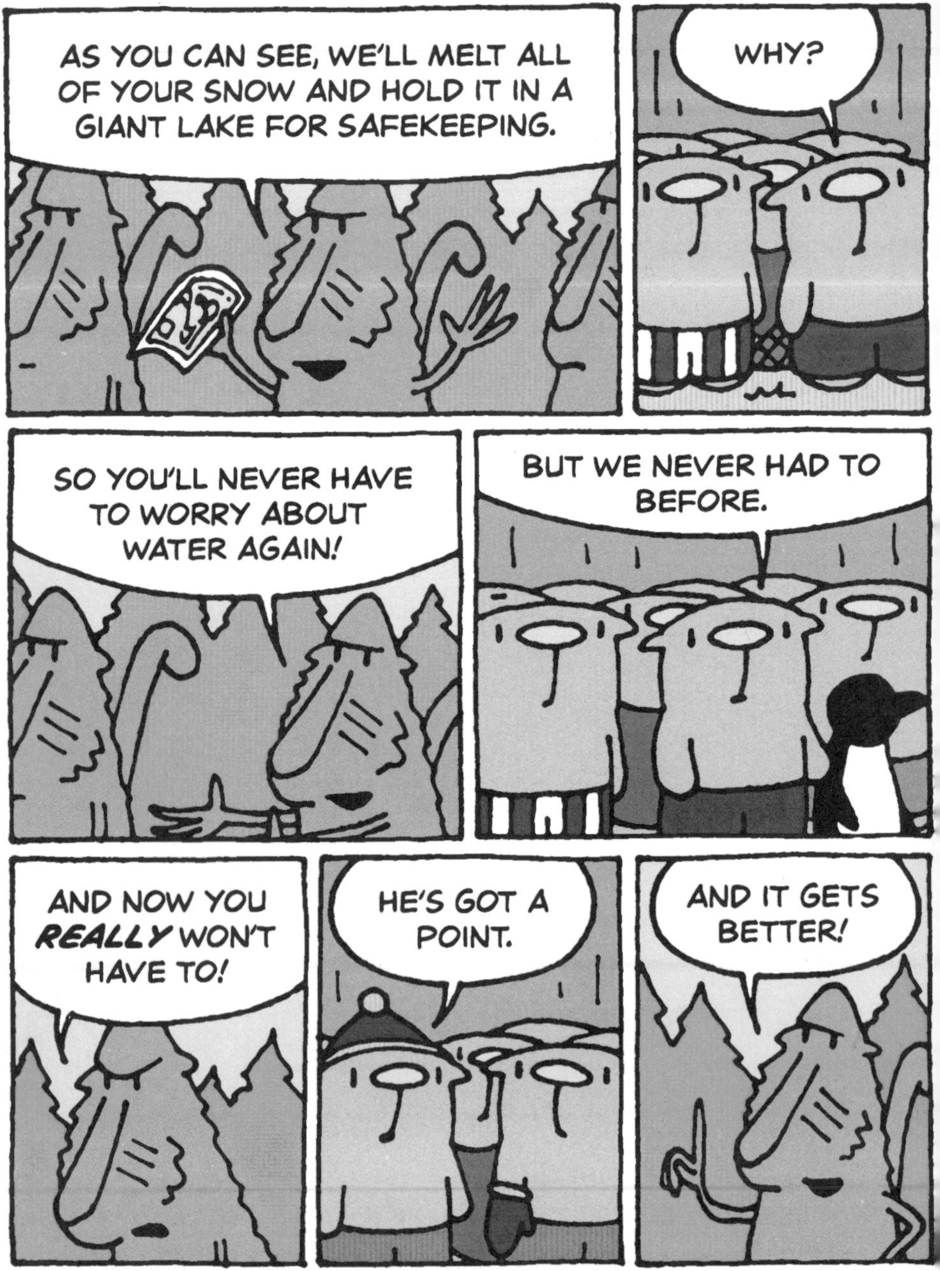
AS YOU CAN SEE, WE'LL MELT ALL OF YOUR SNOW AND HOLD IT IN A GIANT LAKE FOR SAFEKEEPING.
WHY?
SO YOU'LL NEVER HAVE TO WORRY ABOUT WATER AGAIN!
BUT WE NEVER HAD TO BEFORE.
AND NOW YOU *REALLY* WON'T HAVE TO!
HE'S GOT A POINT.
AND IT GETS BETTER!

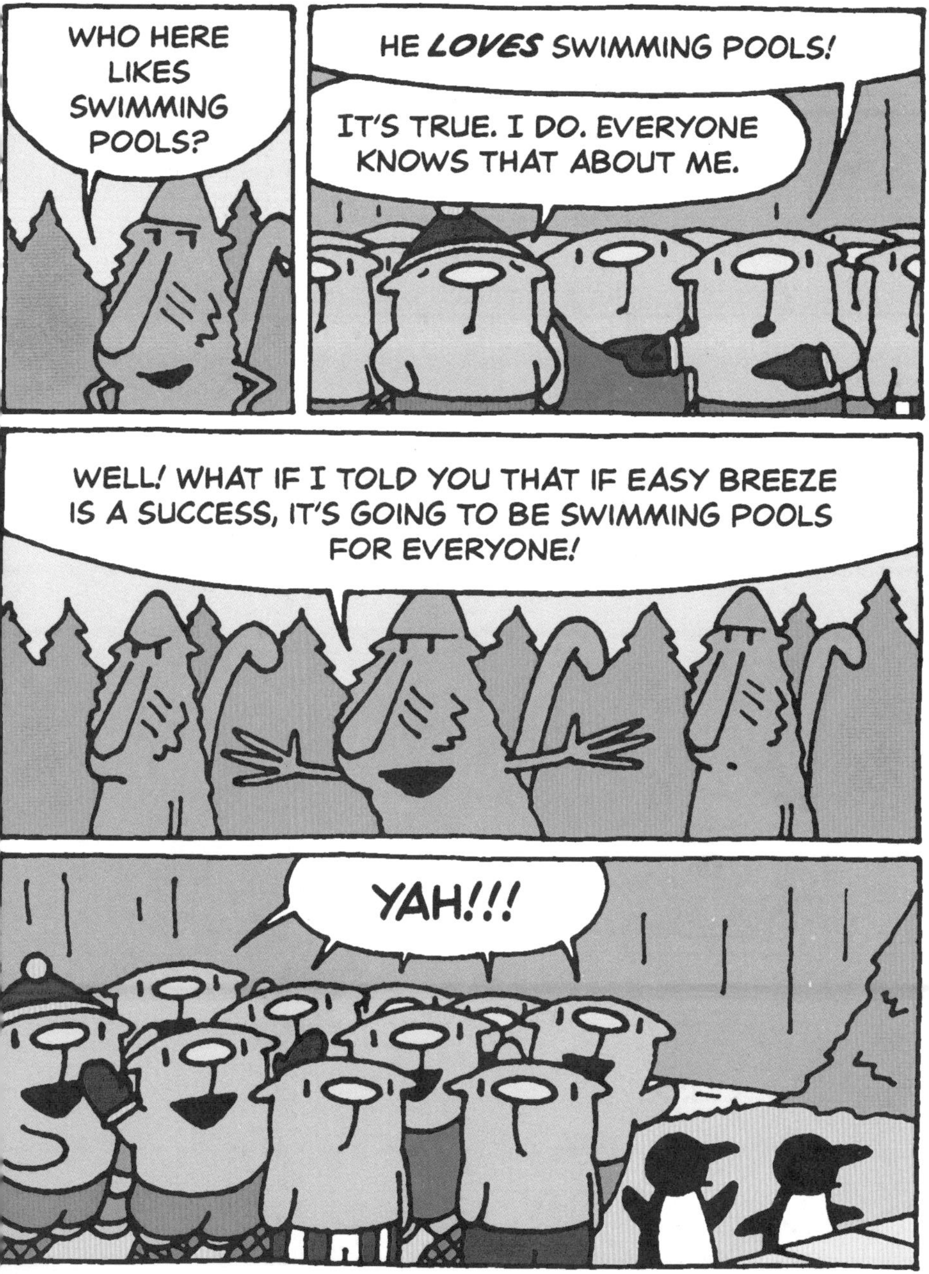
WHO HERE LIKES SWIMMING POOLS?
HE *LOVES* SWIMMING POOLS!
IT'S TRUE. I DO. EVERYONE KNOWS THAT ABOUT ME.
WELL! WHAT IF I TOLD YOU THAT IF EASY BREEZE IS A SUCCESS, IT'S GOING TO BE SWIMMING POOLS FOR EVERYONE!
YAH!!!

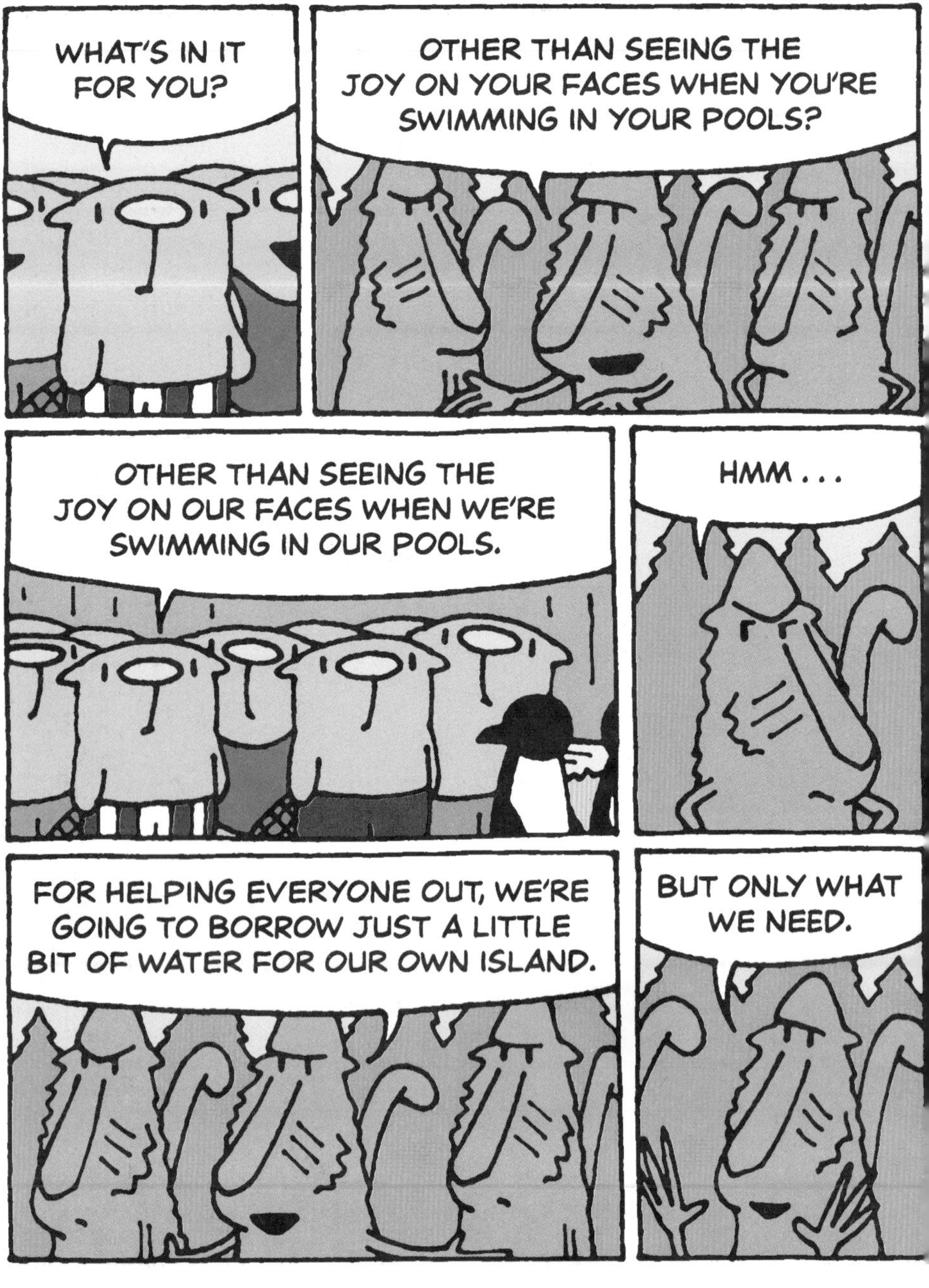
WHAT'S IN IT FOR YOU?
OTHER THAN SEEING THE JOY ON YOUR FACES WHEN YOU'RE SWIMMING IN YOUR POOLS?
OTHER THAN SEEING THE JOY ON OUR FACES WHEN WE'RE SWIMMING IN OUR POOLS.
HMM . . .
FOR HELPING EVERYONE OUT, WE'RE GOING TO BORROW JUST A LITTLE BIT OF WATER FOR OUR OWN ISLAND.
BUT ONLY WHAT WE NEED.

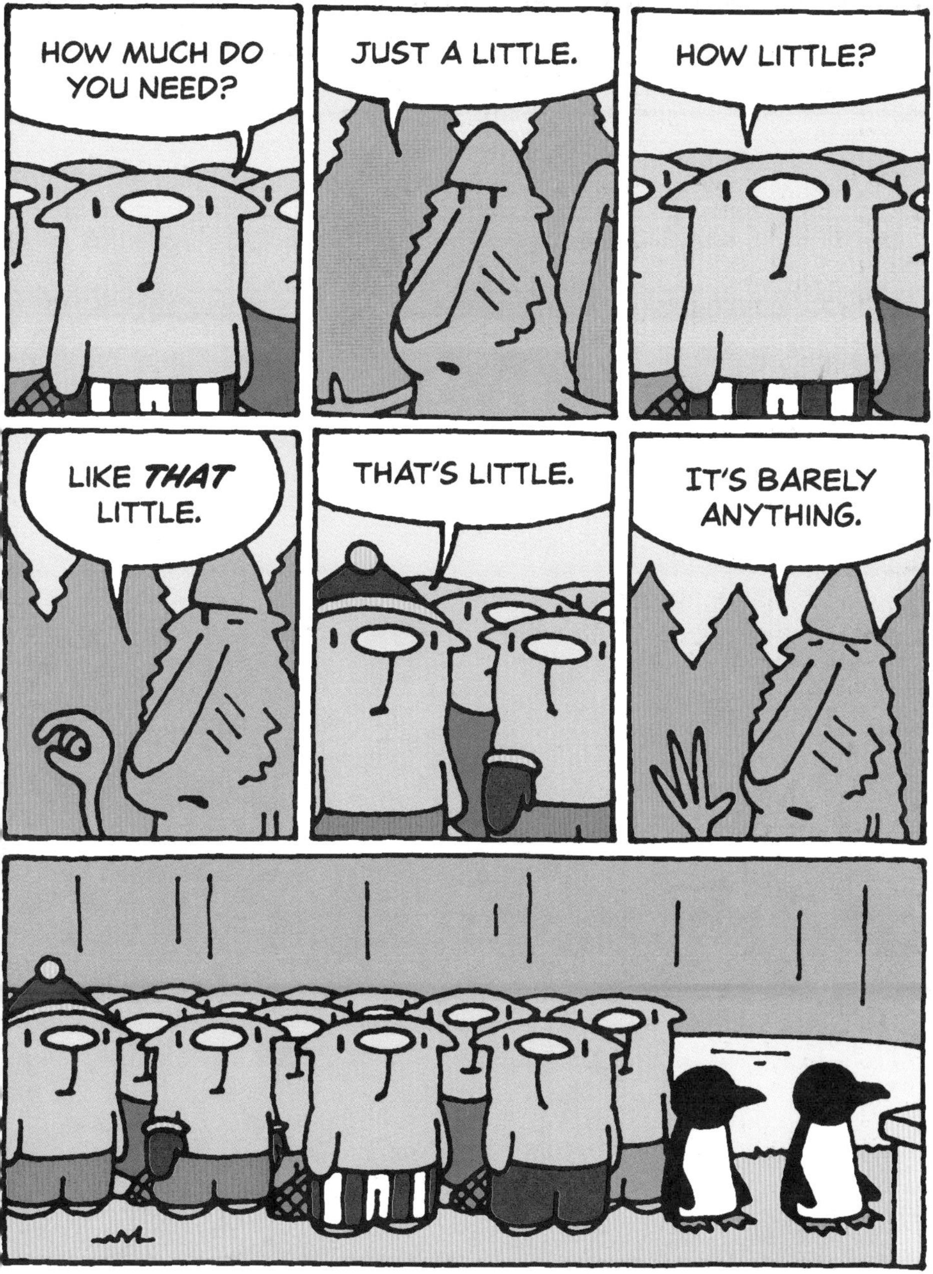
HOW MUCH DO YOU NEED?
JUST A LITTLE.
HOW LITTLE?
LIKE *THAT* LITTLE.
THAT'S LITTLE.
IT'S BARELY ANYTHING.

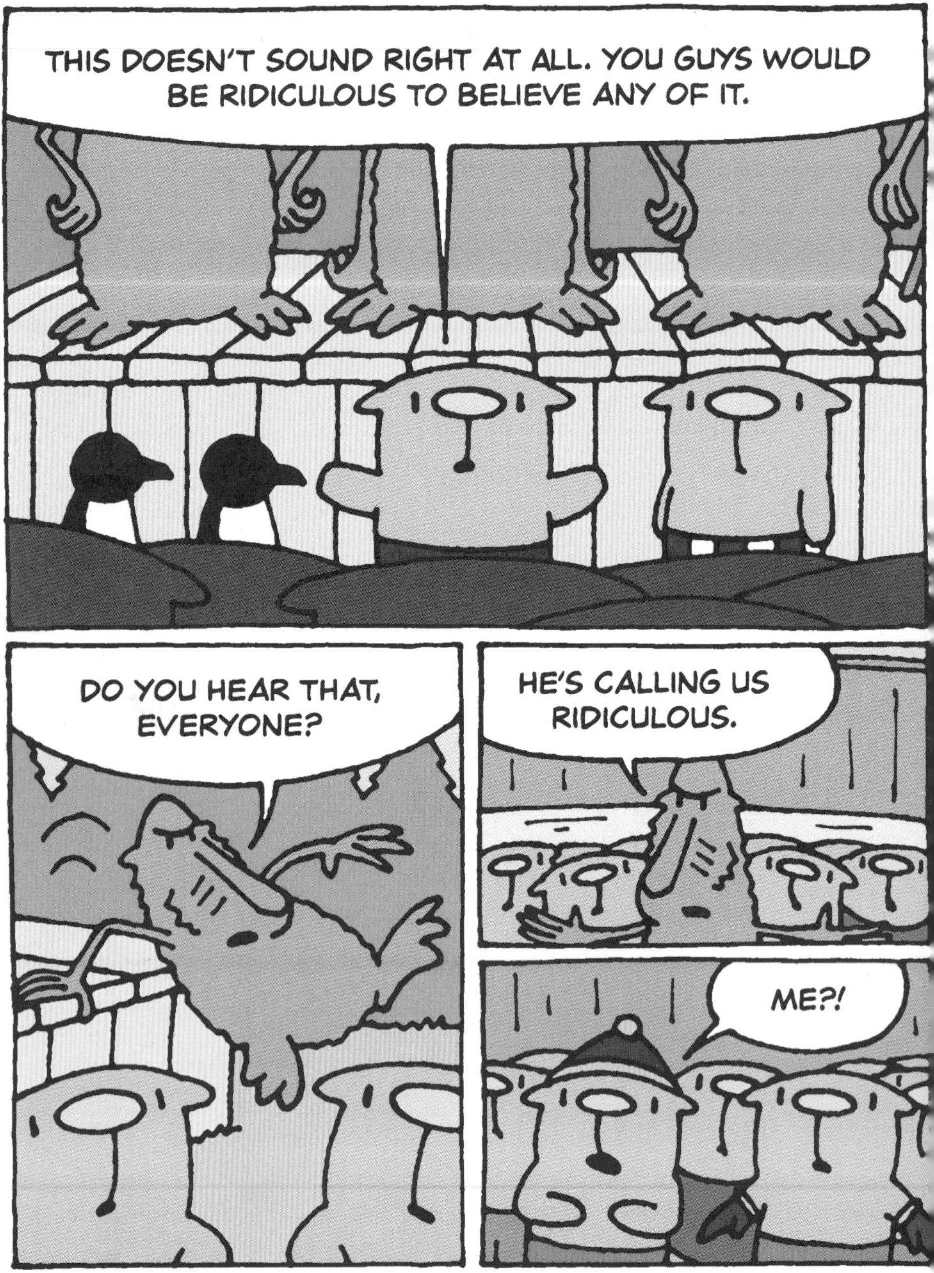
THIS DOESN'T SOUND RIGHT AT ALL. YOU GUYS WOULD BE RIDICULOUS TO BELIEVE ANY OF IT.
DO YOU HEAR THAT, EVERYONE?
HE'S CALLING US RIDICULOUS.
ME?!

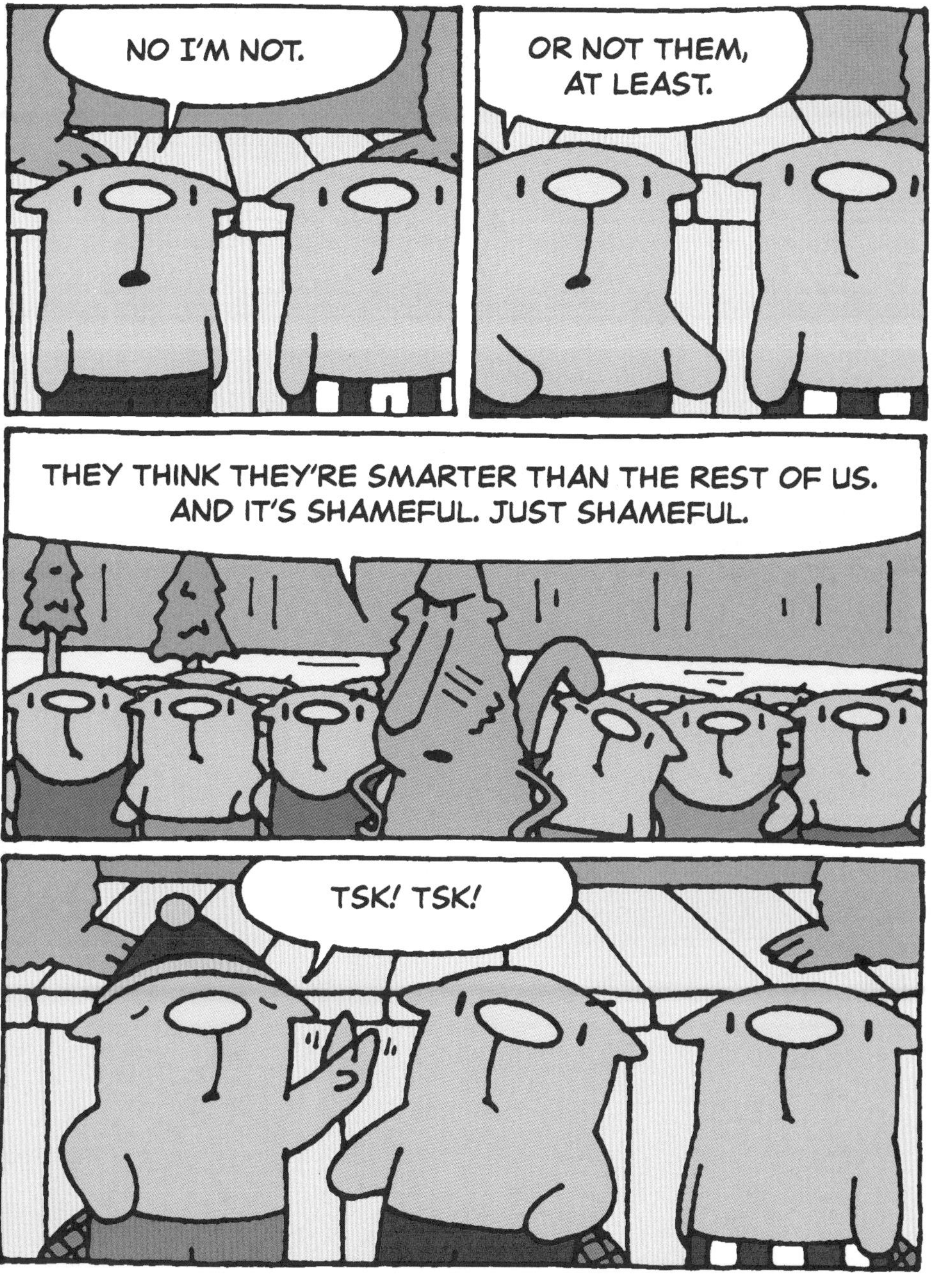
NO I'M NOT.
OR NOT THEM, AT LEAST.
THEY THINK THEY'RE SMARTER THAN THE REST OF US. AND IT'S SHAMEFUL. JUST SHAMEFUL.
TSK! TSK!

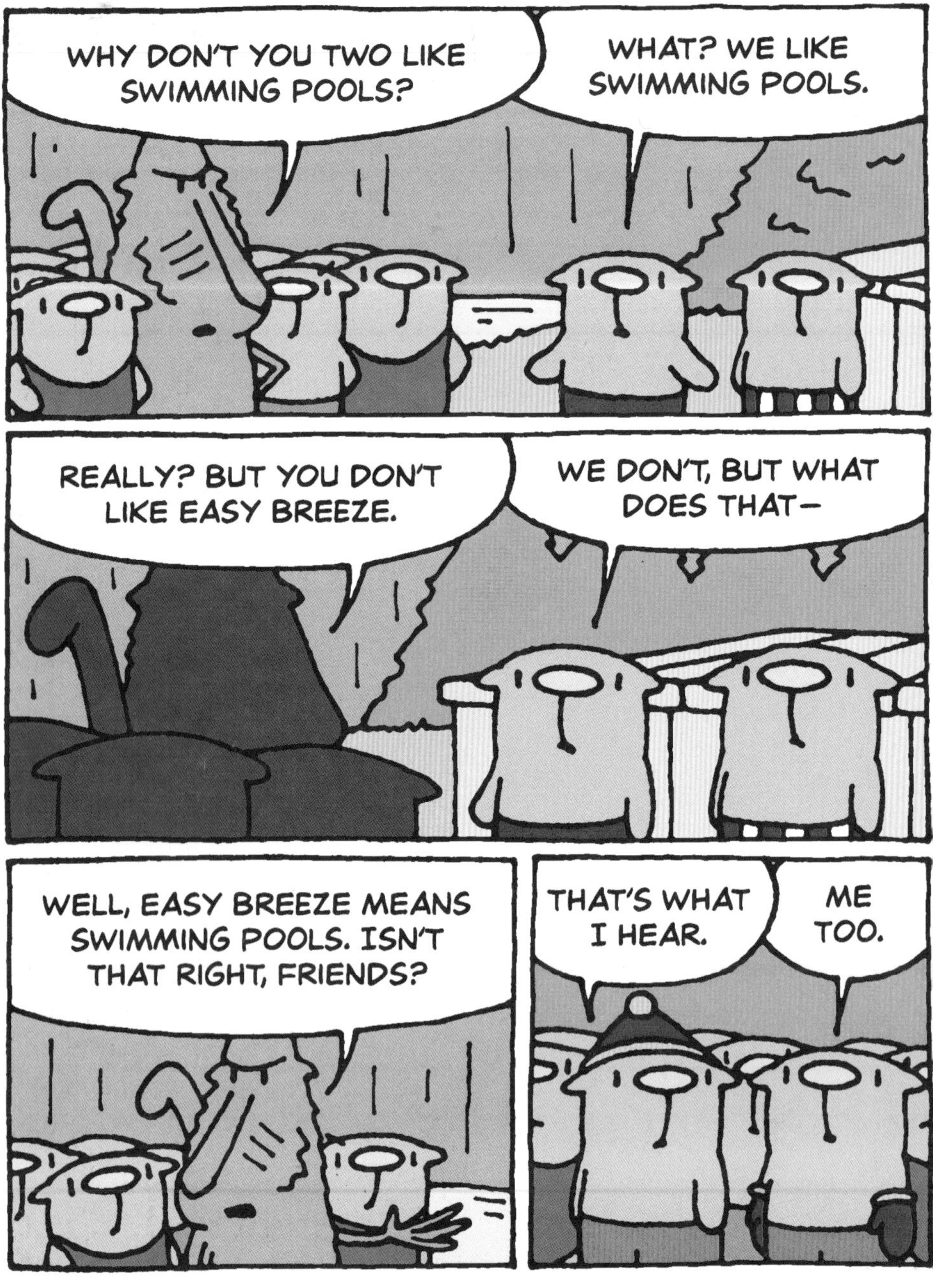
WHY DON'T YOU TWO LIKE SWIMMING POOLS?
WHAT? WE LIKE SWIMMING POOLS.
REALLY? BUT YOU DON'T LIKE EASY BREEZE.
WE DON'T, BUT WHAT DOES THAT—
WELL, EASY BREEZE MEANS SWIMMING POOLS. ISN'T THAT RIGHT, FRIENDS?
THAT'S WHAT I HEAR.
ME TOO.

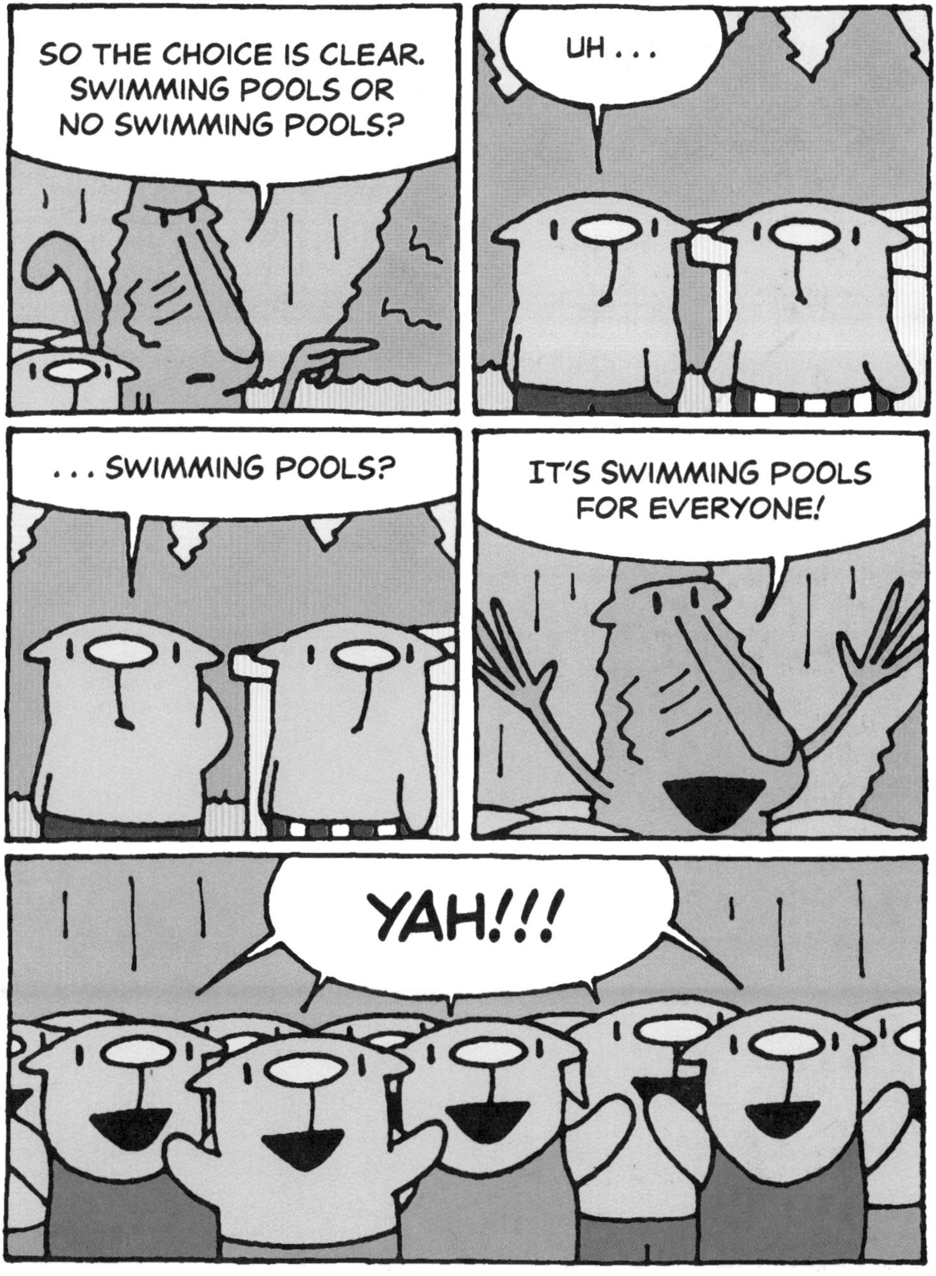
SO THE CHOICE IS CLEAR. SWIMMING POOLS OR NO SWIMMING POOLS?
UH . . .
. . . SWIMMING POOLS?
IT'S SWIMMING POOLS FOR EVERYONE!
YAH!!!

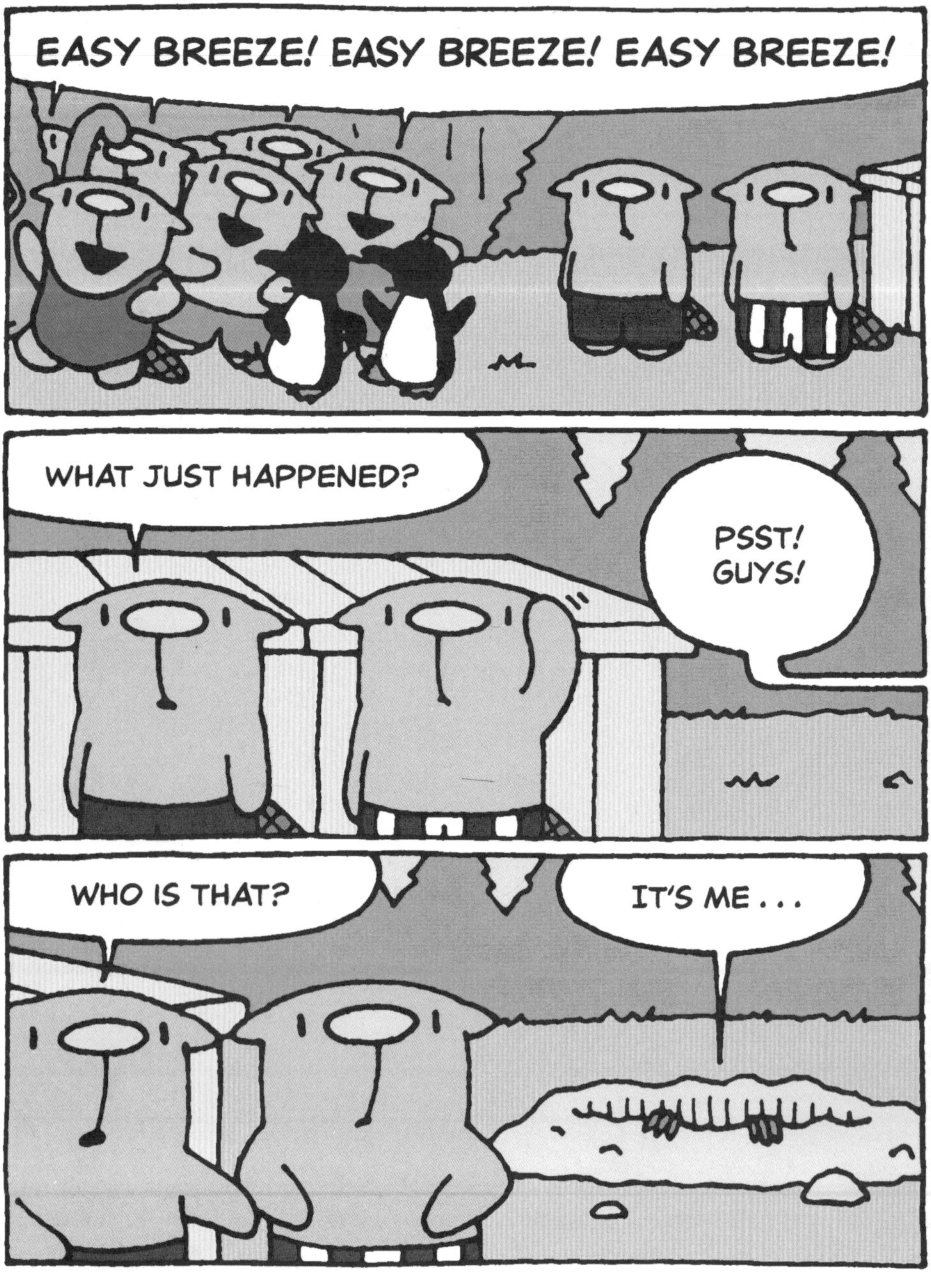
EASY BREEZE! EASY BREEZE! EASY BREEZE!
WHAT JUST HAPPENED?
PSST! GUYS!
WHO IS THAT?
IT'S ME . . .

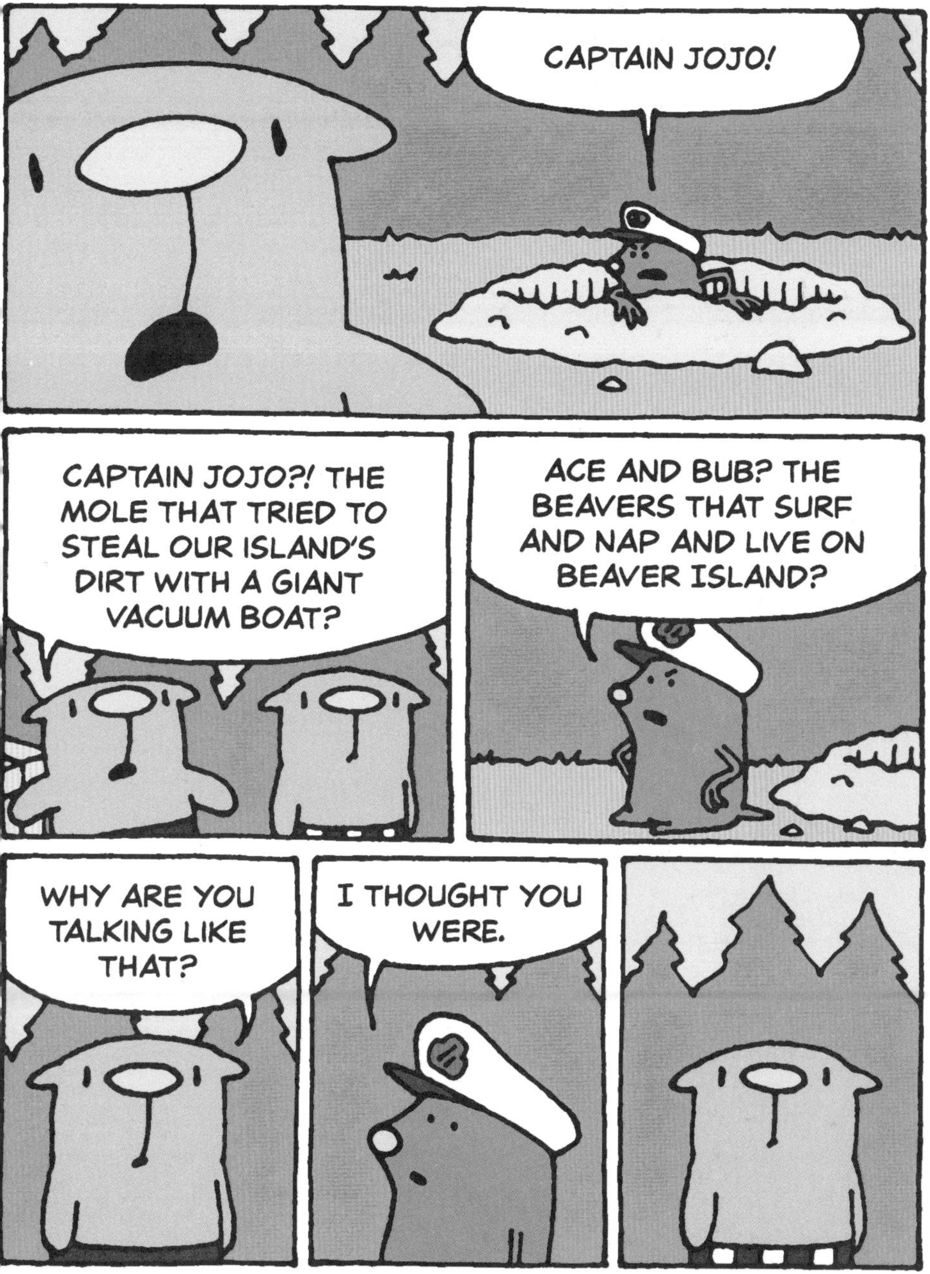
CAPTAIN JOJO!
CAPTAIN JOJO?! THE MOLE THAT TRIED TO STEAL OUR ISLAND'S DIRT WITH A GIANT VACUUM BOAT?
ACE AND BUB? THE BEAVERS THAT SURF AND NAP AND LIVE ON BEAVER ISLAND?
WHY ARE YOU TALKING LIKE THAT?
I THOUGHT YOU WERE.

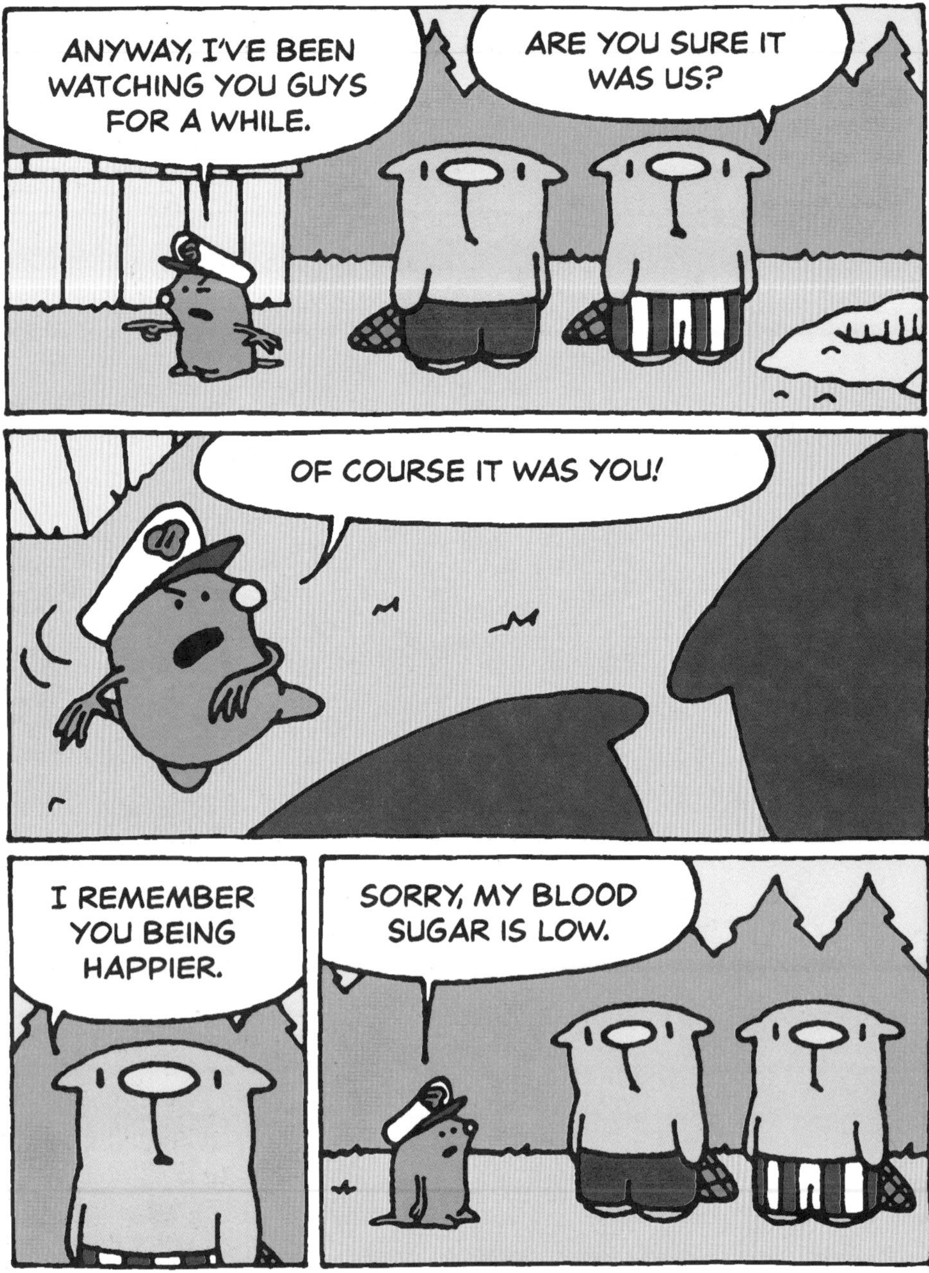
ANYWAY, I'VE BEEN WATCHING YOU GUYS FOR A WHILE.
ARE YOU SURE IT WAS US?
OF COURSE IT WAS YOU!
I REMEMBER YOU BEING HAPPIER.
SORRY, MY BLOOD SUGAR IS LOW.

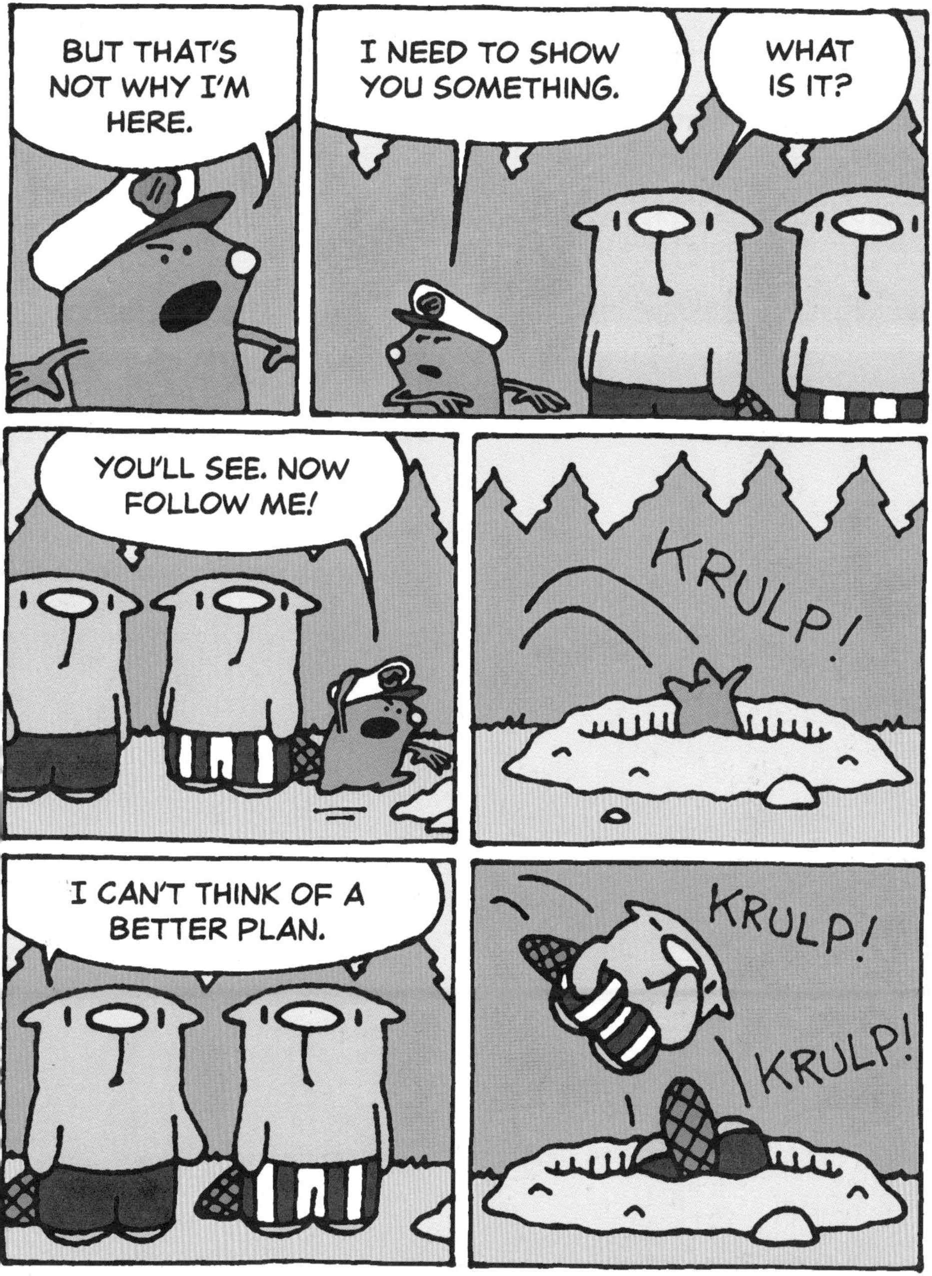
BUT THAT'S NOT WHY I'M HERE.
I NEED TO SHOW YOU SOMETHING.
WHAT IS IT?
YOU'LL SEE. NOW FOLLOW ME!
KRULP!
I CAN'T THINK OF A BETTER PLAN.
KRULP!
KRULP!

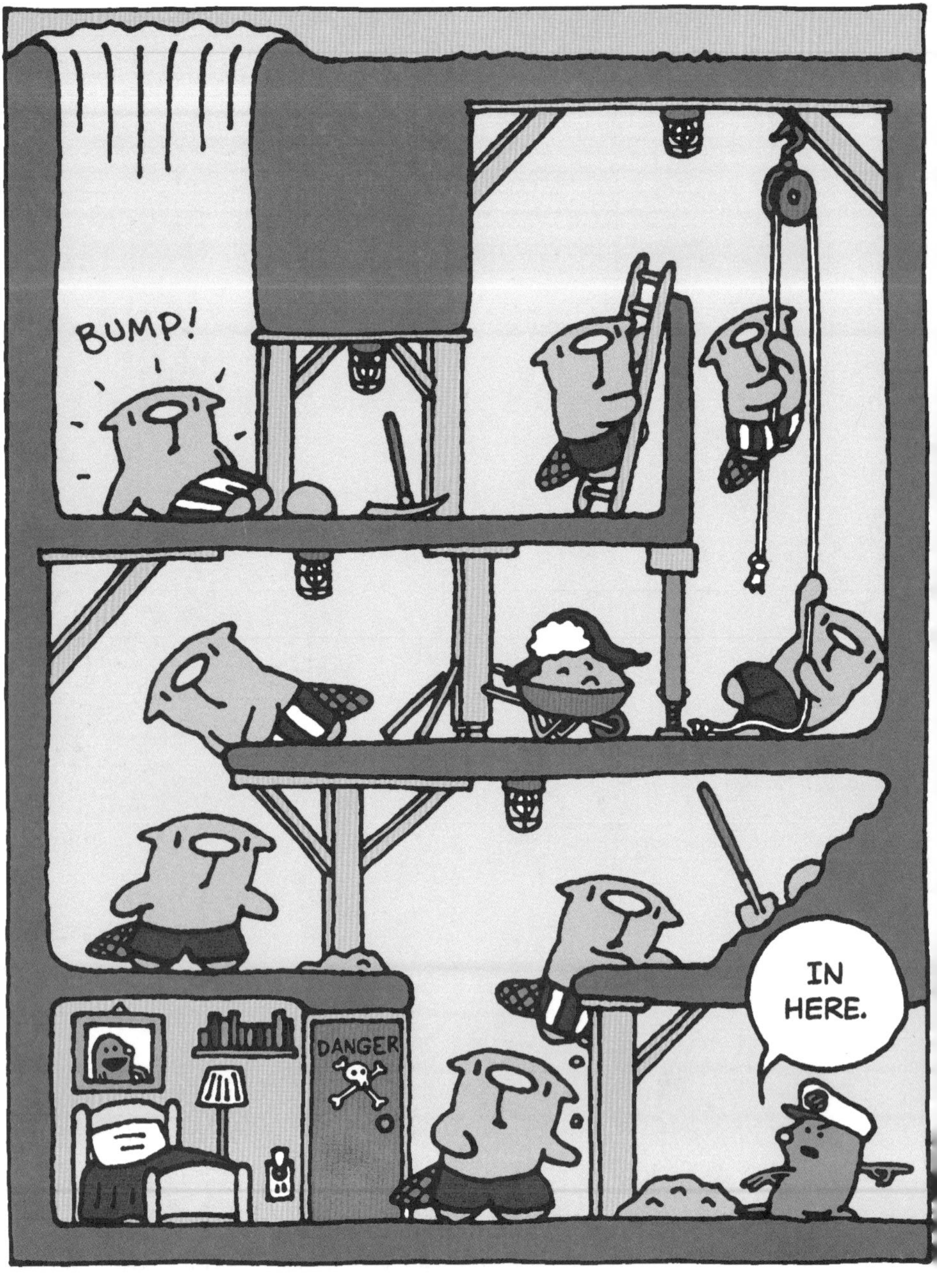
BUMP!
DANGER
IN HERE.

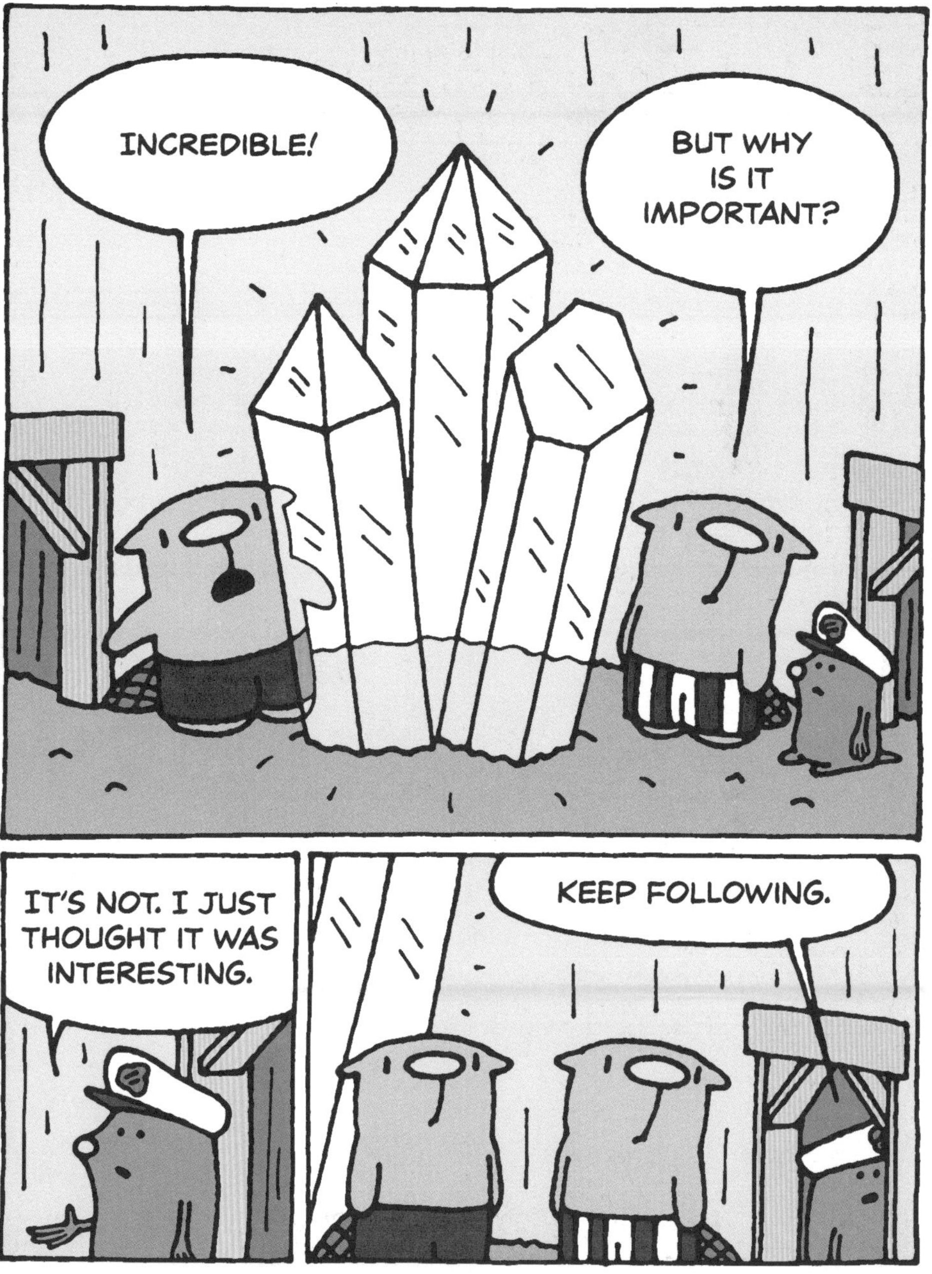
INCREDIBLE!
BUT WHY IS IT IMPORTANT?
IT'S NOT. I JUST THOUGHT IT WAS INTERESTING.
KEEP FOLLOWING.

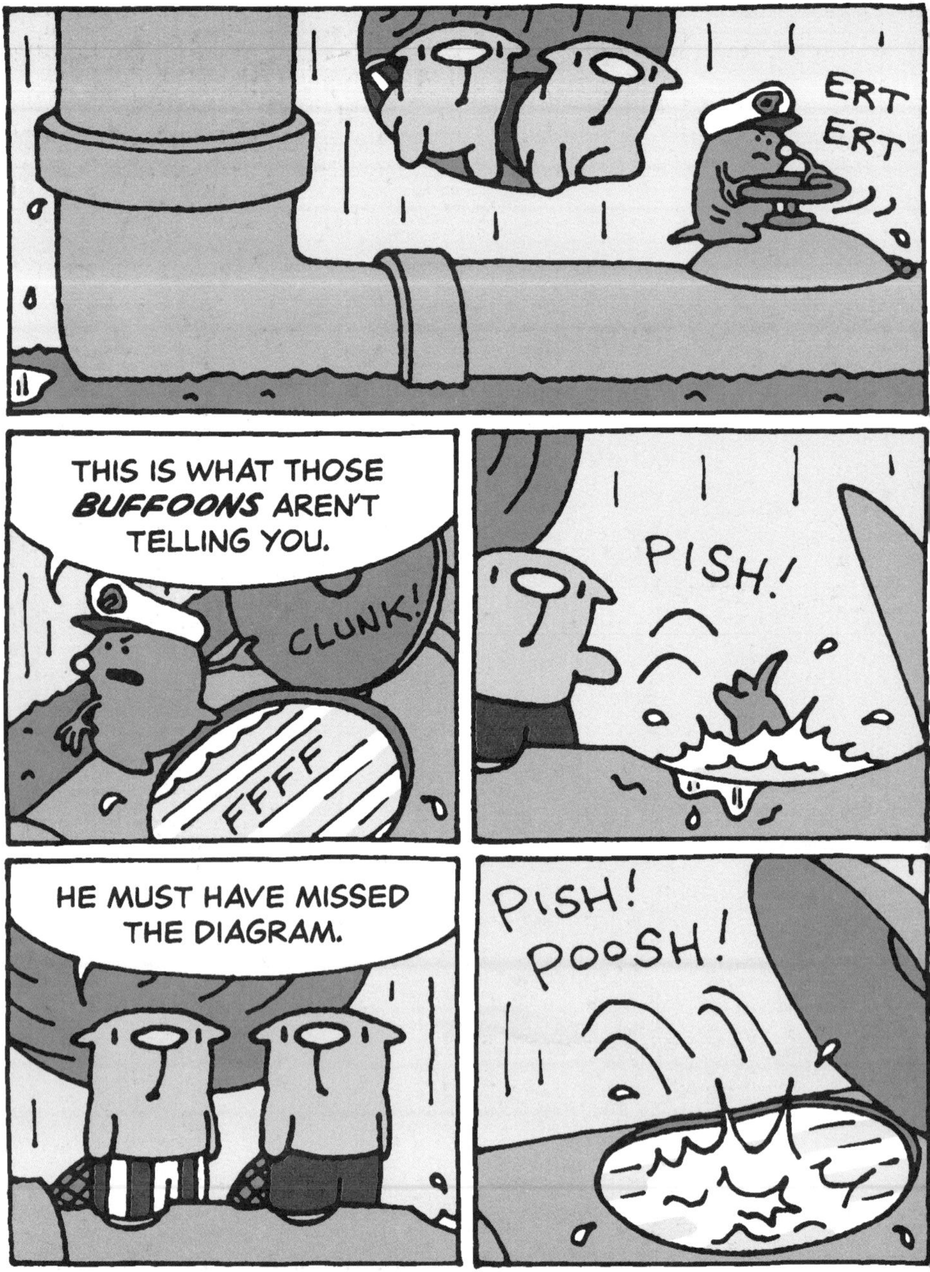
ERT
ERT
THIS IS WHAT THOSE *BUFFOONS* AREN'T TELLING YOU.
CLUNK!
FFFF
PISH!
HE MUST HAVE MISSED THE DIAGRAM.
PISH!
POOSH!

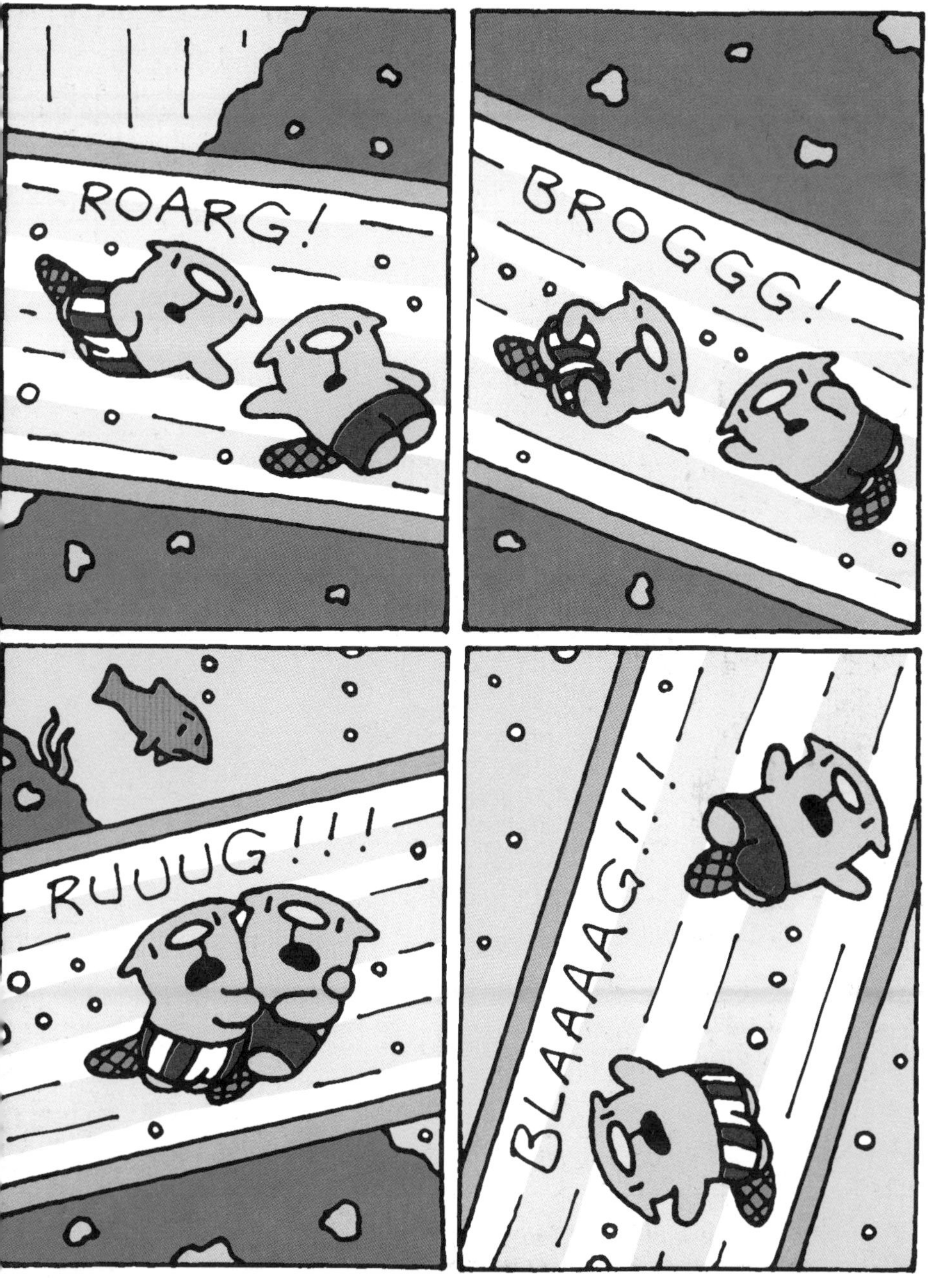
ROARG!
BROGGG!
RUUUG!!!
BLAAAG!!!

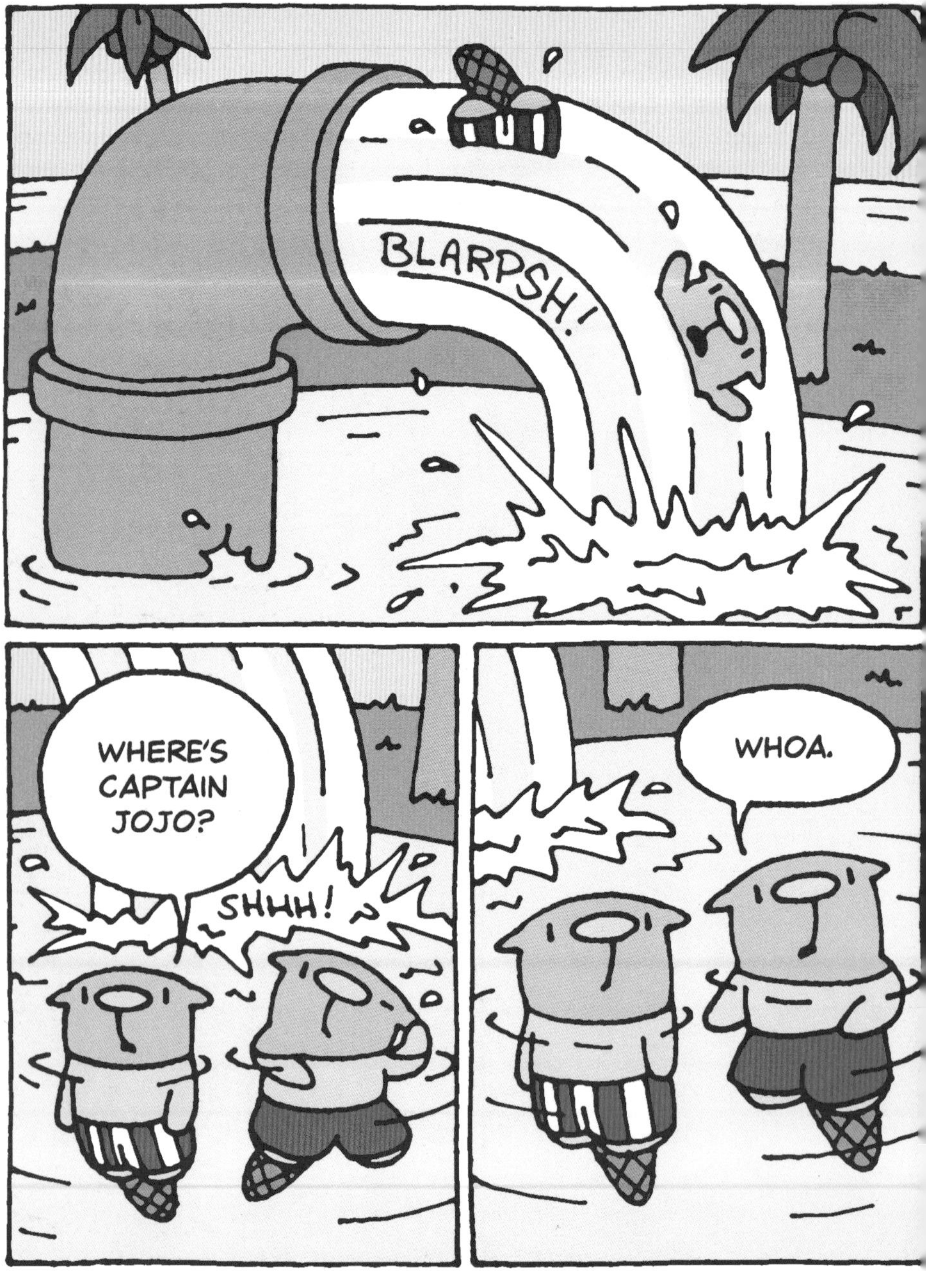
BLARPSH!
WHERE'S CAPTAIN JOJO?
SHHH!
WHOA.

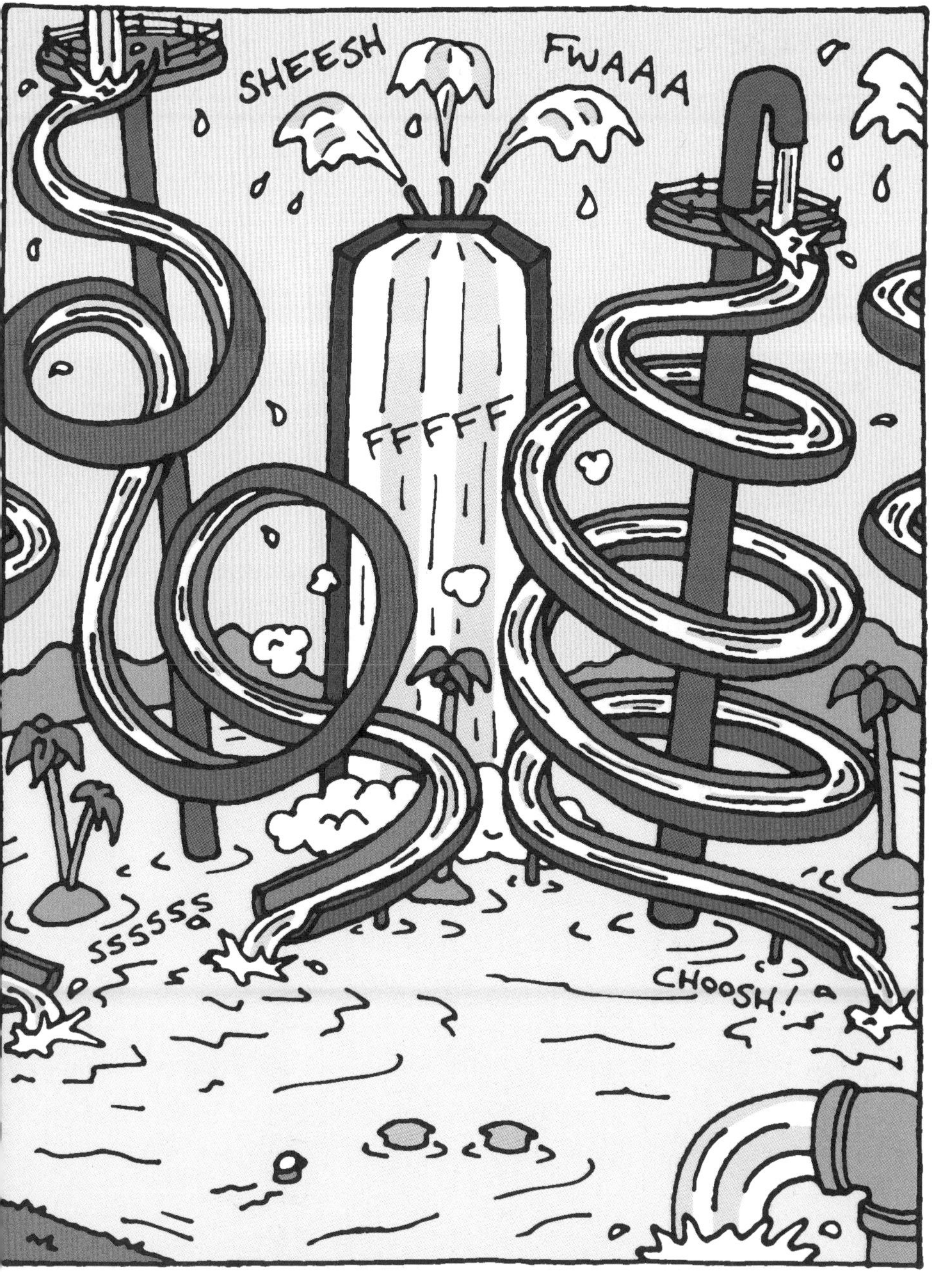
SHEESH
FWAAAA
FFFFF
SSSSSS
CHOOSH!

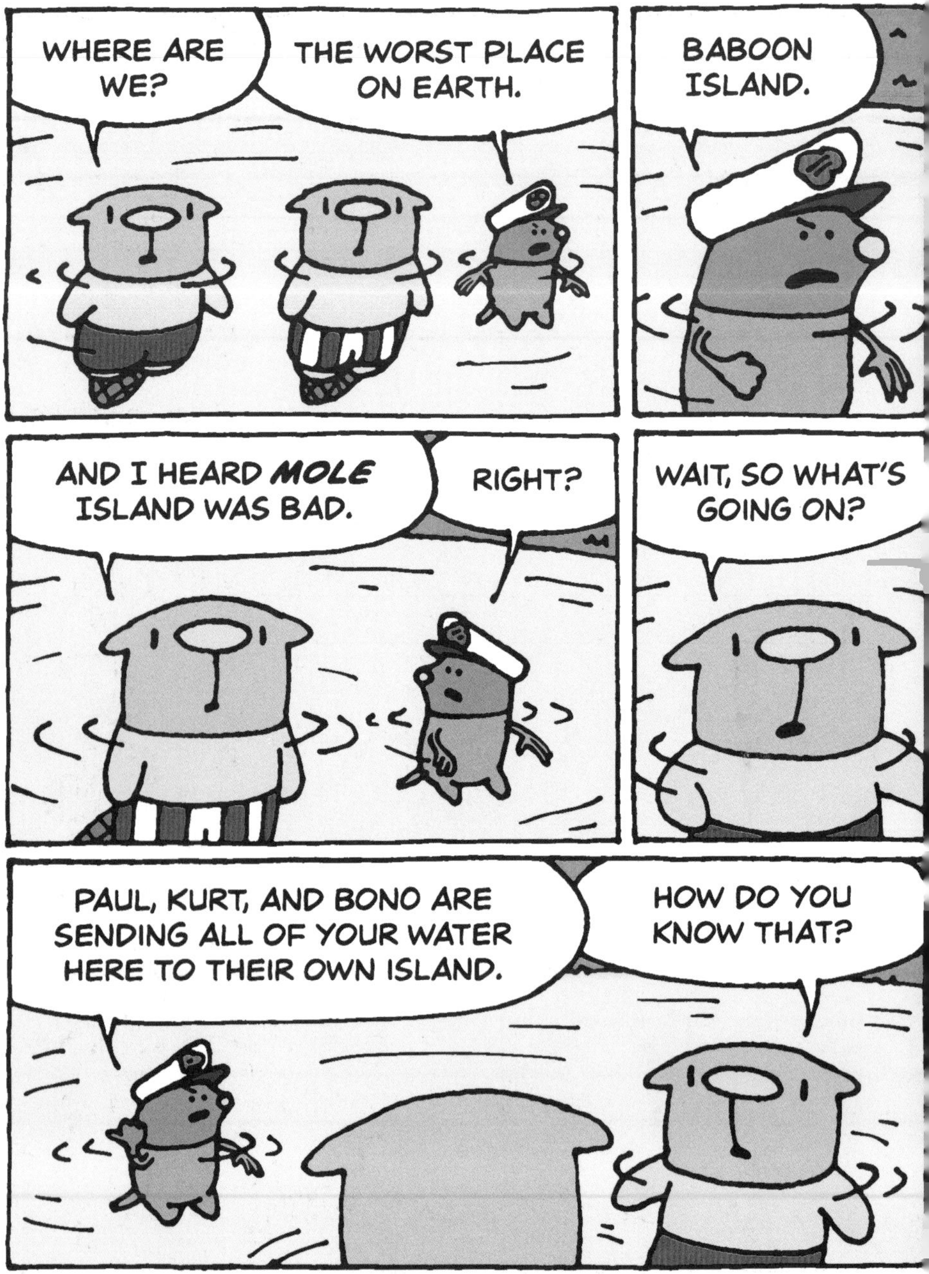
WHERE ARE WE?
THE WORST PLACE ON EARTH.
BABOON ISLAND.
AND I HEARD *MOLE* ISLAND WAS BAD.
RIGHT?
WAIT, SO WHAT'S GOING ON?
PAUL, KURT, AND BONO ARE SENDING ALL OF YOUR WATER HERE TO THEIR OWN ISLAND.
HOW DO YOU KNOW THAT?

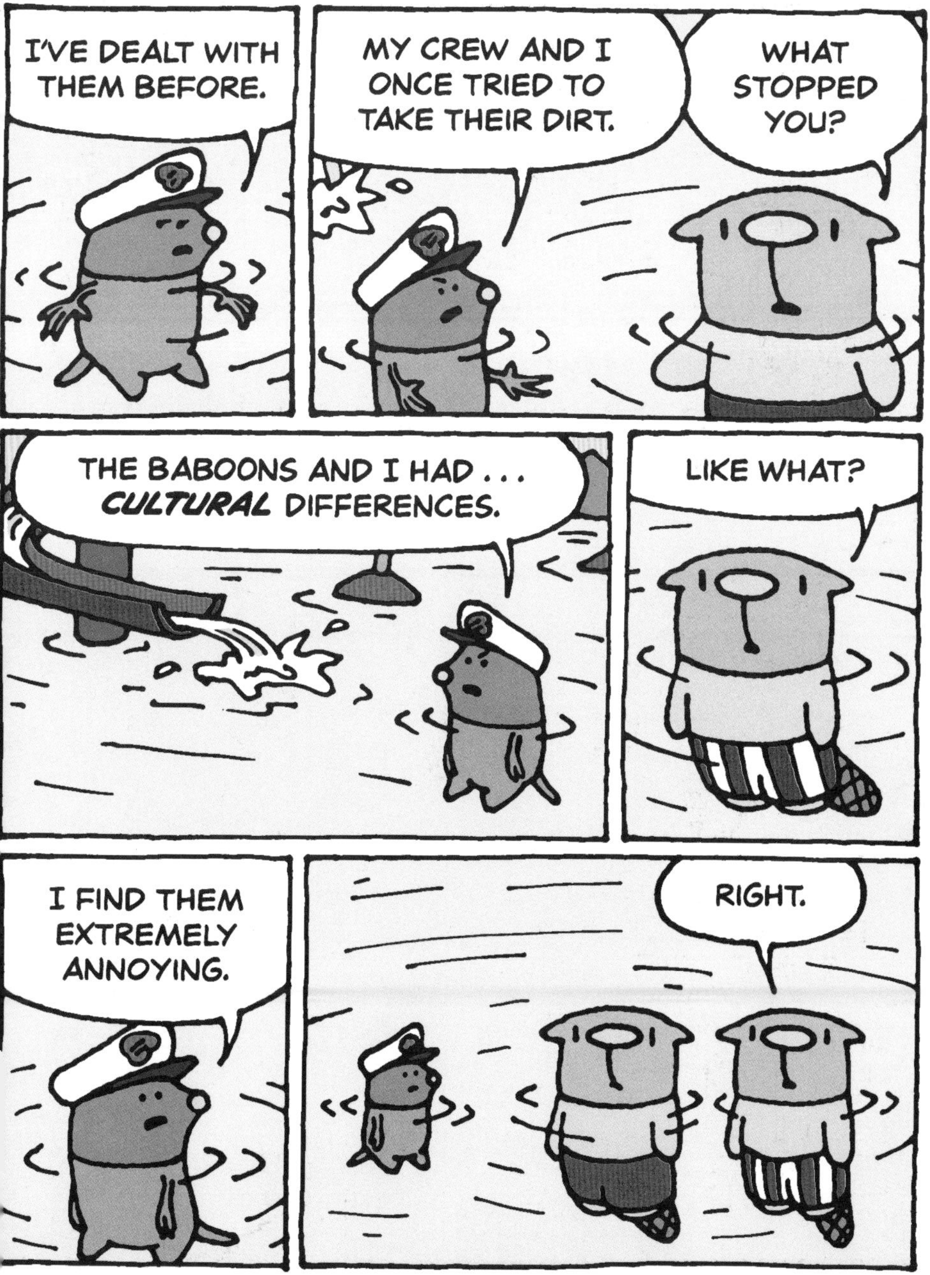
I'VE DEALT WITH THEM BEFORE.
MY CREW AND I ONCE TRIED TO TAKE THEIR DIRT.
WHAT STOPPED YOU?
THE BABOONS AND I HAD . . . *CULTURAL* DIFFERENCES.
LIKE WHAT?
I FIND THEM EXTREMELY ANNOYING.
RIGHT.

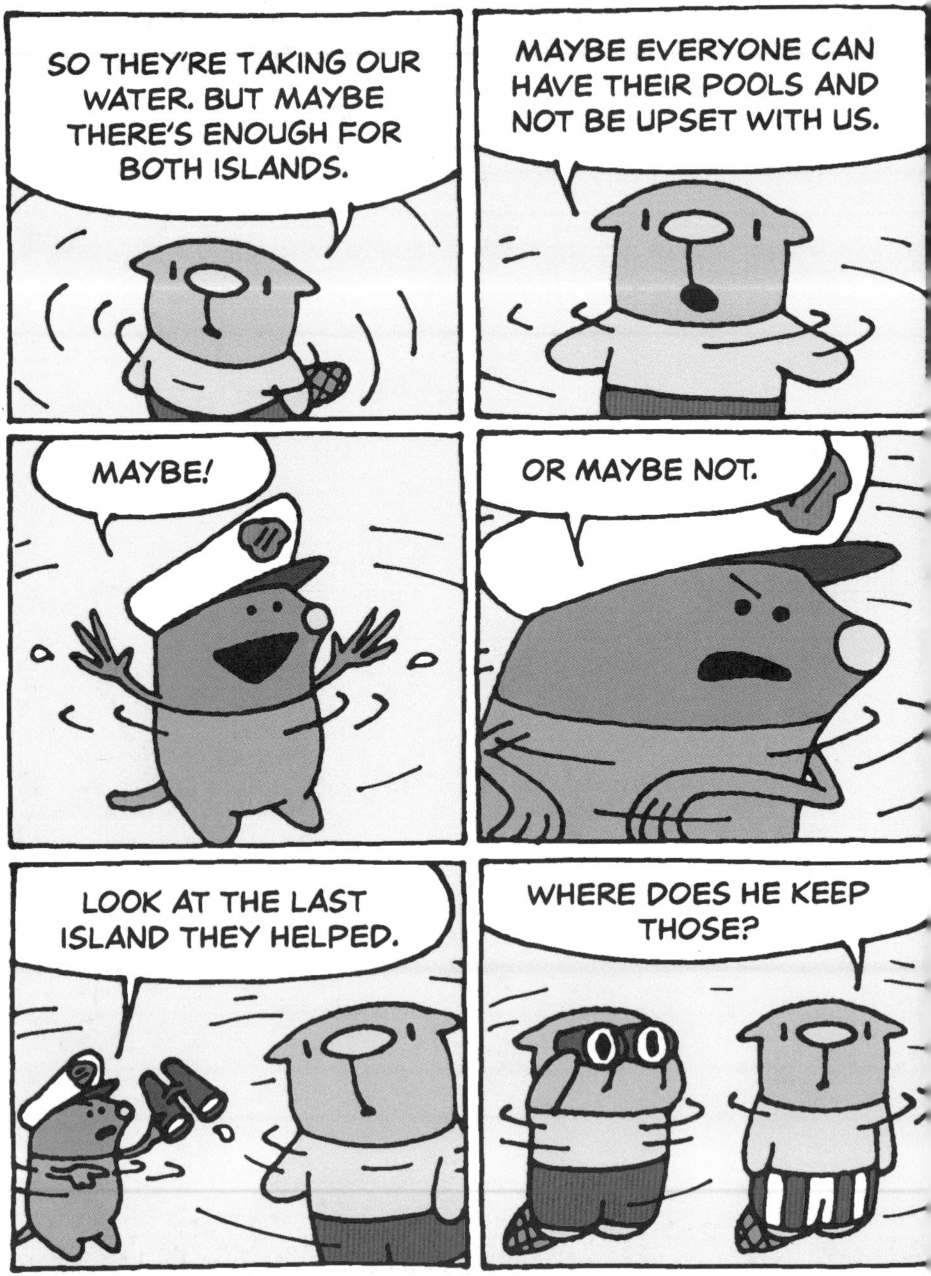
SO THEY'RE TAKING OUR WATER. BUT MAYBE THERE'S ENOUGH FOR BOTH ISLANDS.
MAYBE EVERYONE CAN HAVE THEIR POOLS AND NOT BE UPSET WITH US.
MAYBE!
OR MAYBE NOT.
LOOK AT THE LAST ISLAND THEY HELPED.
WHERE DOES HE KEEP THOSE?

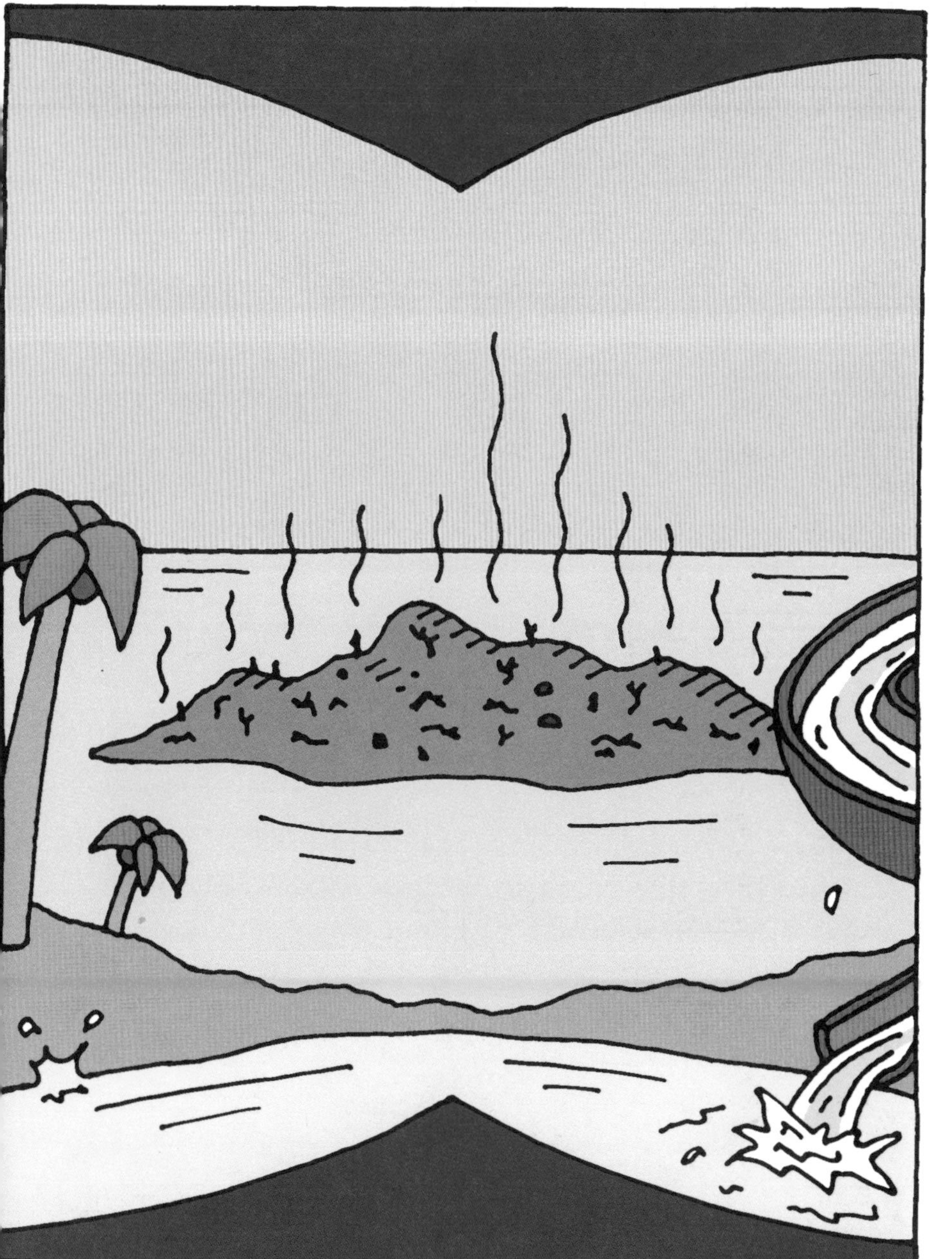

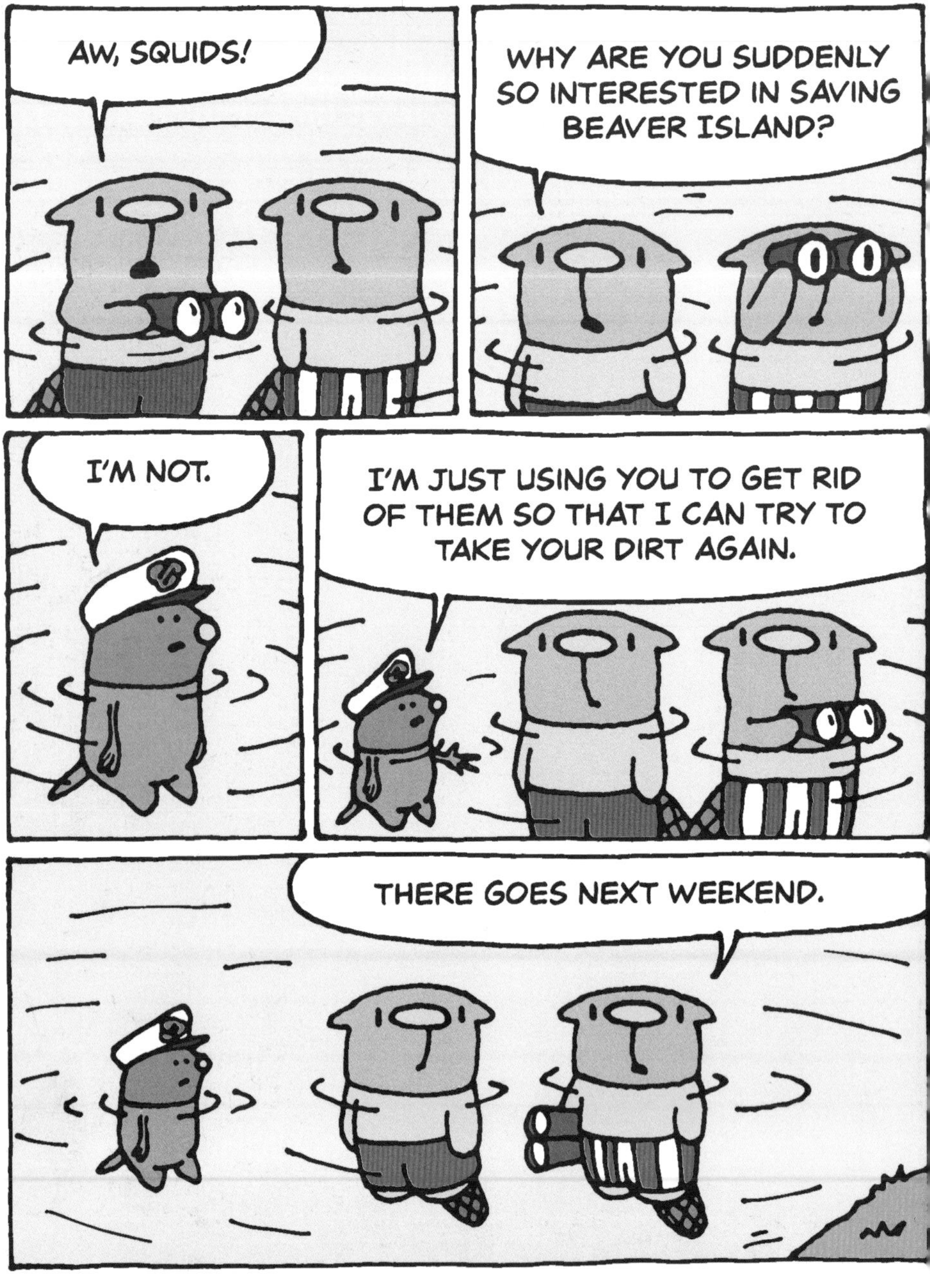
AW, SQUIDS!
WHY ARE YOU SUDDENLY SO INTERESTED IN SAVING BEAVER ISLAND?
I'M NOT.
I'M JUST USING YOU TO GET RID OF THEM SO THAT I CAN TRY TO TAKE YOUR DIRT AGAIN.
THERE GOES NEXT WEEKEND.

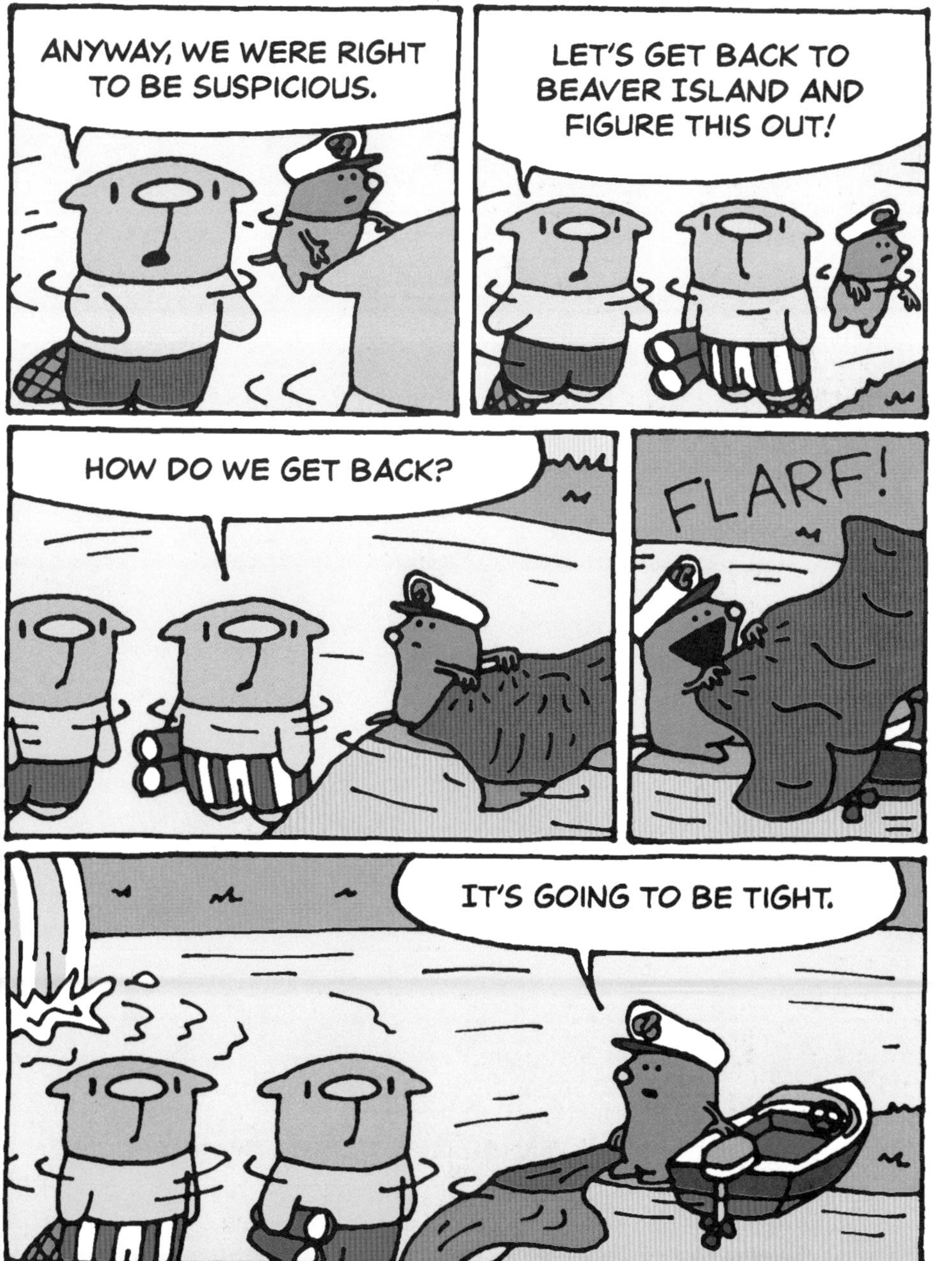
ANYWAY, WE WERE RIGHT TO BE SUSPICIOUS.
LET'S GET BACK TO BEAVER ISLAND AND FIGURE THIS OUT!
HOW DO WE GET BACK?
FLARF!
IT'S GOING TO BE TIGHT.

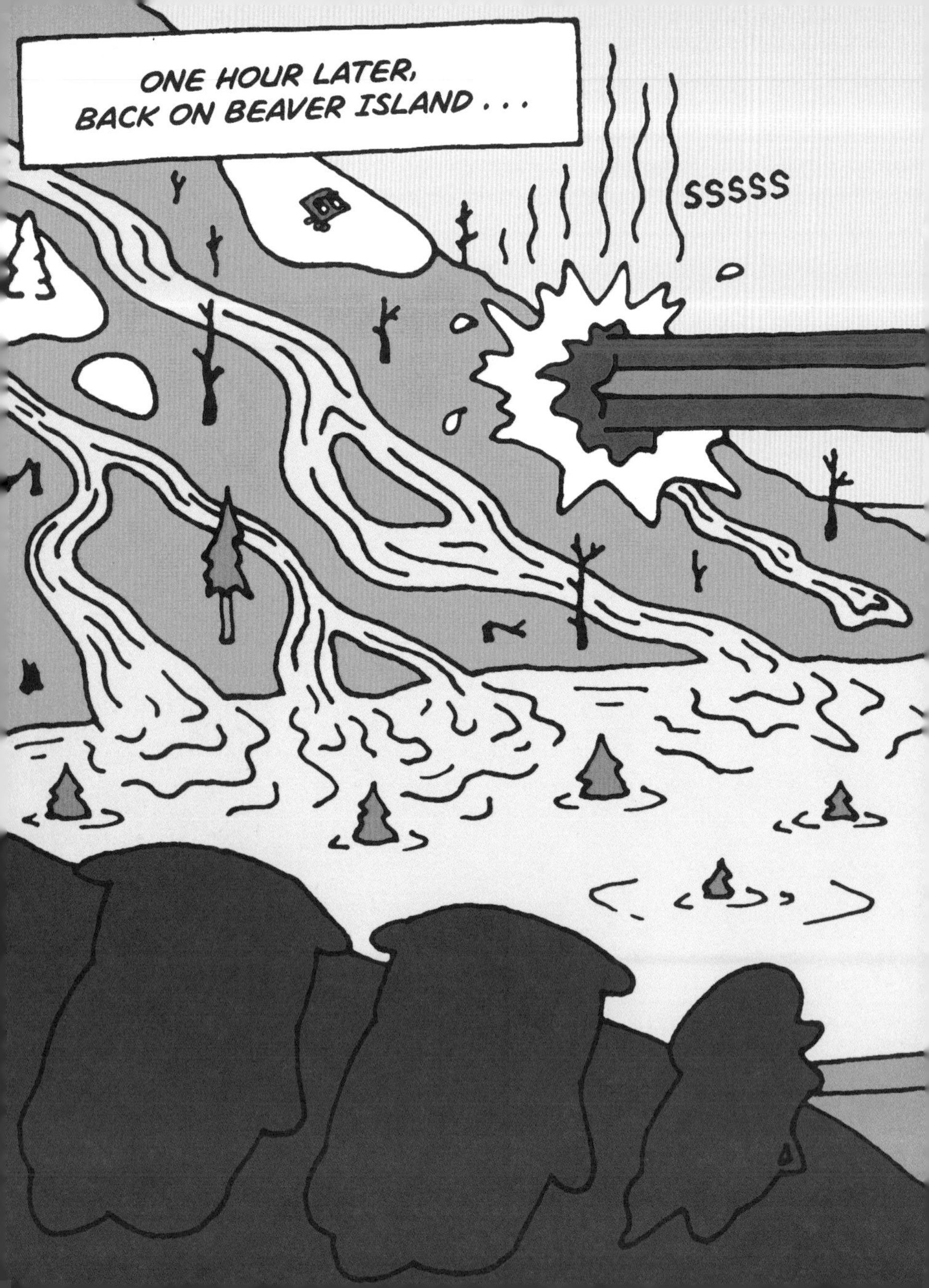
ONE HOUR LATER,
BACK ON BEAVER ISLAND . . .
SSSSS

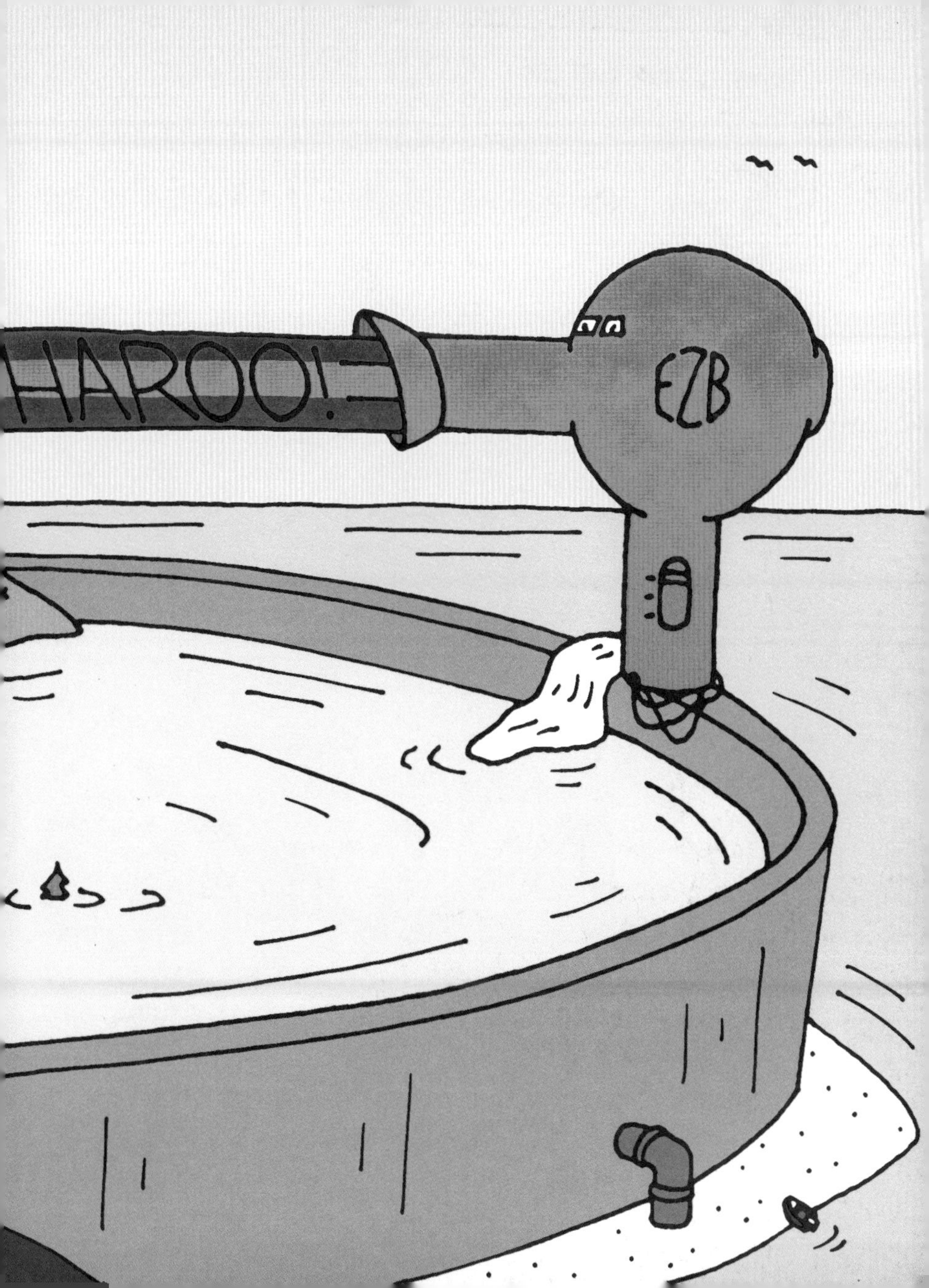
HAROO!
EZB

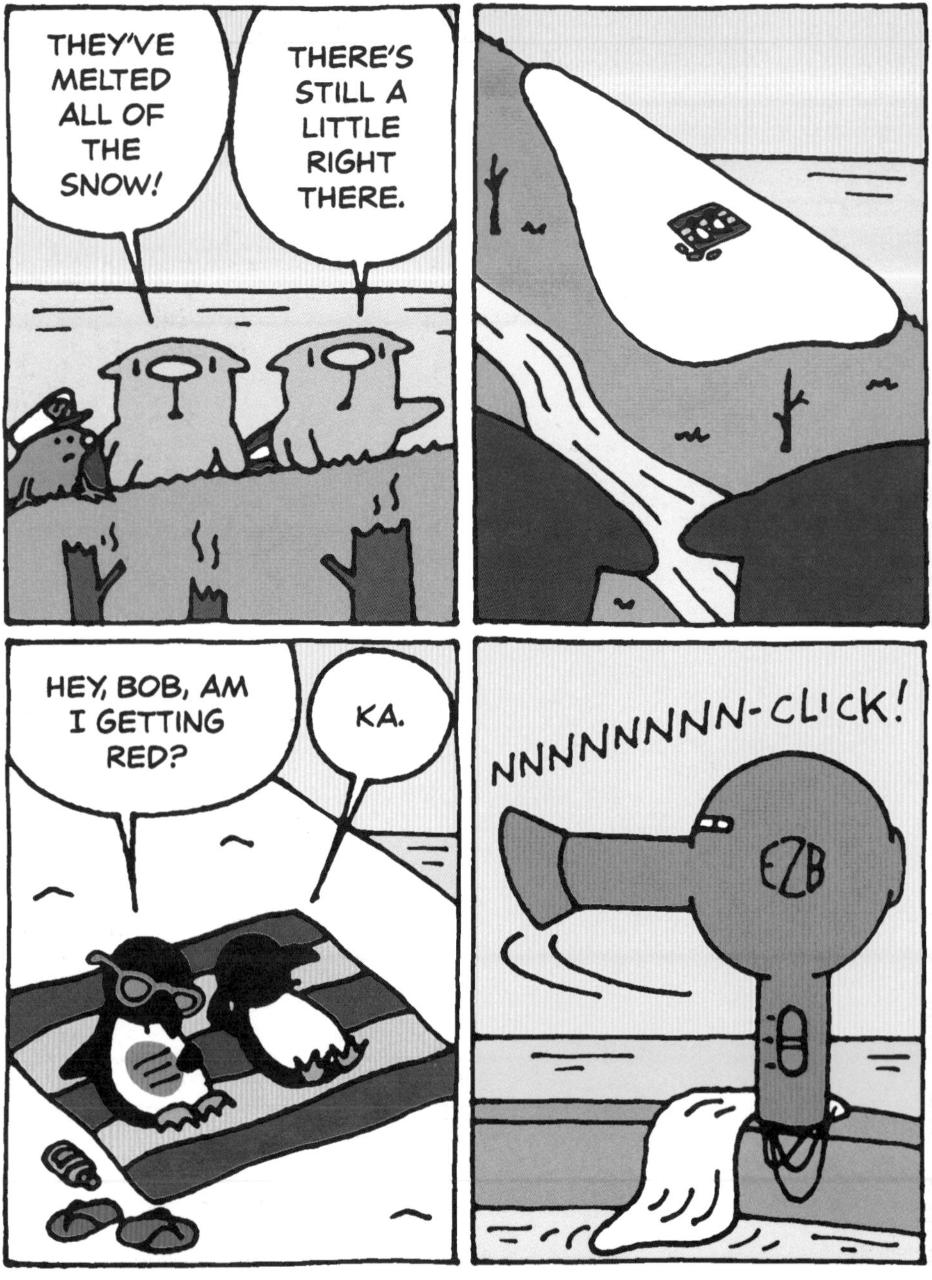
THEY'VE MELTED ALL OF THE SNOW!
THERE'S STILL A LITTLE RIGHT THERE.
HEY, BOB, AM I GETTING RED?
KA.
NNNNNNNNN-CLICK!
EZB

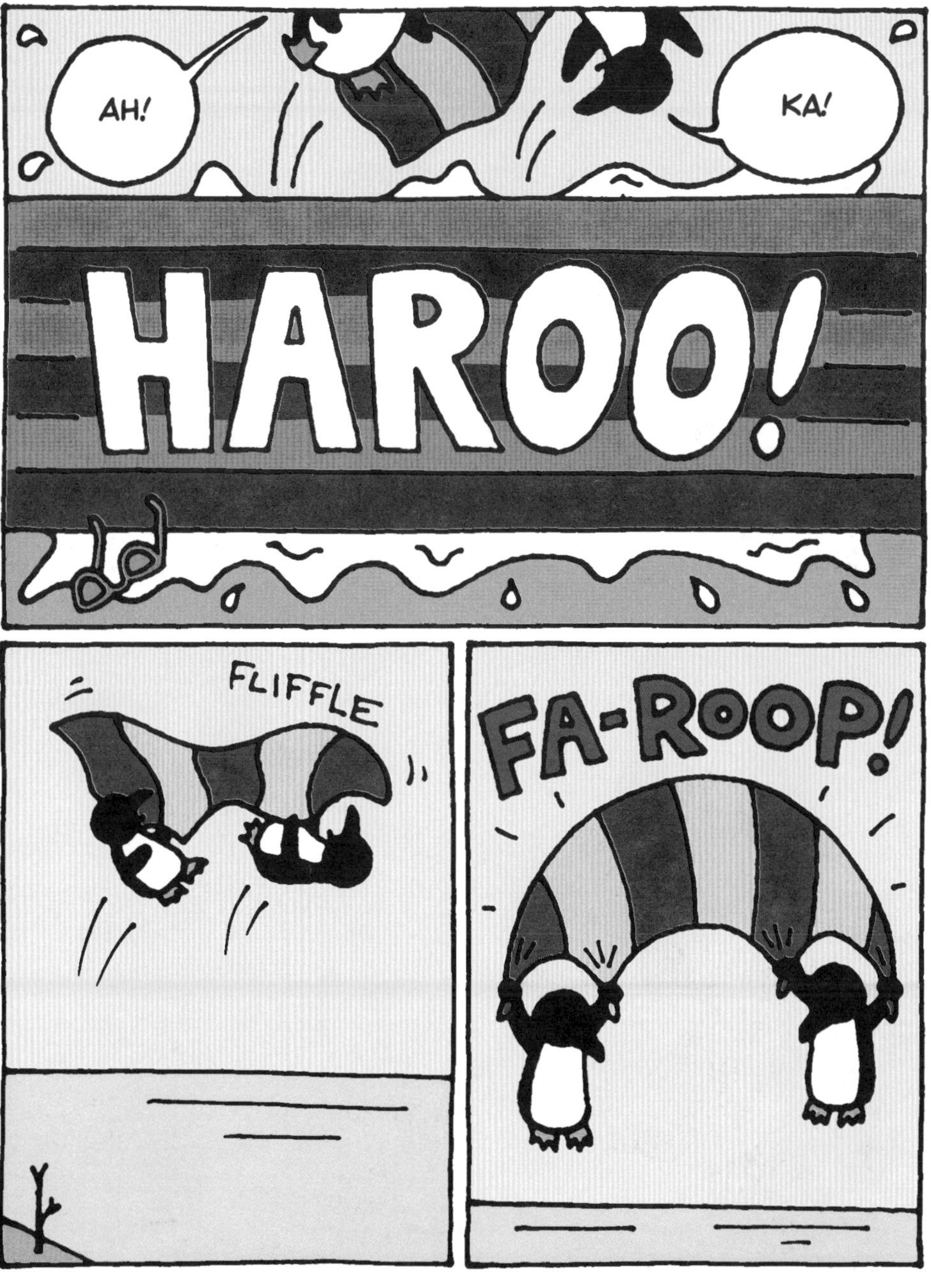
AH!
KA!
HAROO!
FLIFFLE
FA-ROOP!

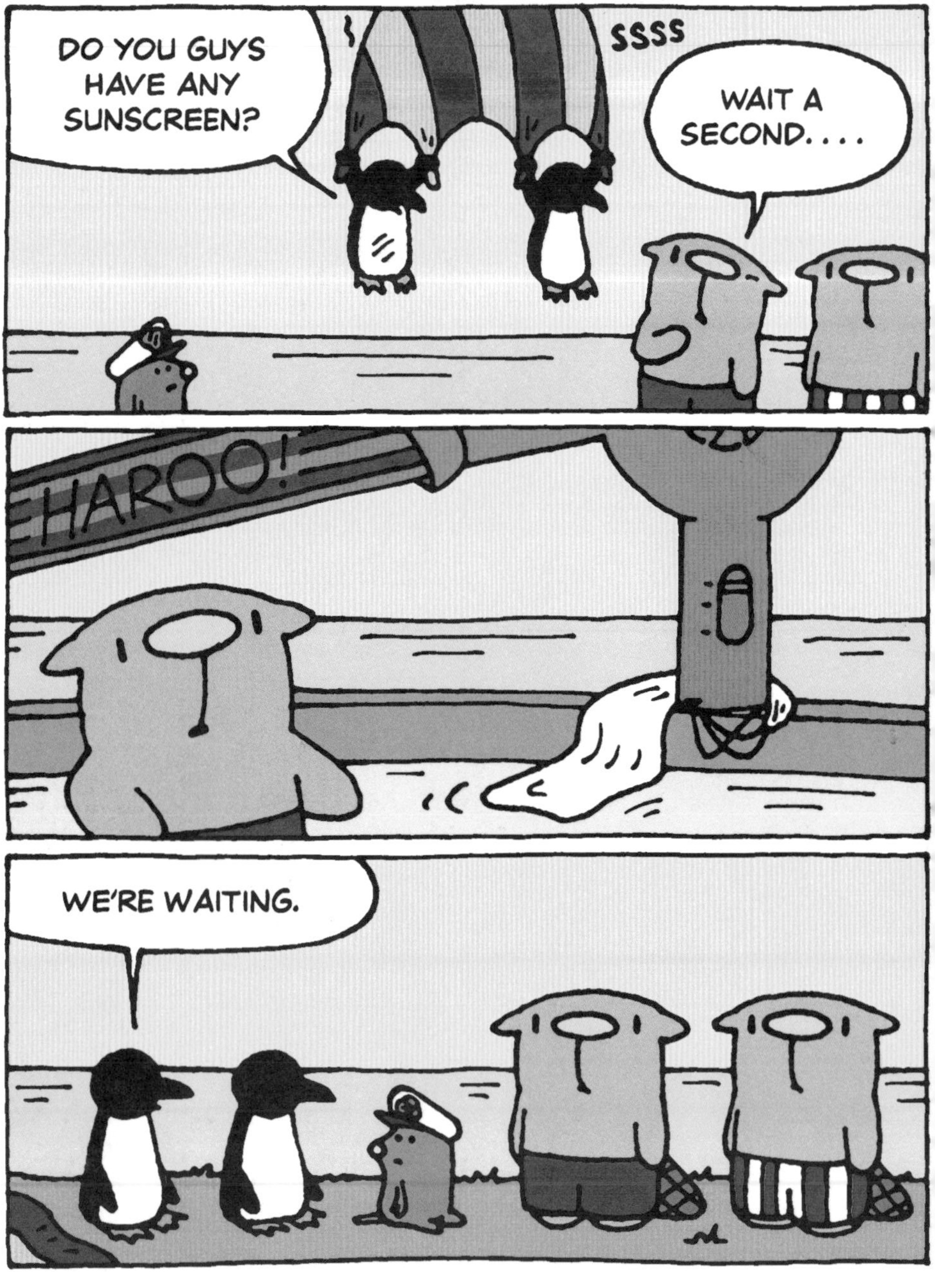
DO YOU GUYS HAVE ANY SUNSCREEN?
SSSS
WAIT A SECOND. . . .
HAROO!
WE'RE WAITING.

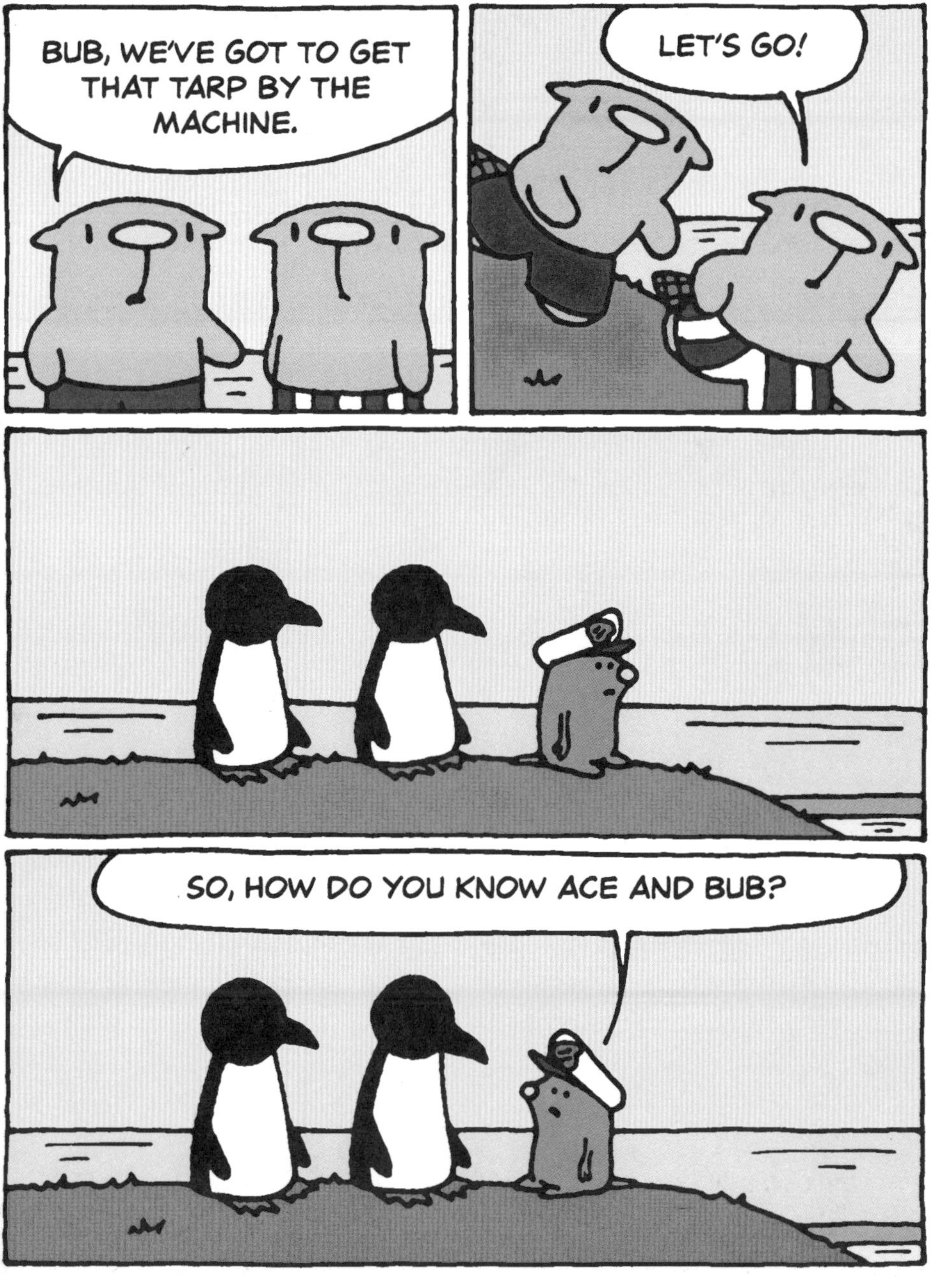
BUB, WE'VE GOT TO GET THAT TARP BY THE MACHINE.
LET'S GO!
SO, HOW DO YOU KNOW ACE AND BUB?

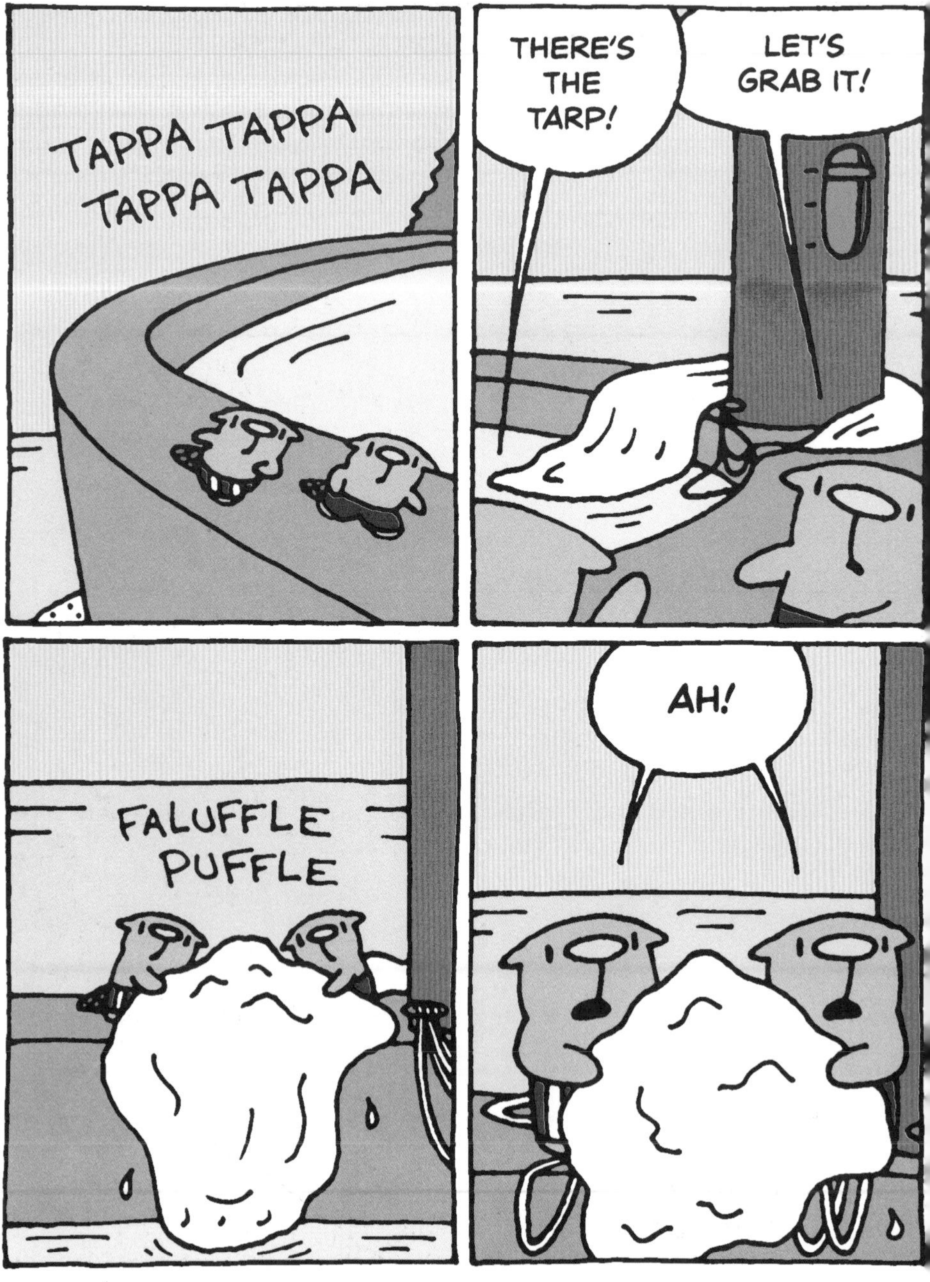
TAPPA TAPPA
TAPPA TAPPA
THERE'S THE TARP!
LET'S GRAB IT!
FALUFFLE
PUFFLE
AH!

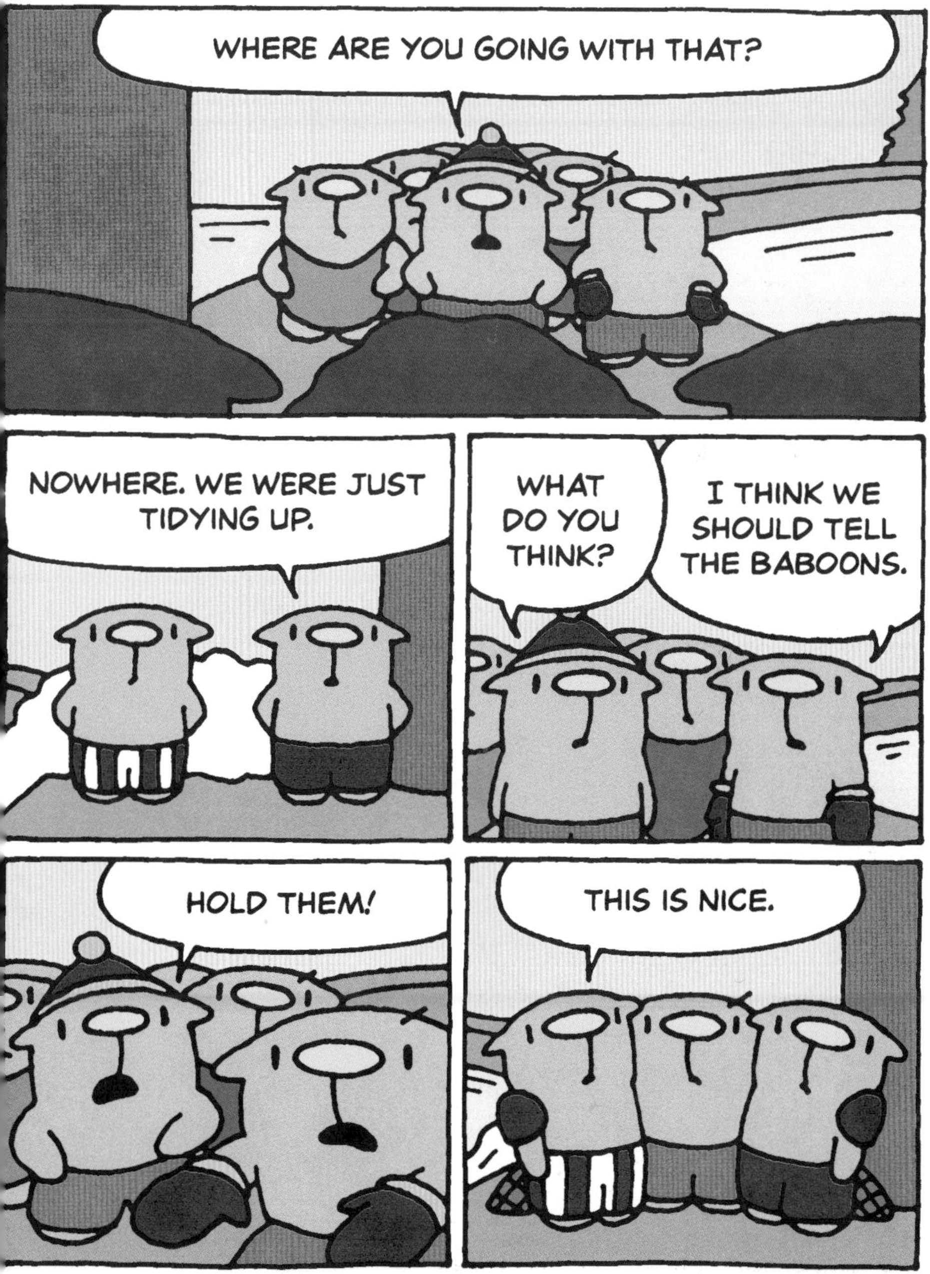
WHERE ARE YOU GOING WITH THAT?
NOWHERE. WE WERE JUST TIDYING UP.
WHAT DO YOU THINK?
I THINK WE SHOULD TELL THE BABOONS.
HOLD THEM!
THIS IS NICE.

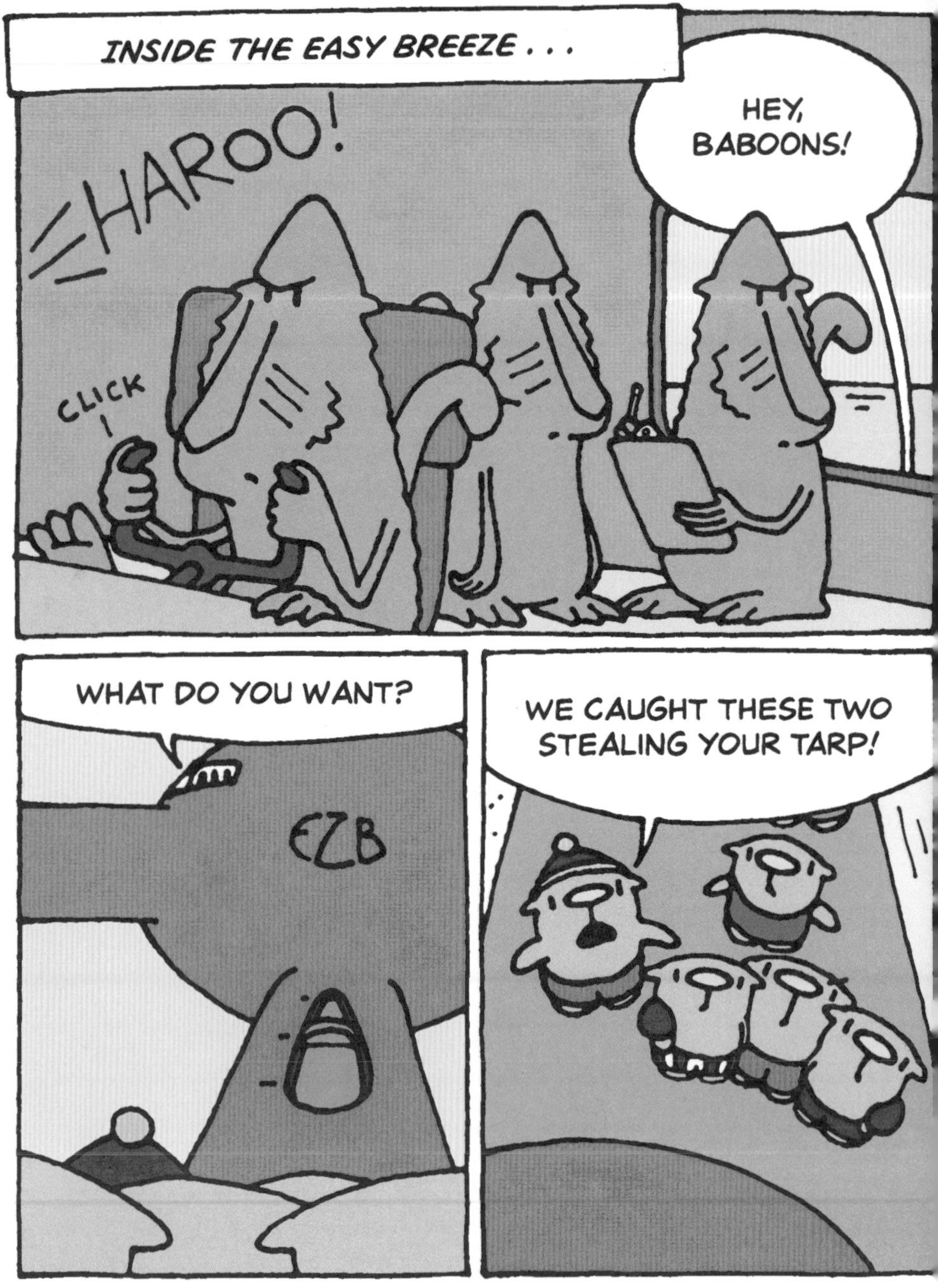
INSIDE THE EASY BREEZE . . .
HAROO!
HEY, BABOONS!
CLICK
WHAT DO YOU WANT?
EZB
WE CAUGHT THESE TWO STEALING YOUR TARP!

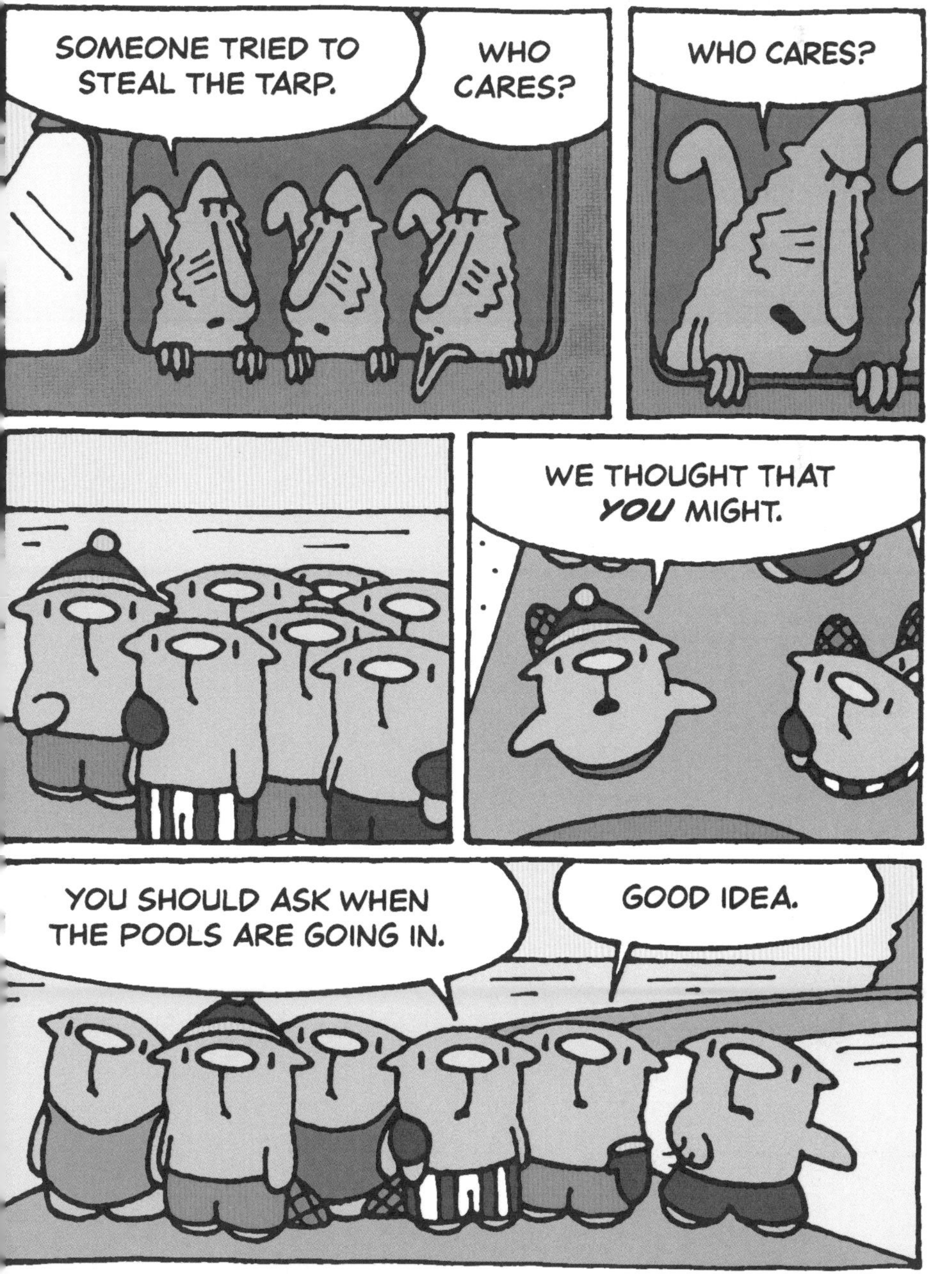
SOMEONE TRIED TO STEAL THE TARP.
WHO CARES?
WHO CARES?
WE THOUGHT THAT *YOU* MIGHT.
YOU SHOULD ASK WHEN THE POOLS ARE GOING IN.
GOOD IDEA.

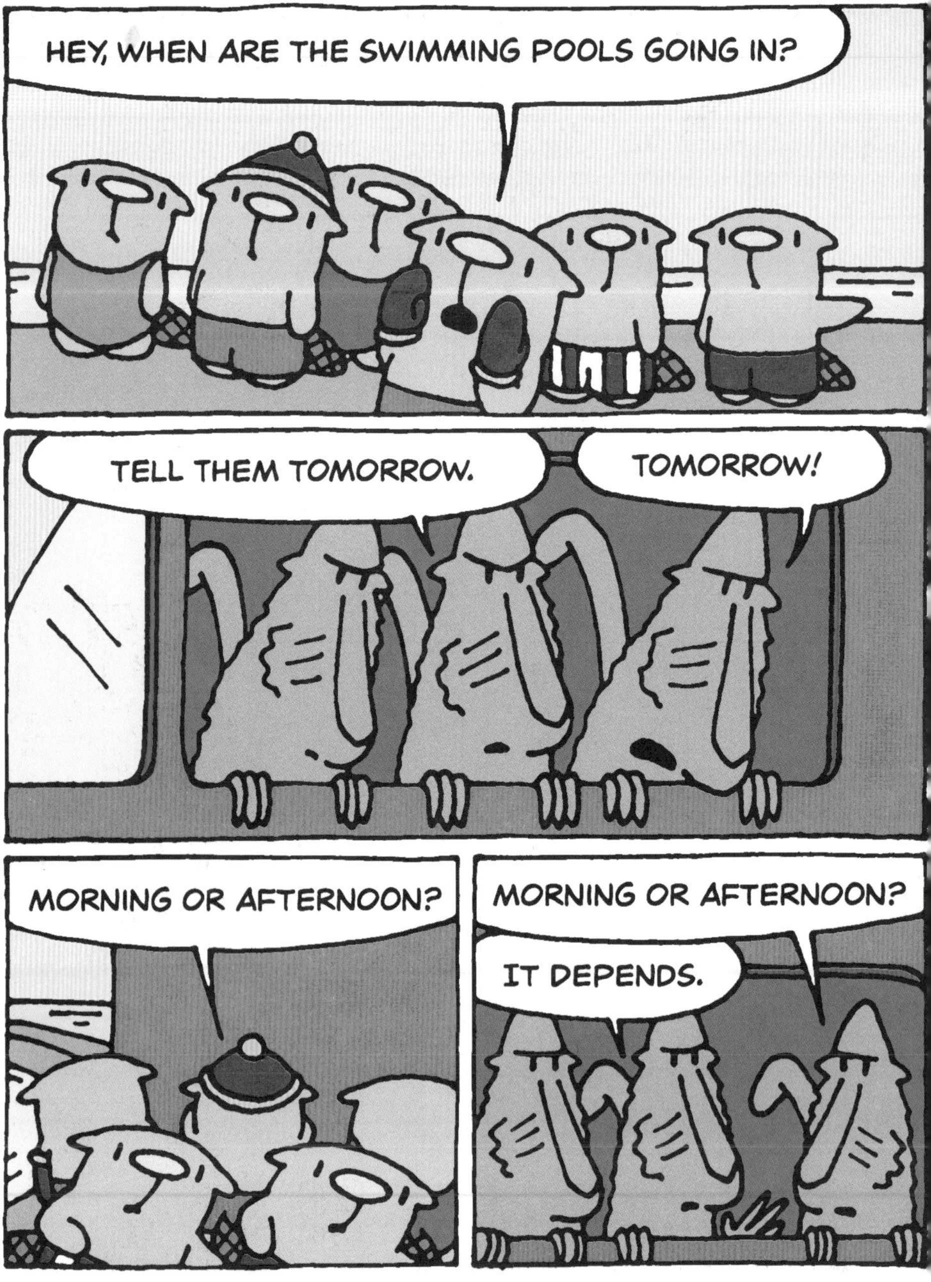
HEY, WHEN ARE THE SWIMMING POOLS GOING IN?
TELL THEM TOMORROW.
TOMORROW!
MORNING OR AFTERNOON?
MORNING OR AFTERNOON?
IT DEPENDS.

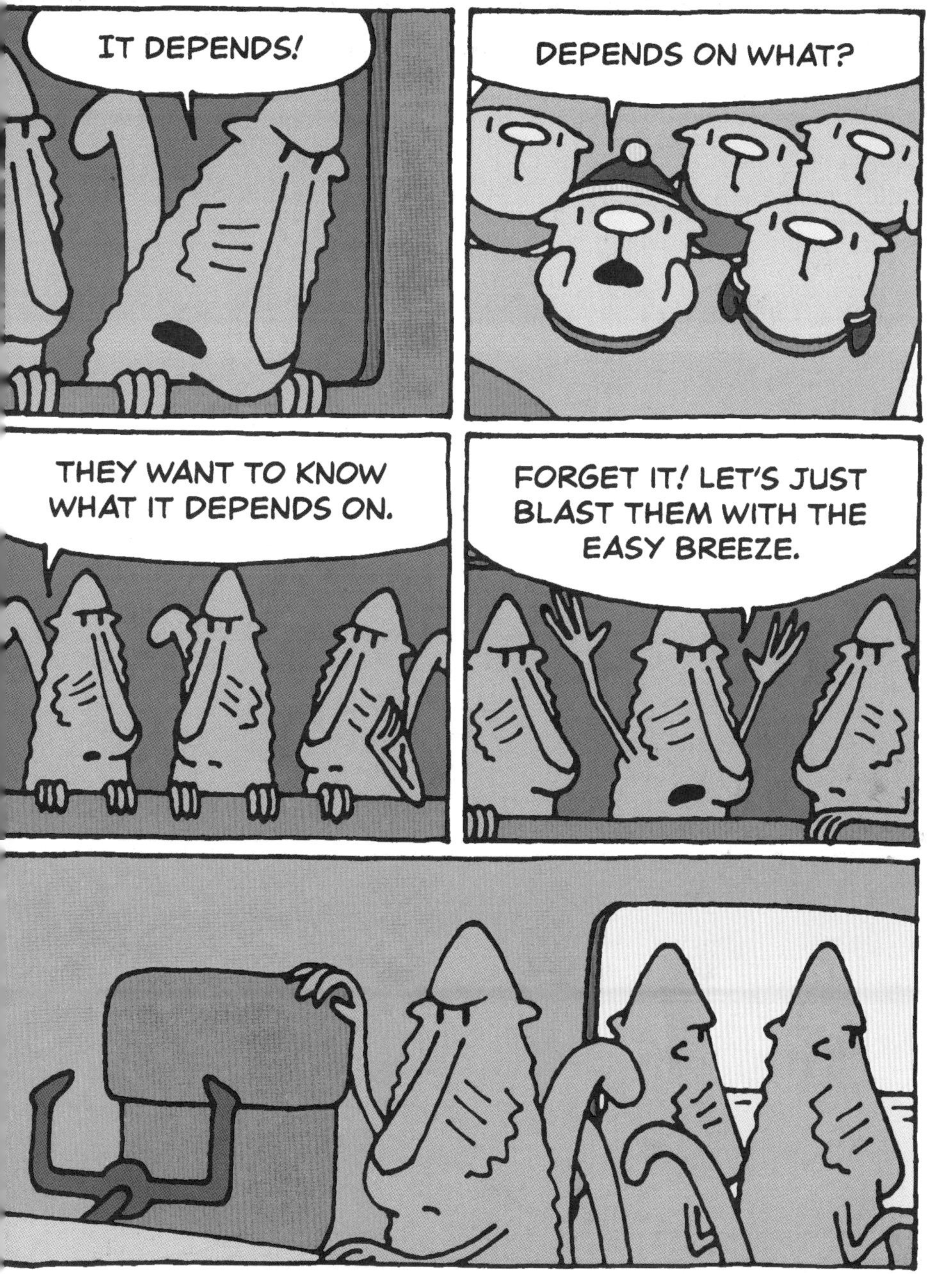
IT DEPENDS!
DEPENDS ON WHAT?
THEY WANT TO KNOW WHAT IT DEPENDS ON.
FORGET IT! LET'S JUST BLAST THEM WITH THE EASY BREEZE.

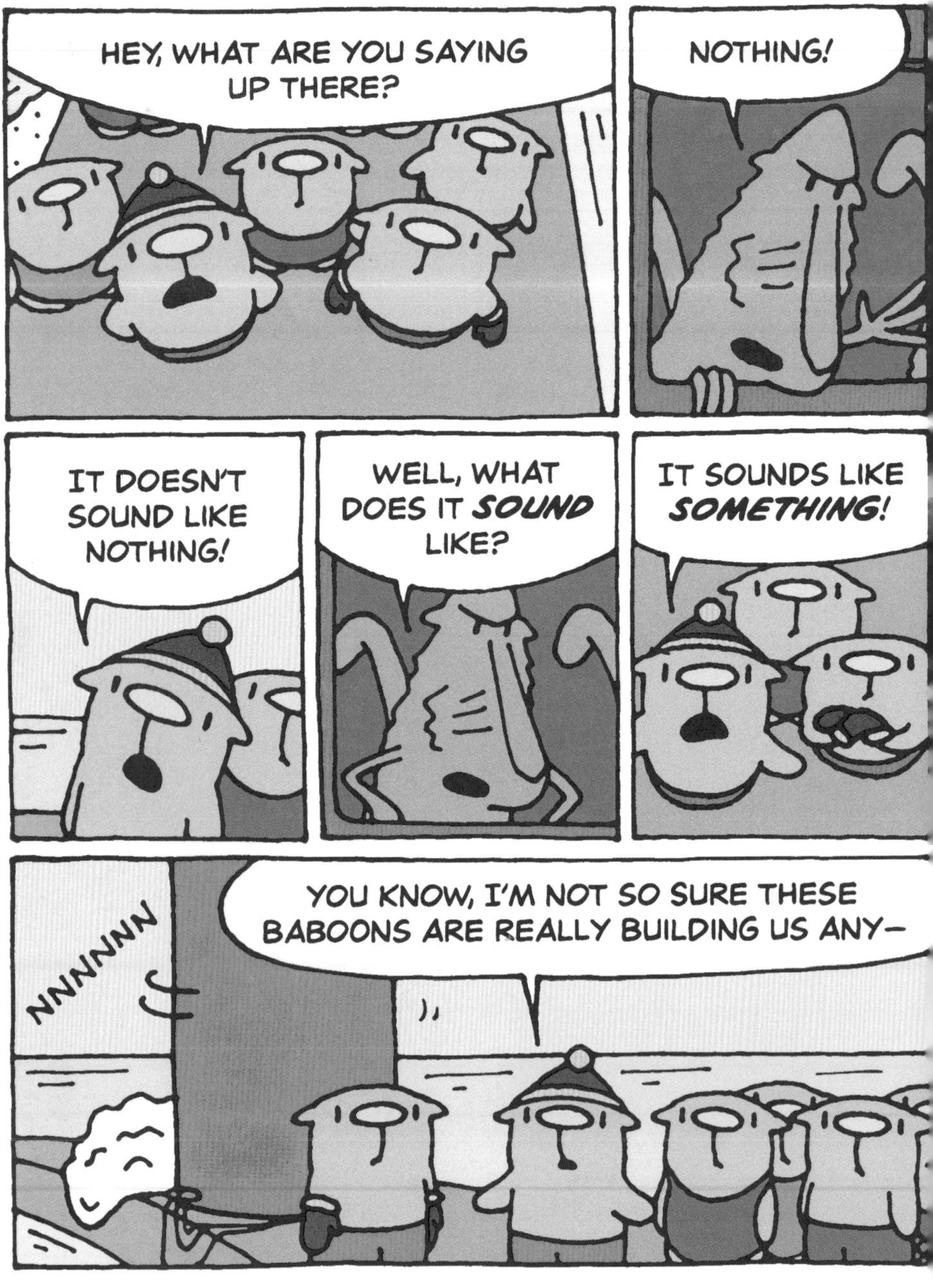
HEY, WHAT ARE YOU SAYING UP THERE?
NOTHING!
IT DOESN'T SOUND LIKE NOTHING!
WELL, WHAT DOES IT *SOUND* LIKE?
IT SOUNDS LIKE *SOMETHING!*
YOU KNOW, I'M NOT SO SURE THESE BABOONS ARE REALLY BUILDING US ANY—
NNNNNN

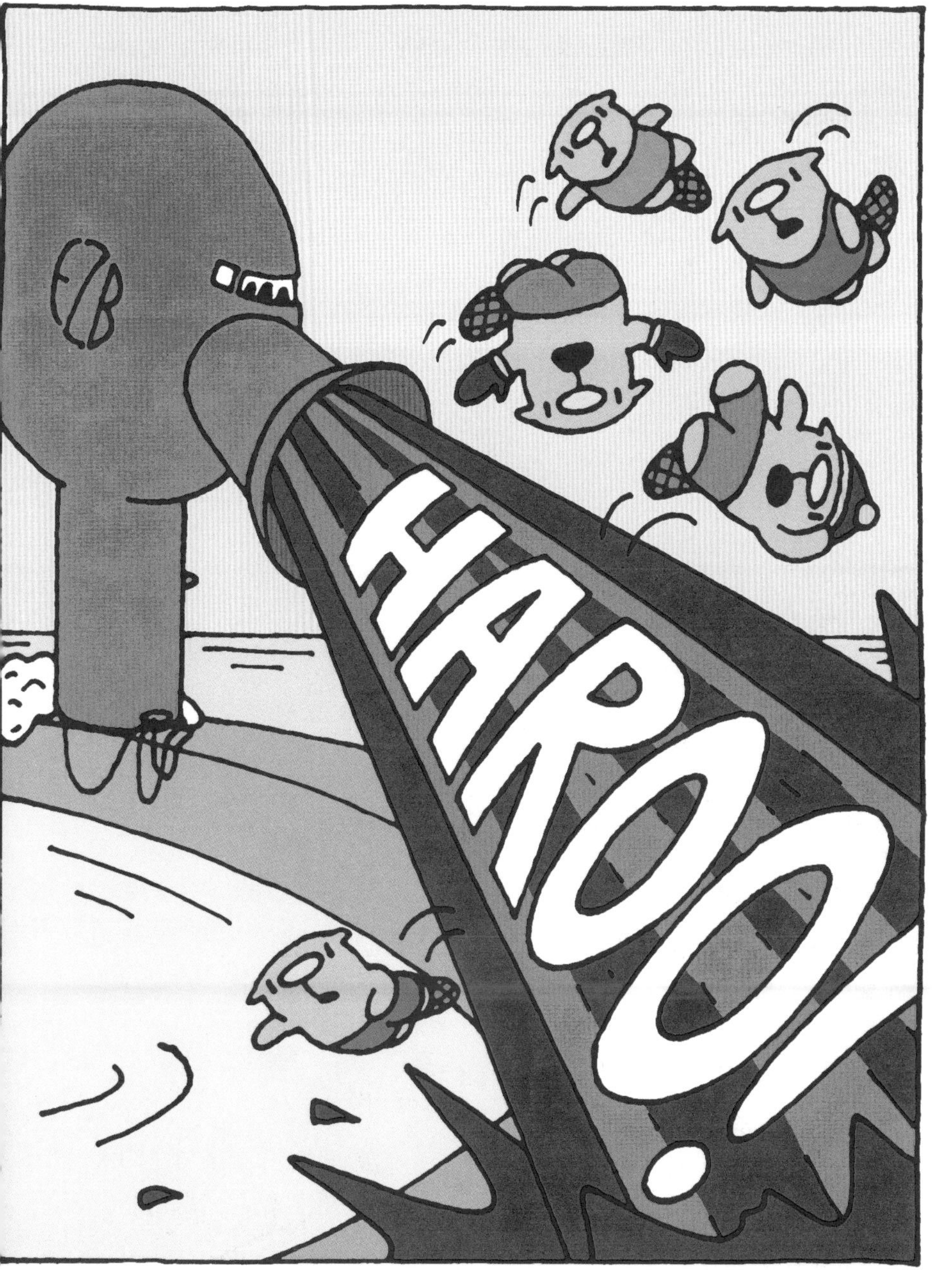
HAROO!

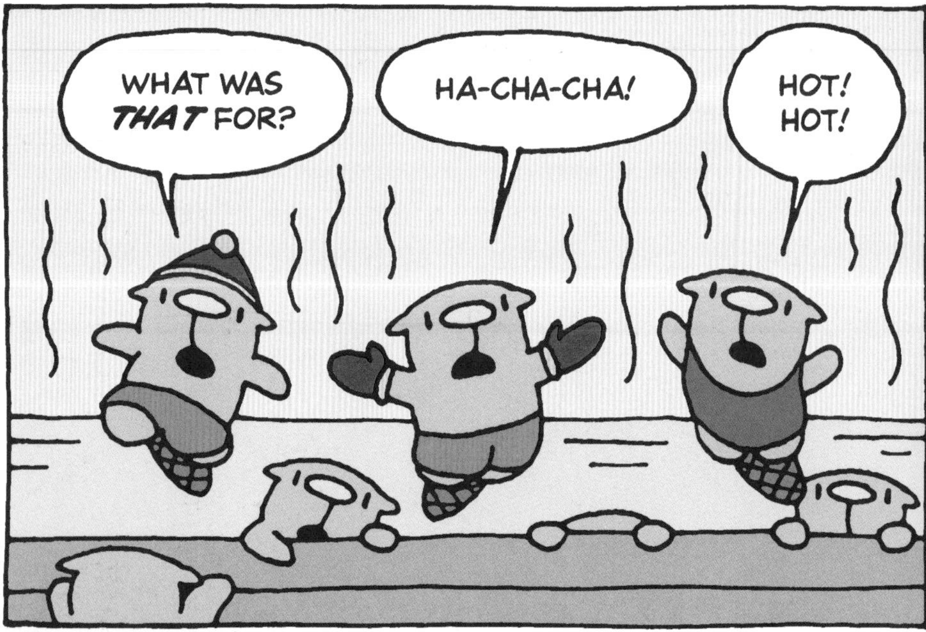
WHAT WAS *THAT* FOR?
HA-CHA-CHA!
HOT! HOT!

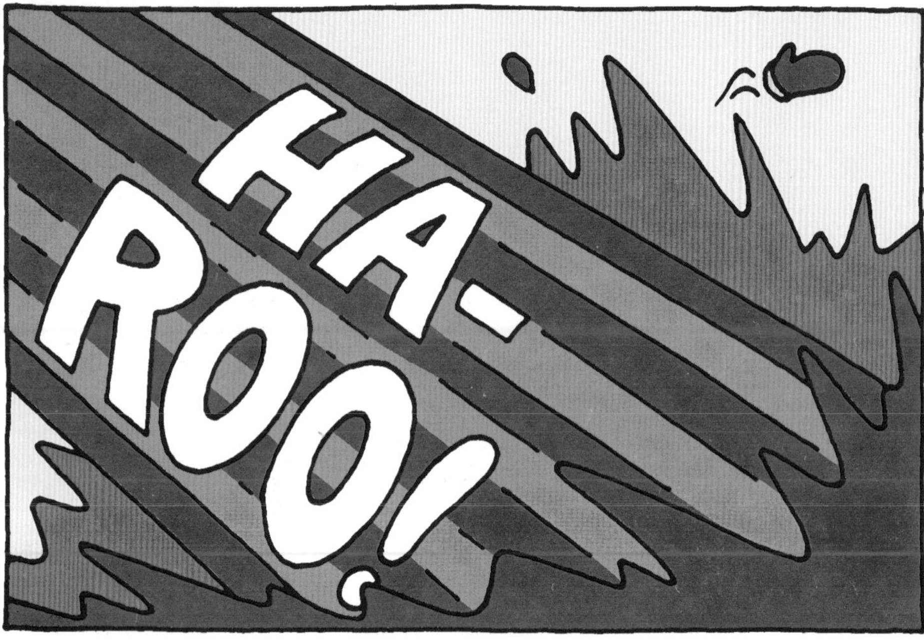
HA-ROO!

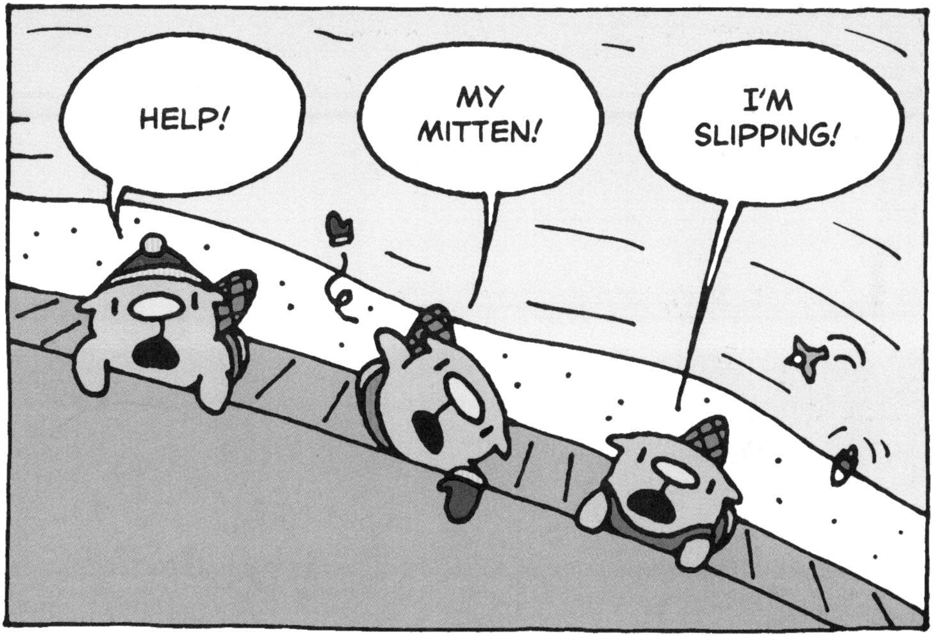
HELP!
MY MITTEN!
I'M SLIPPING!

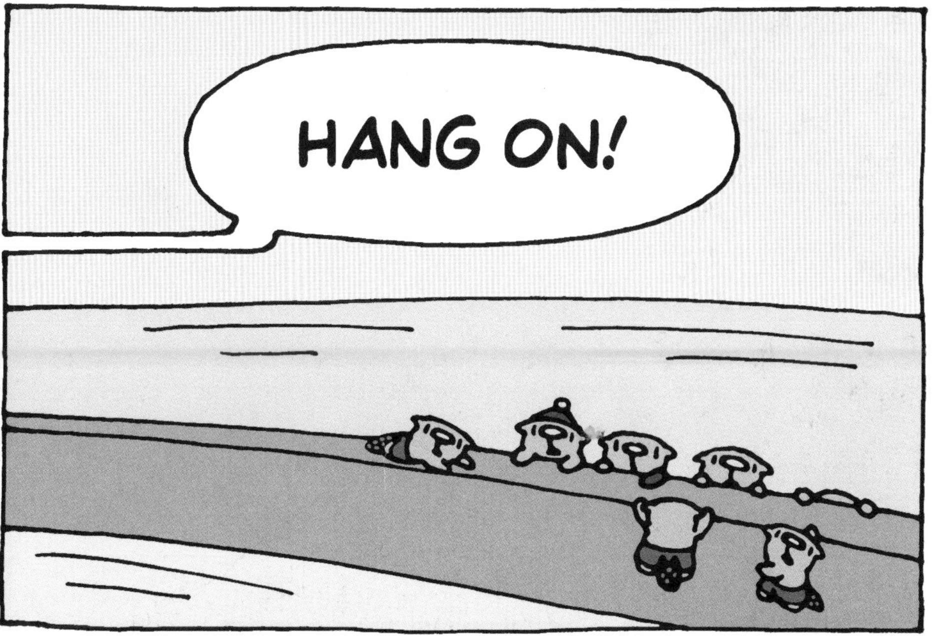
HANG ON!

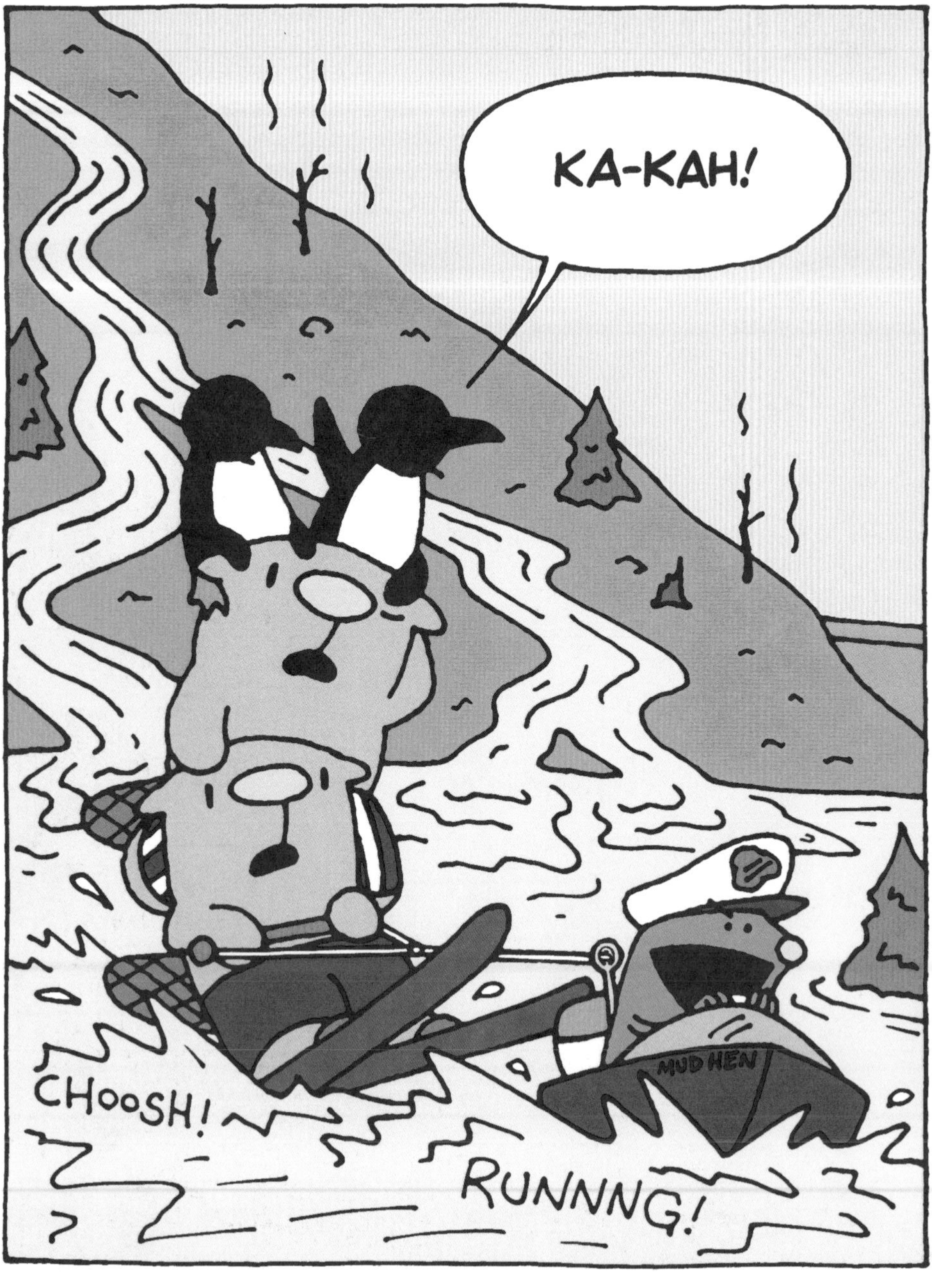
KA-KAH!
MUDHEN
CHOOSH!
RUNNNG!

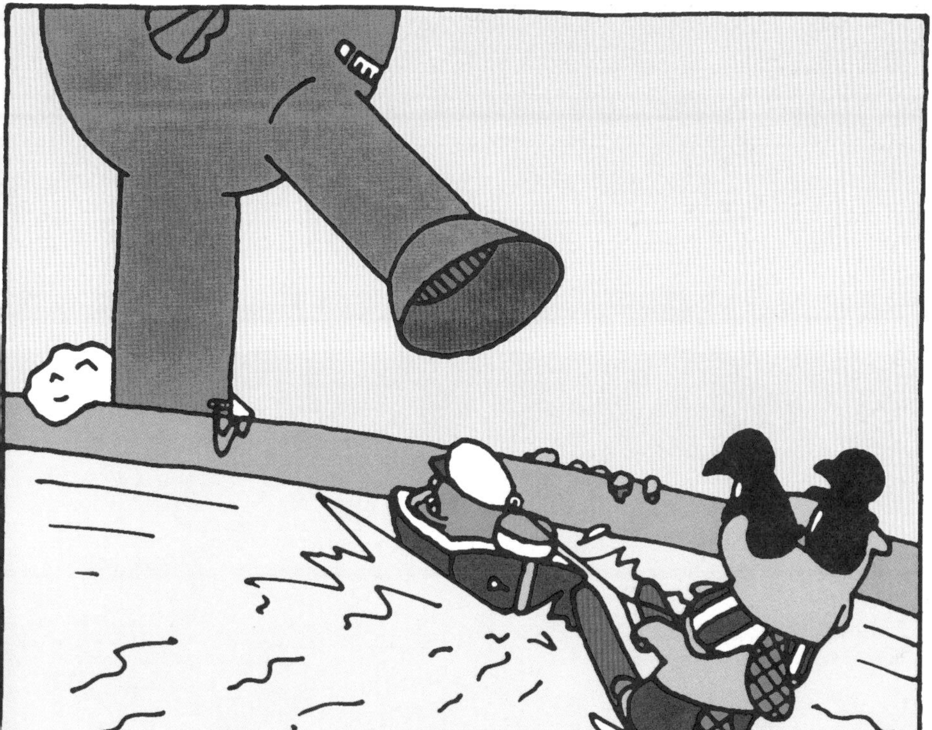
CROOSH!
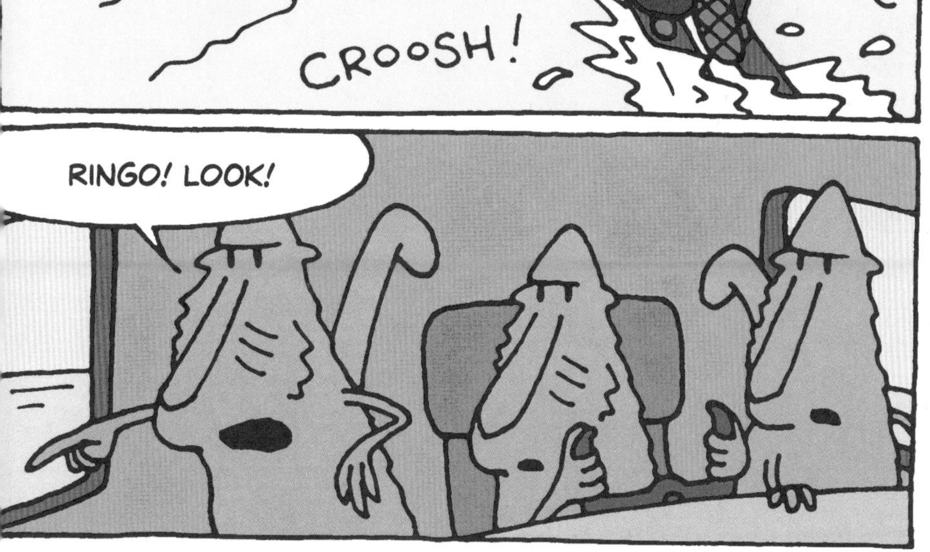
RINGO! LOOK!

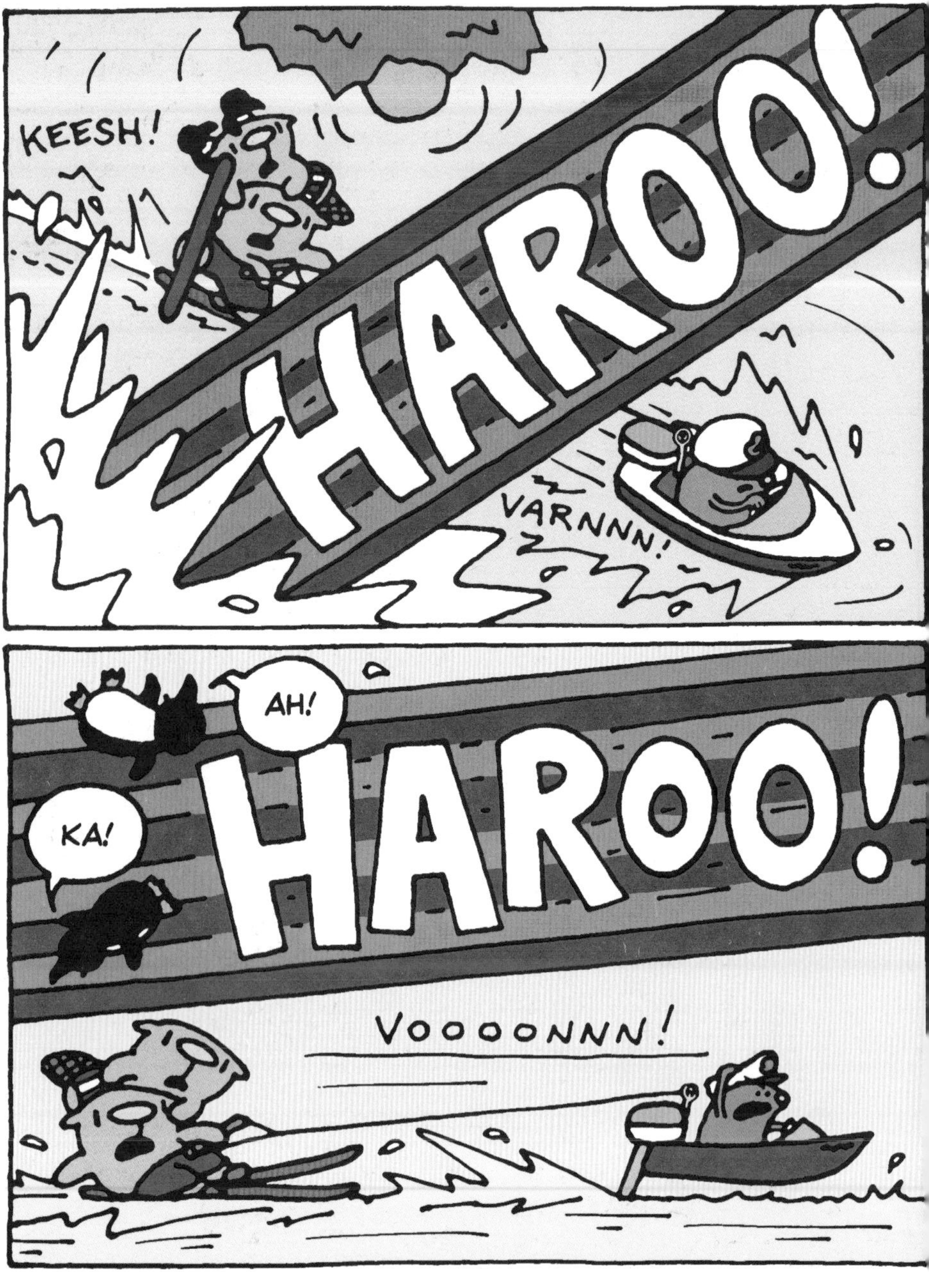
KEESH!
HAROO!
VARNNN!
AH!
KA!
HAROO!
VOOOONNN!

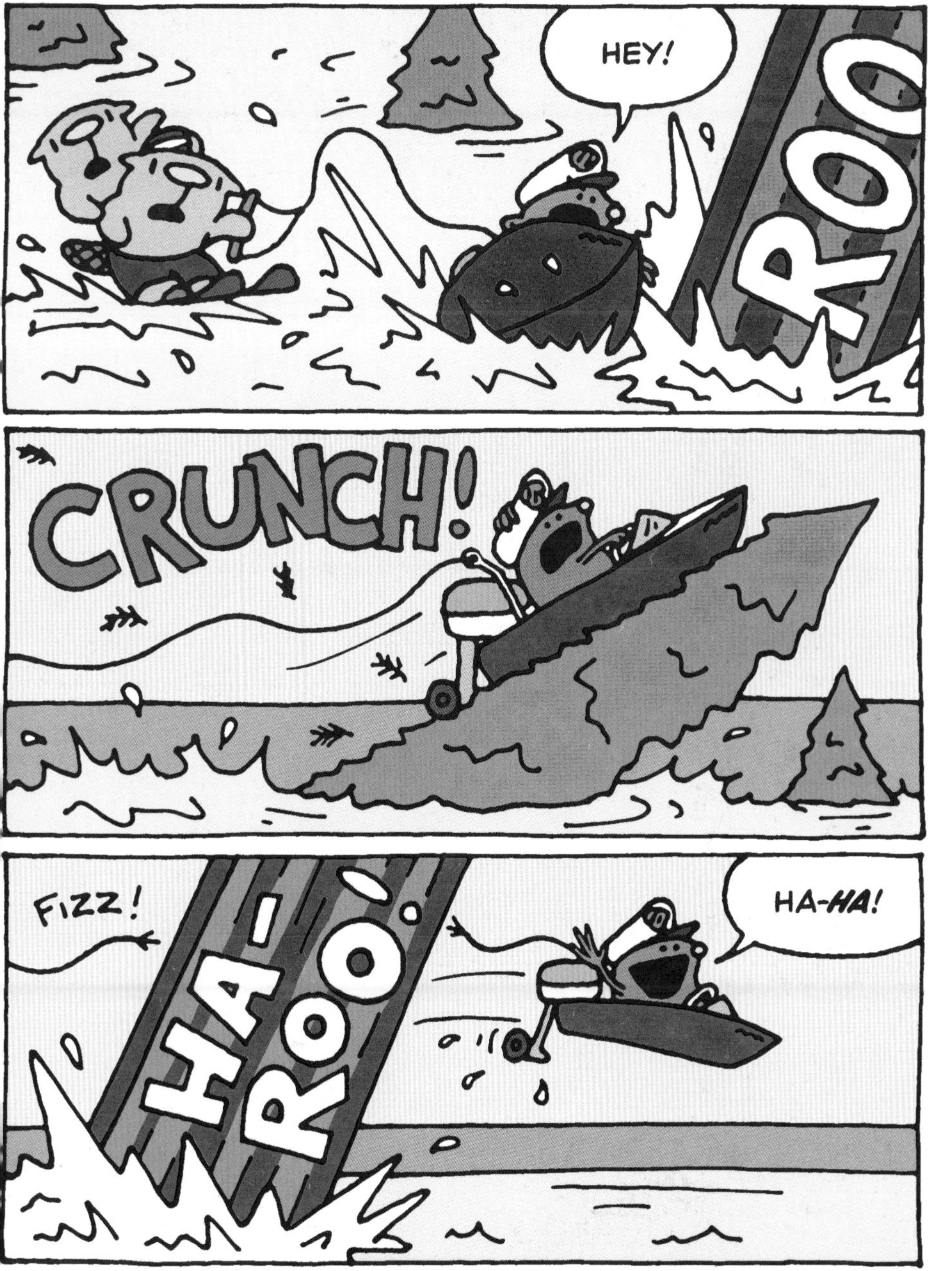
HEY!
ROO
CRUNCH!
FIZZ!
HA-ROO!
HA-HA!

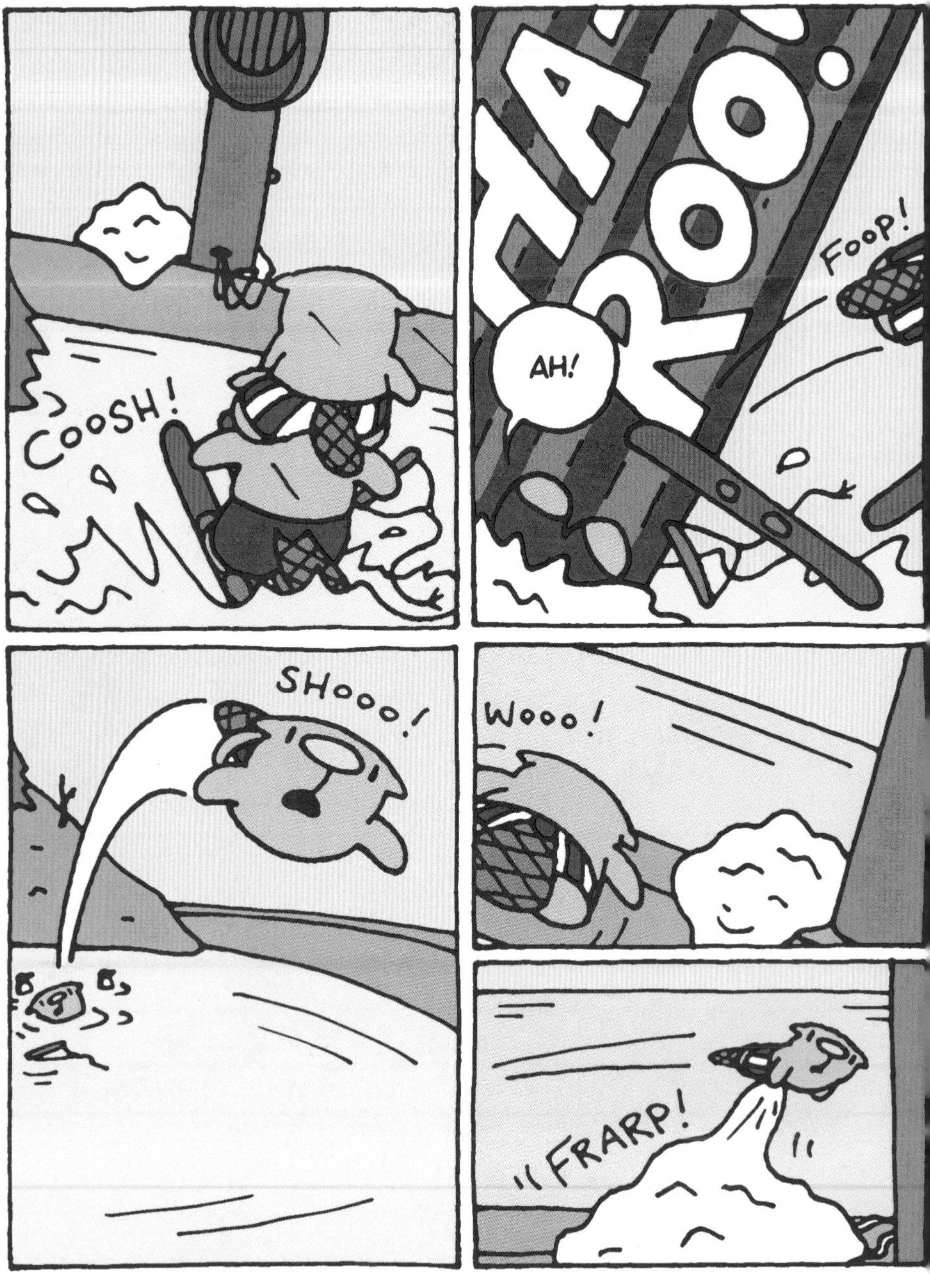

COOSH!
TA-ROO!
AH!
FOOP!
SHOOO!
WOOO!
FRARP!

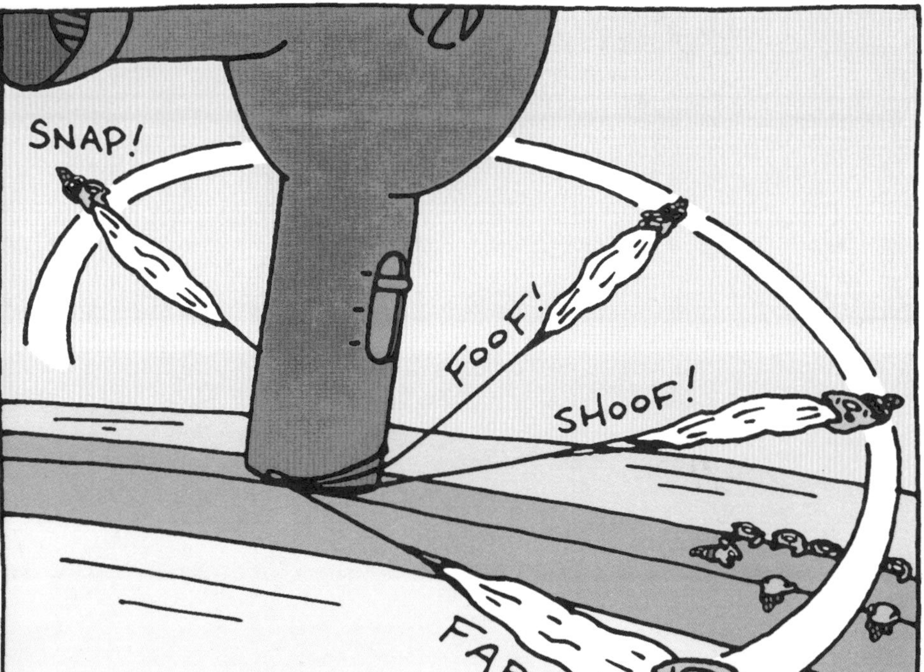
SNAP!
FOOF!
SHOOF!
FARF!
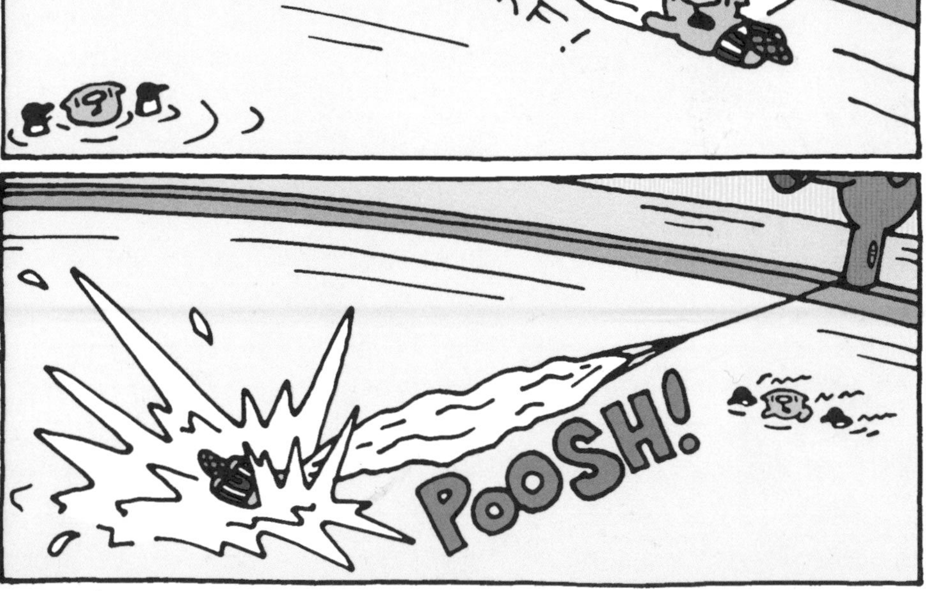
POOSH!

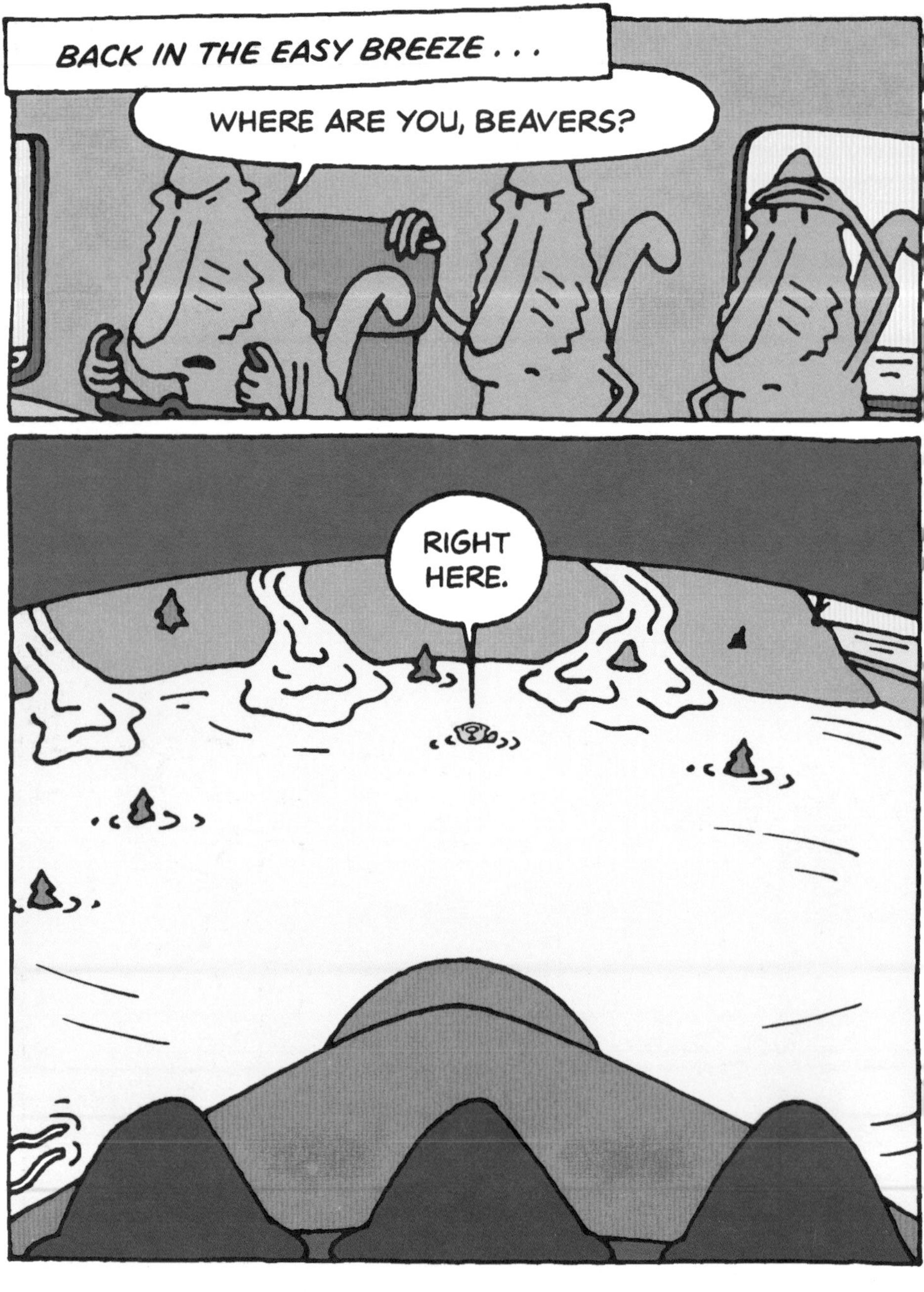
BACK IN THE EASY BREEZE . . .
WHERE ARE YOU, BEAVERS?
RIGHT HERE.

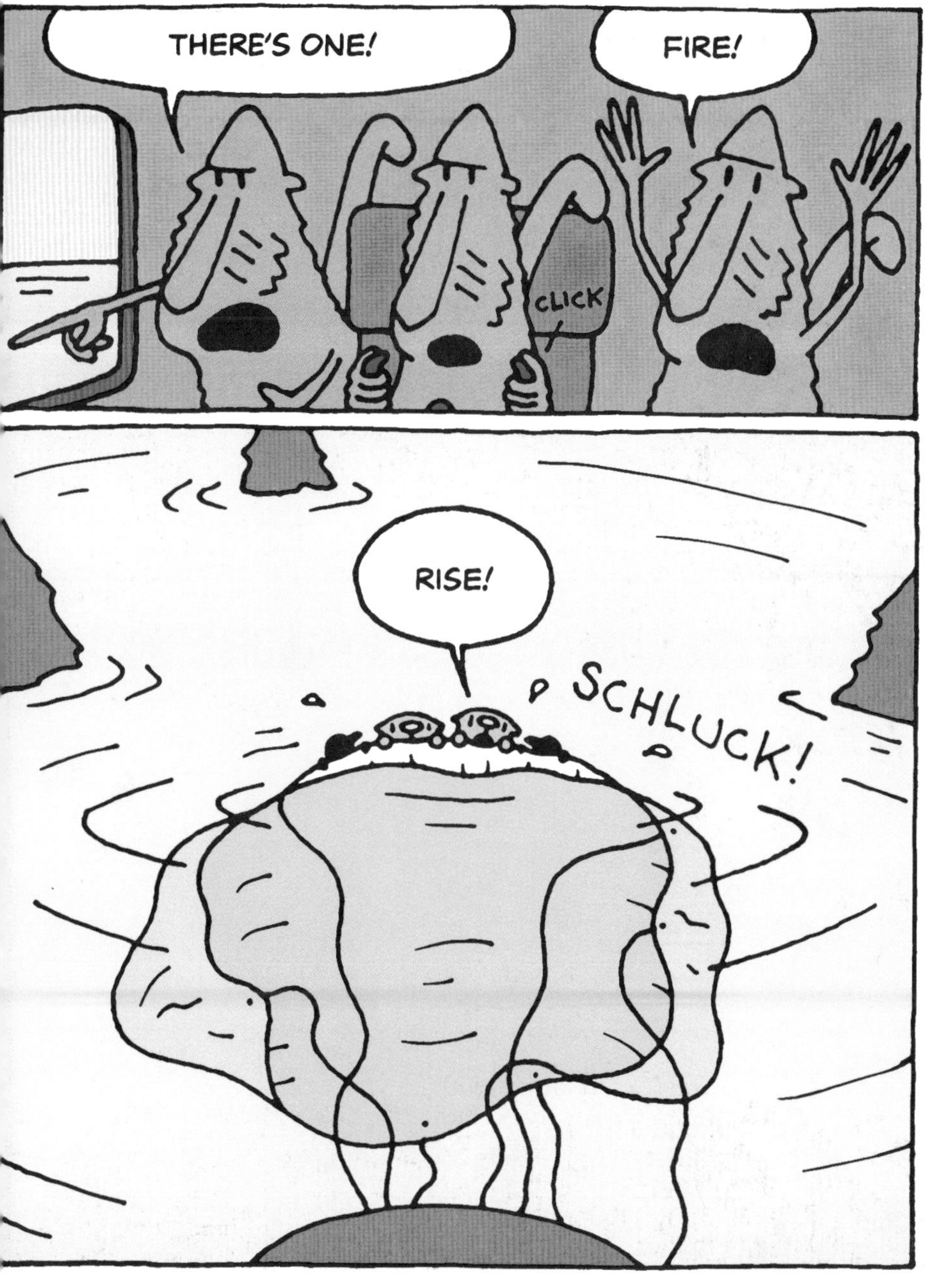
THERE'S ONE!
FIRE!
CLICK
RISE!
SCHLUCK!

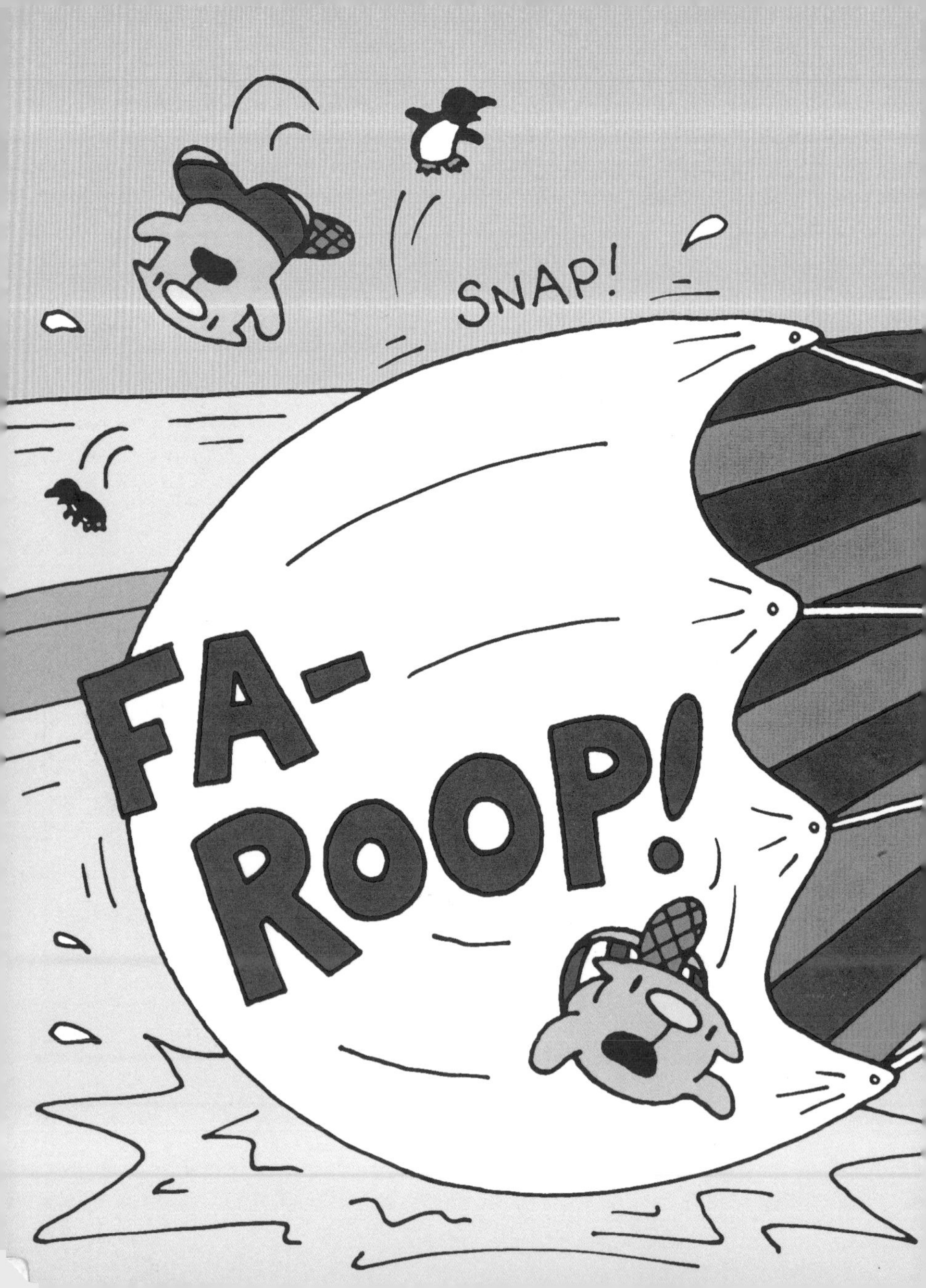
SNAP!
FA-
ROOP!

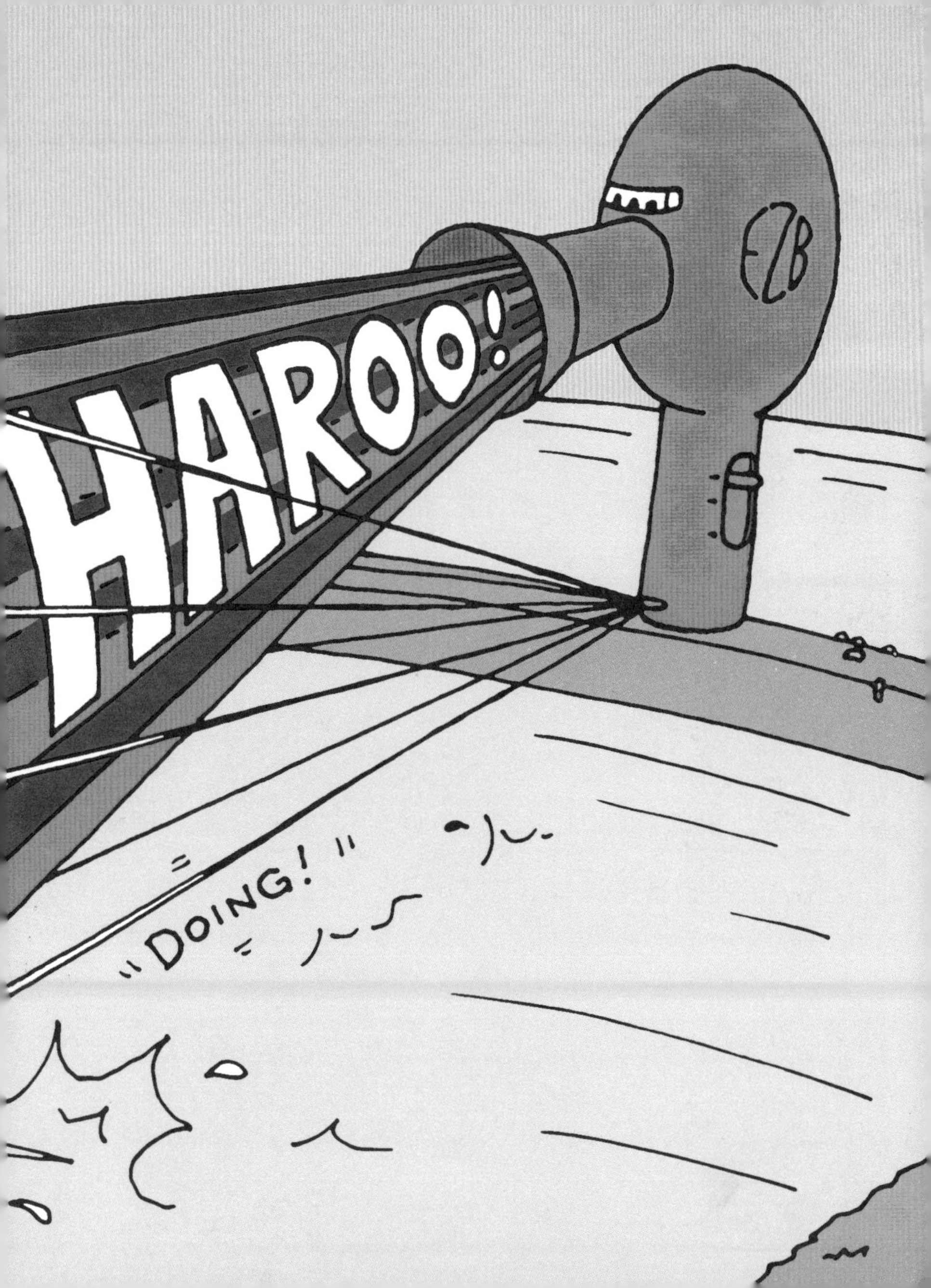
HAROO!
"DOING!"
EZB

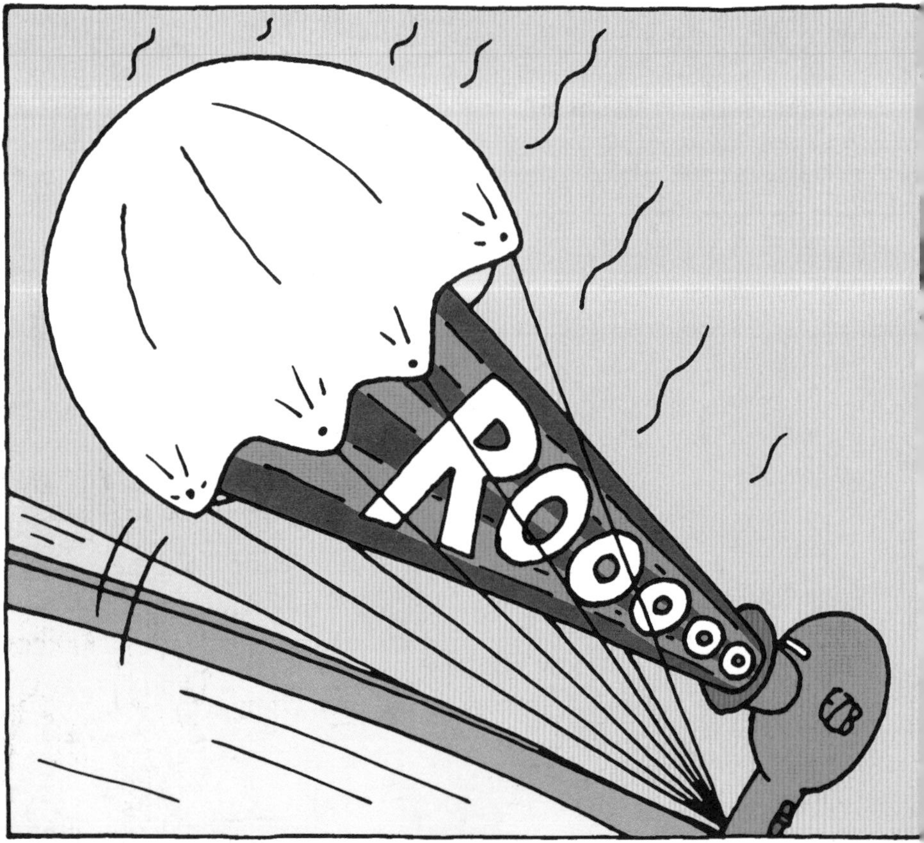
ROOooooo

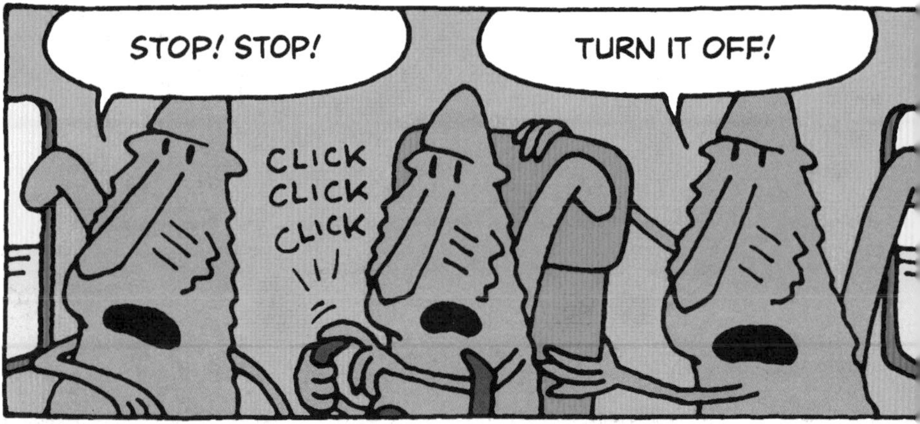
STOP! STOP!
CLICK
CLICK
CLICK
TURN IT OFF!

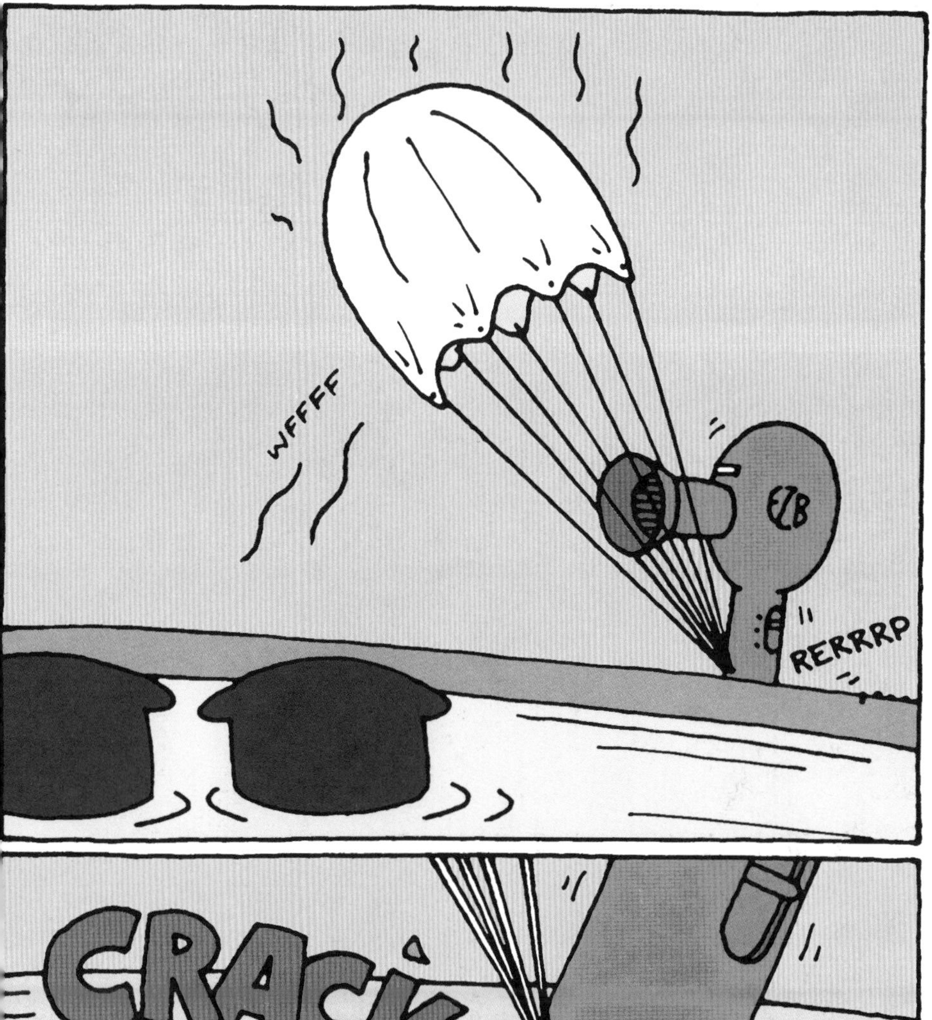
WFFFF
EZB
RERRRP

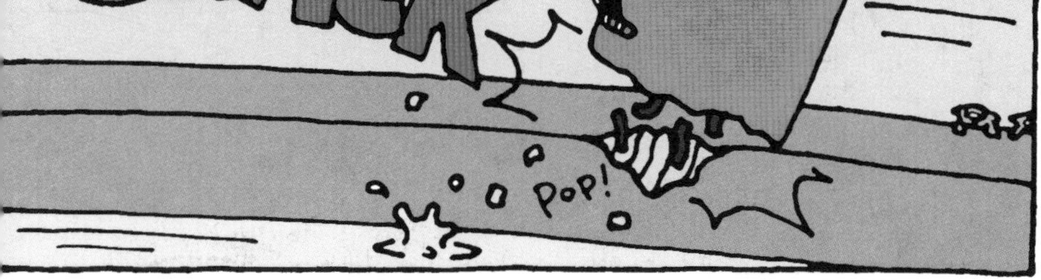
CRACK
POP!

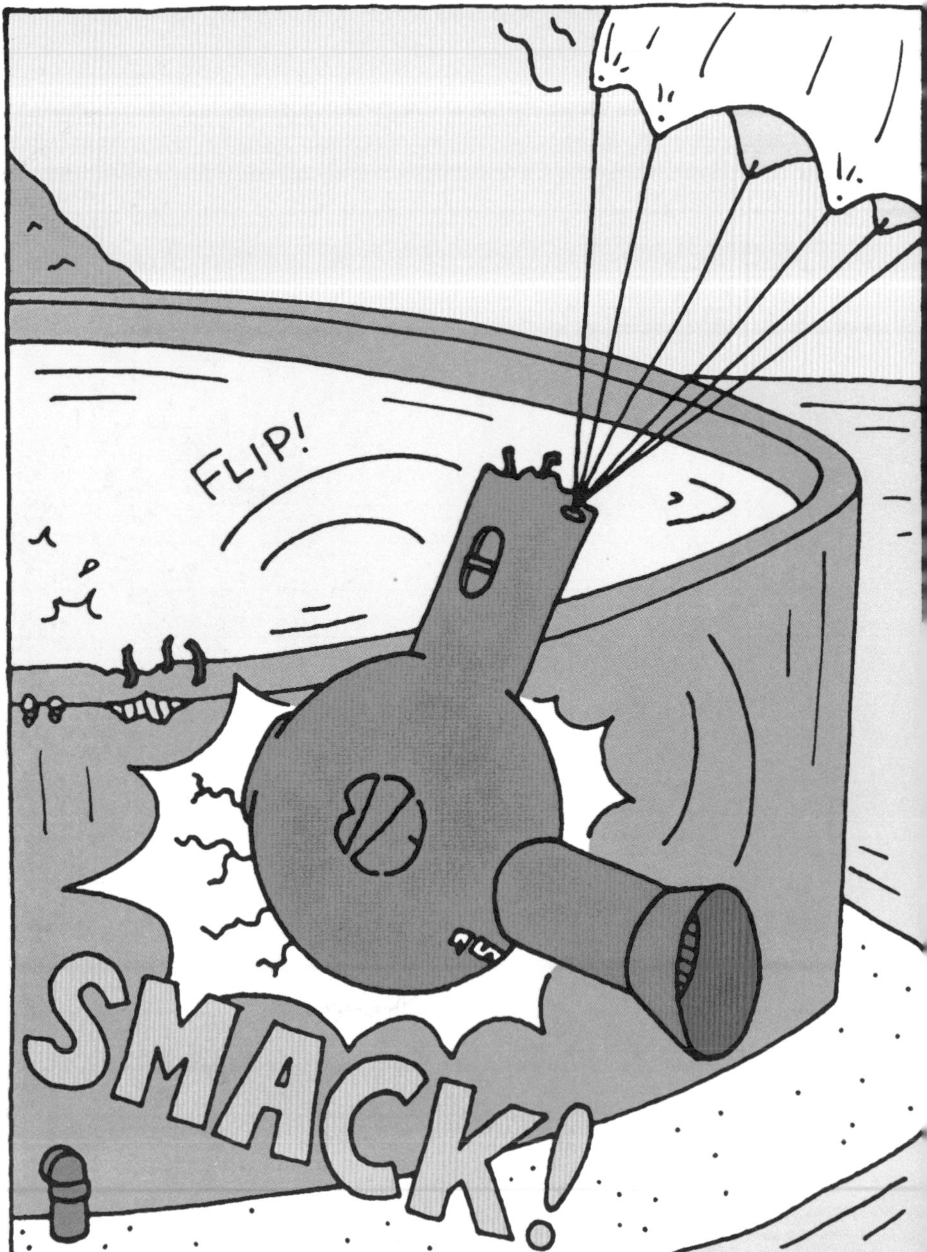
FLIP!
SMACK!

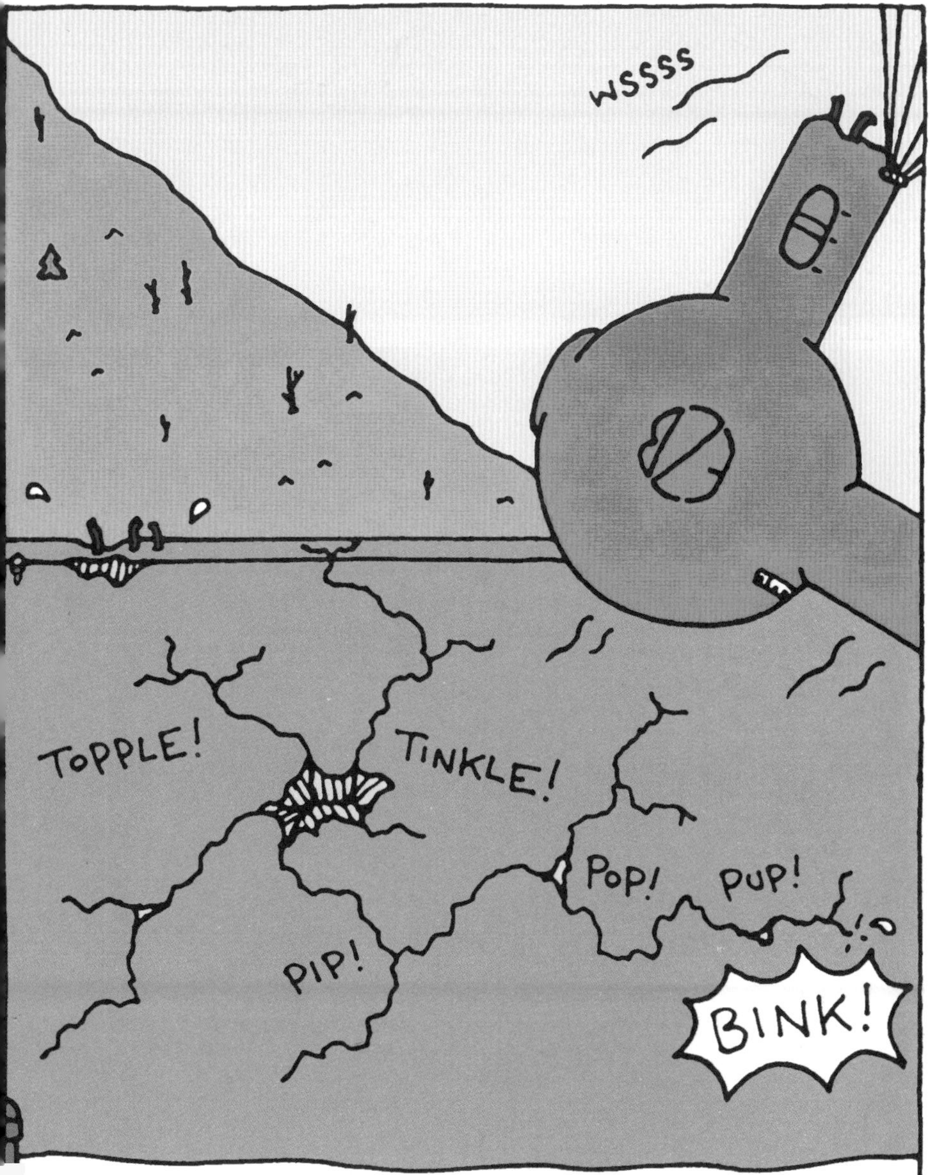
WSSSS
TOPPLE!
TINKLE!
POP!
PUP!
PIP!
BINK!

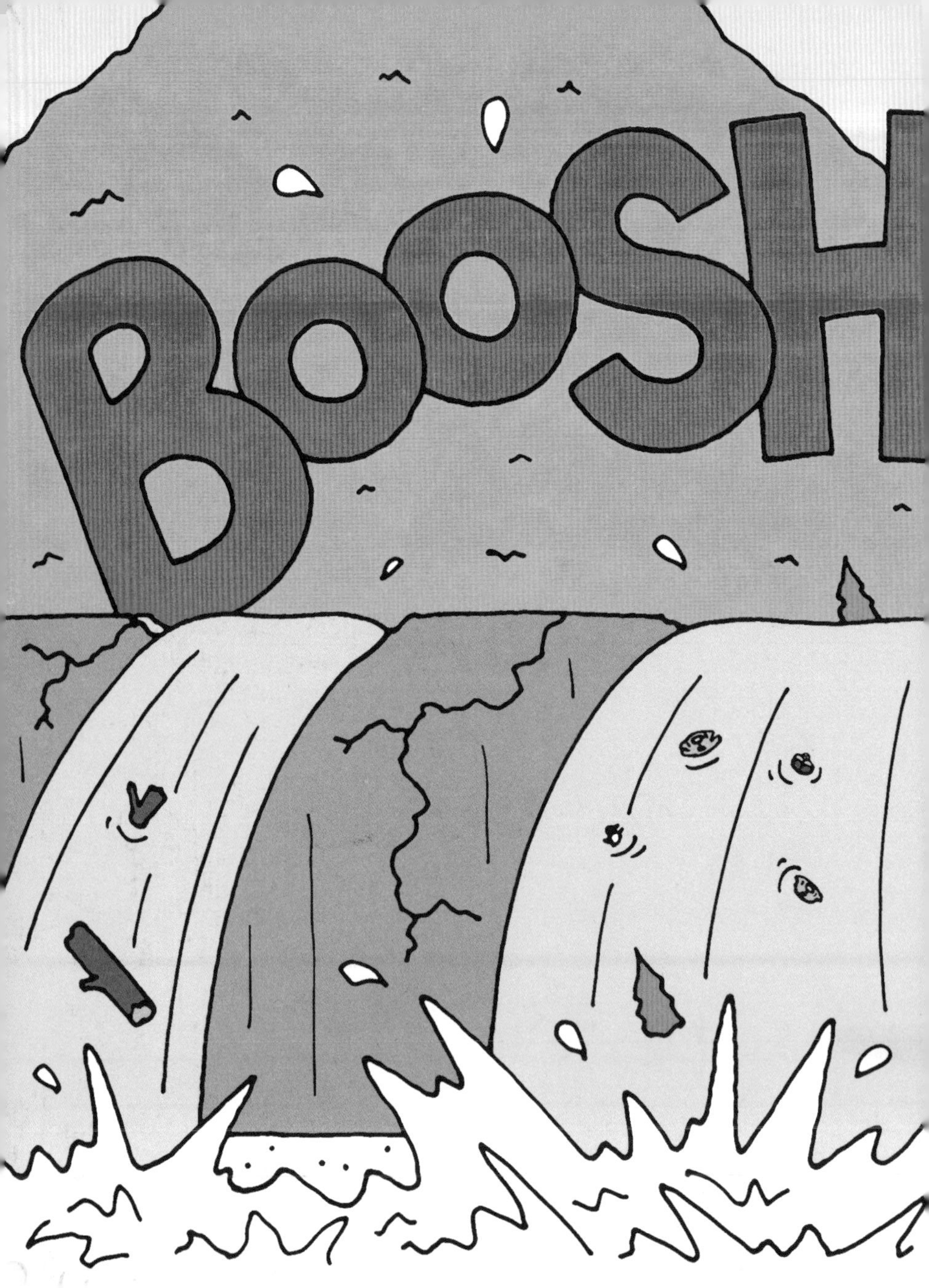
BOOSH

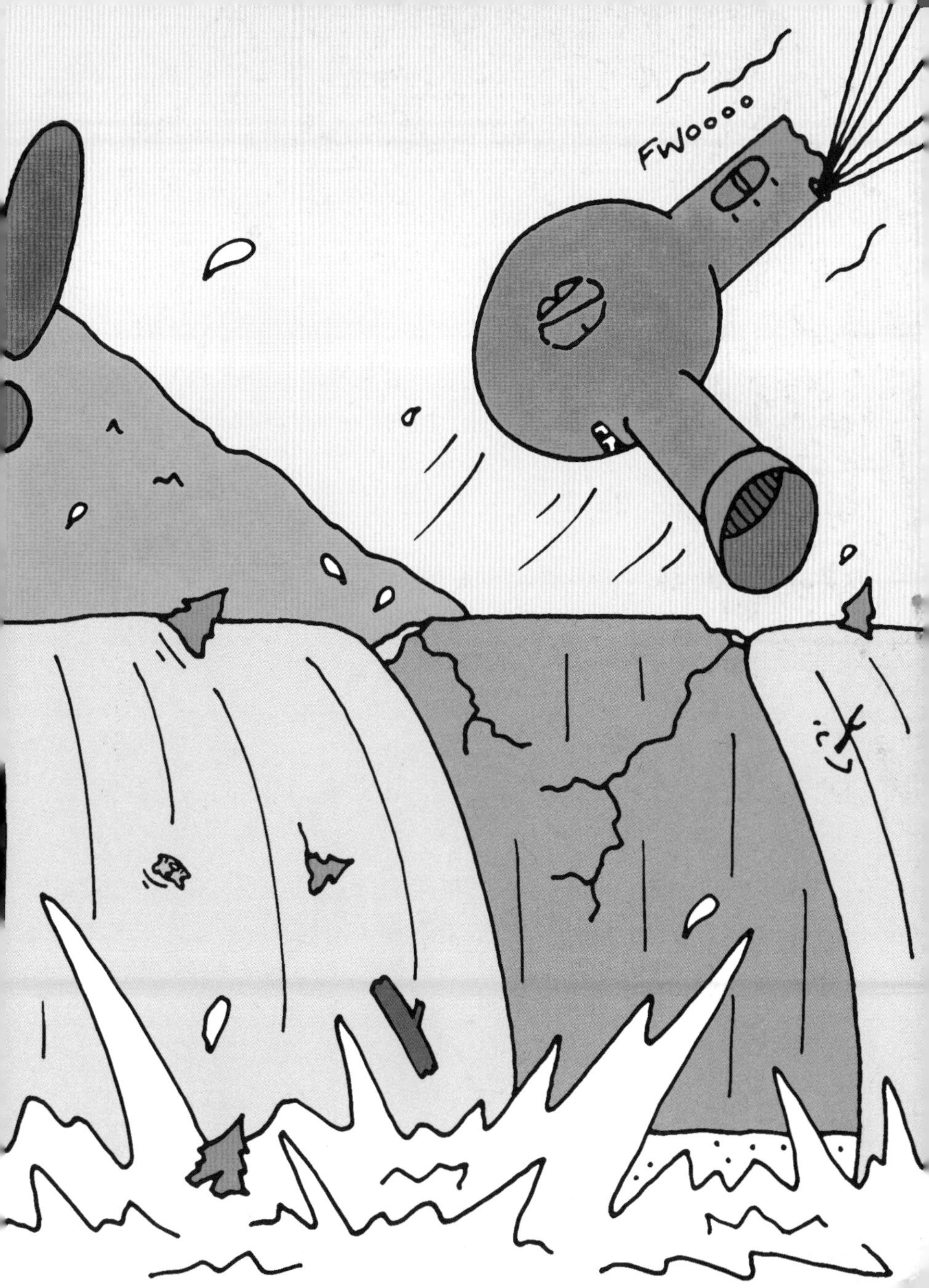
FWoooo

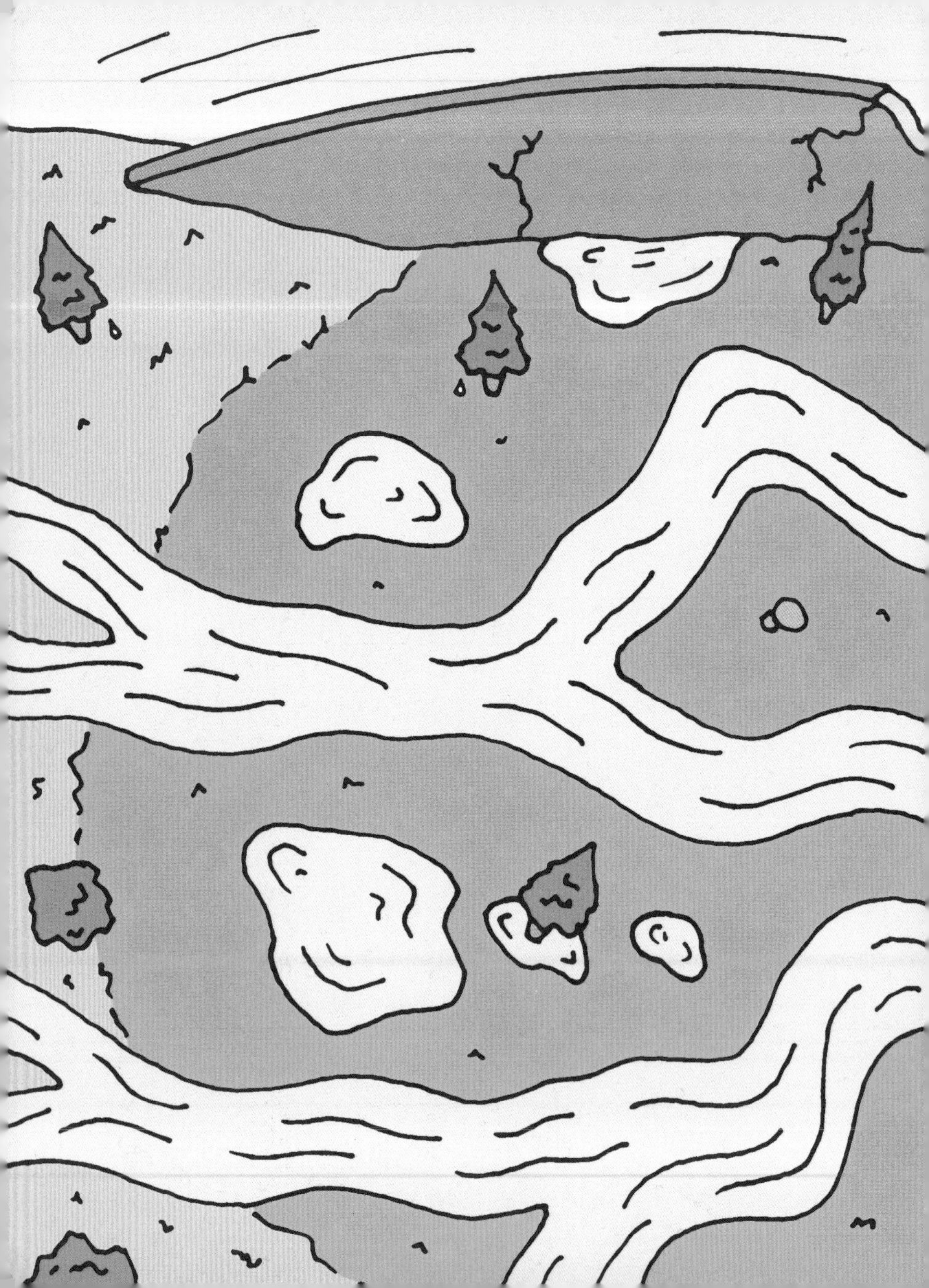

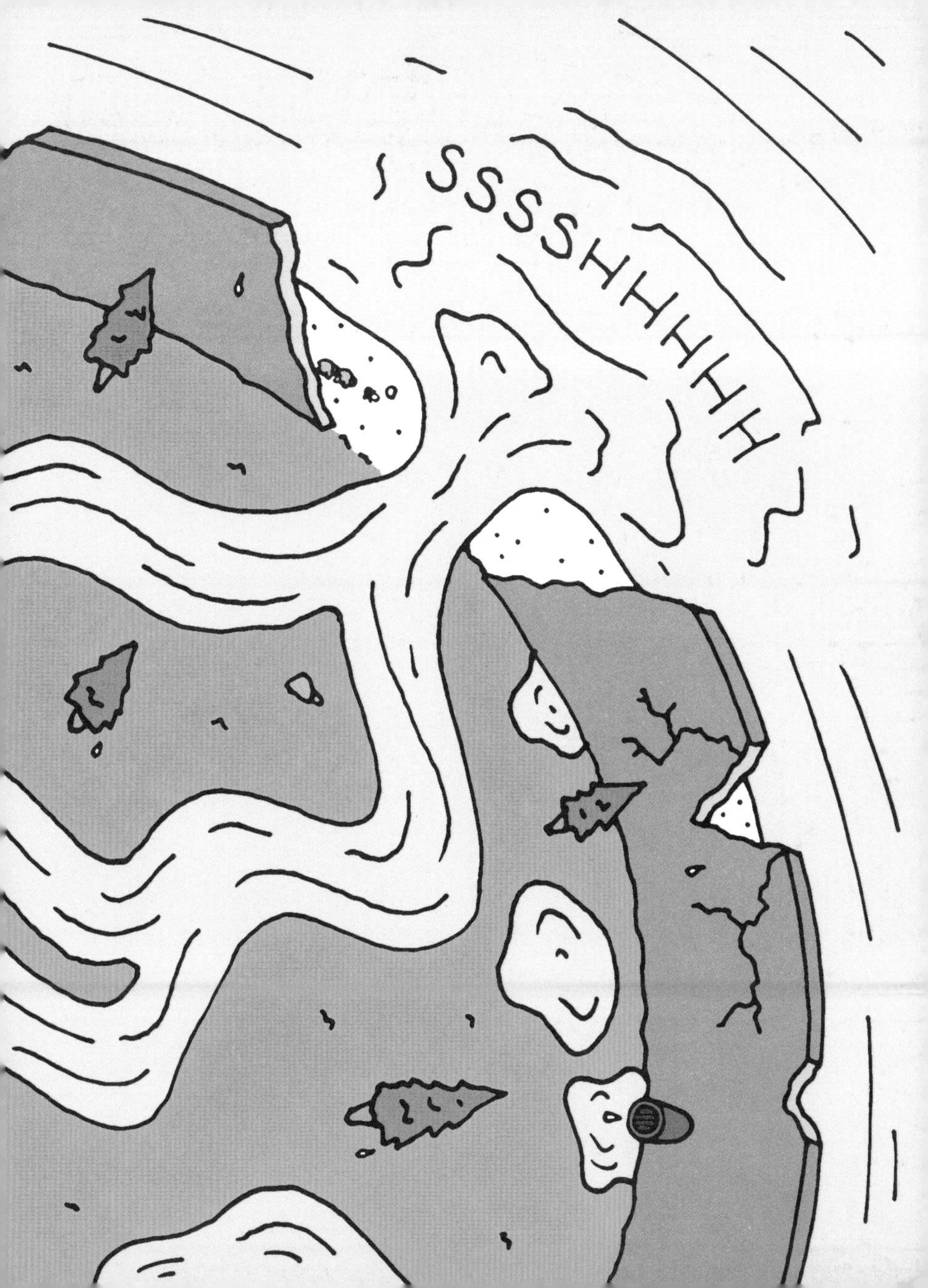
SSSSHHHHHH

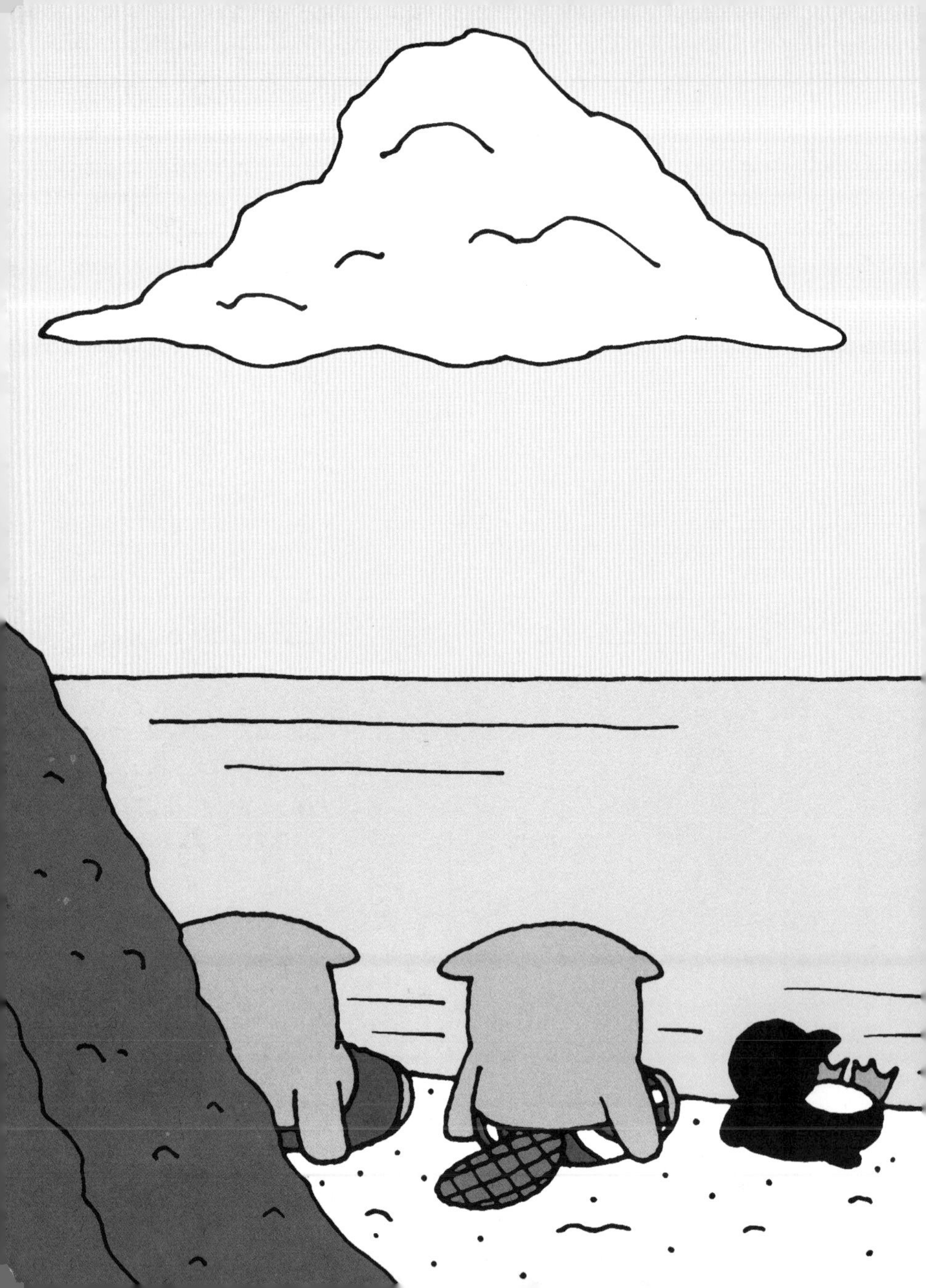

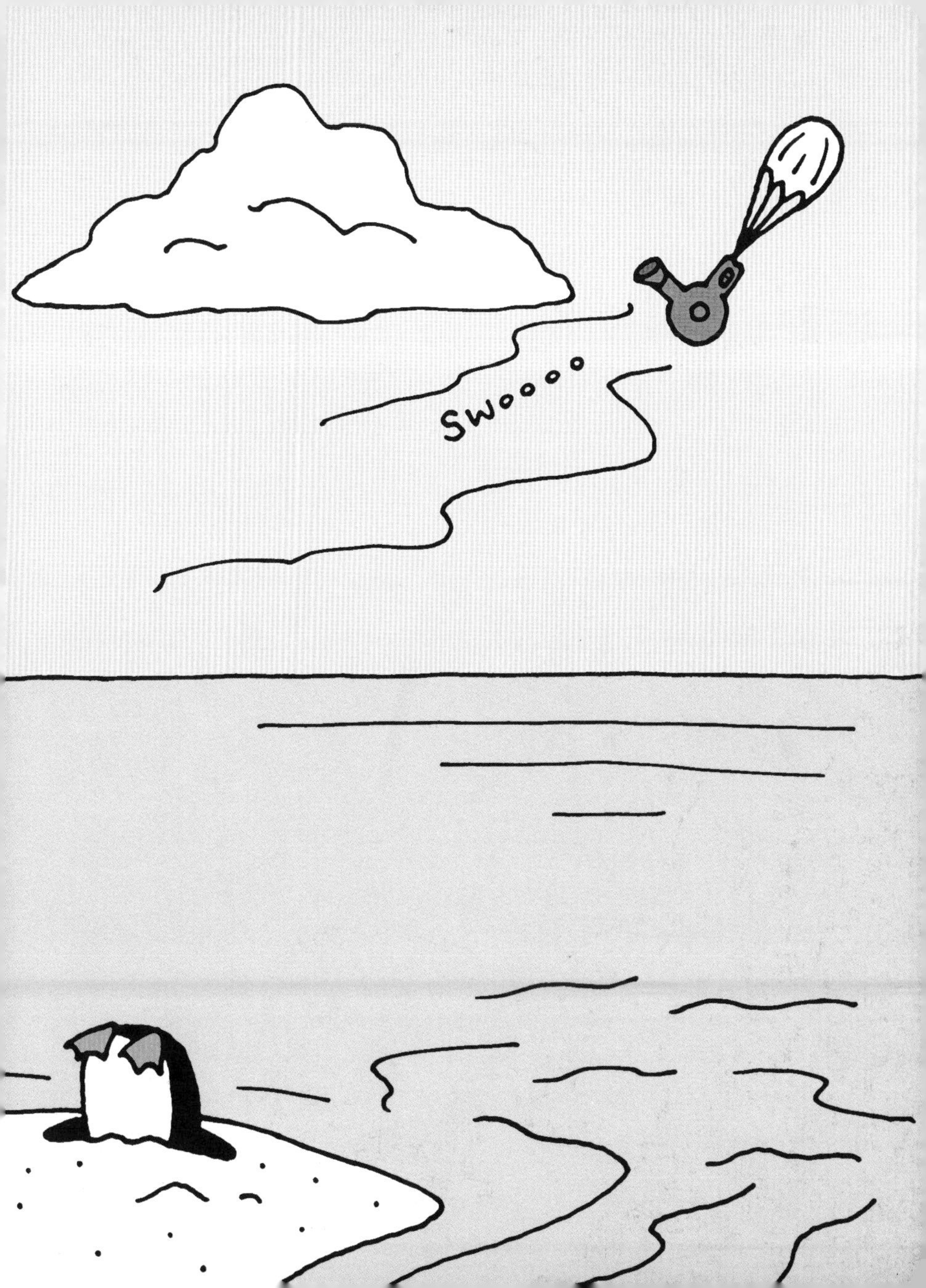
SWOOOO

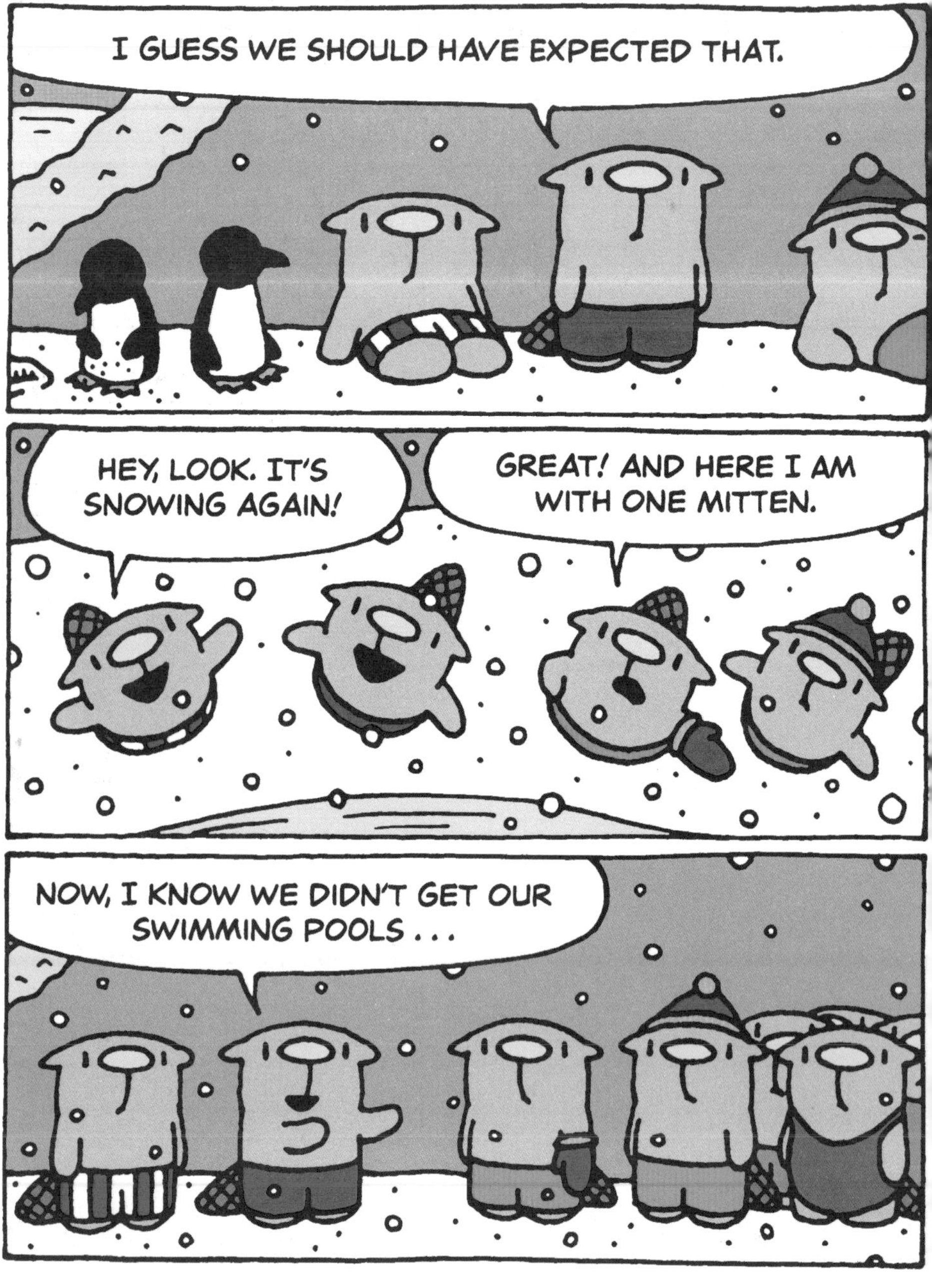
I GUESS WE SHOULD HAVE EXPECTED THAT.
HEY, LOOK. IT'S SNOWING AGAIN!
GREAT! AND HERE I AM WITH ONE MITTEN.
NOW, I KNOW WE DIDN'T GET OUR SWIMMING POOLS . . .

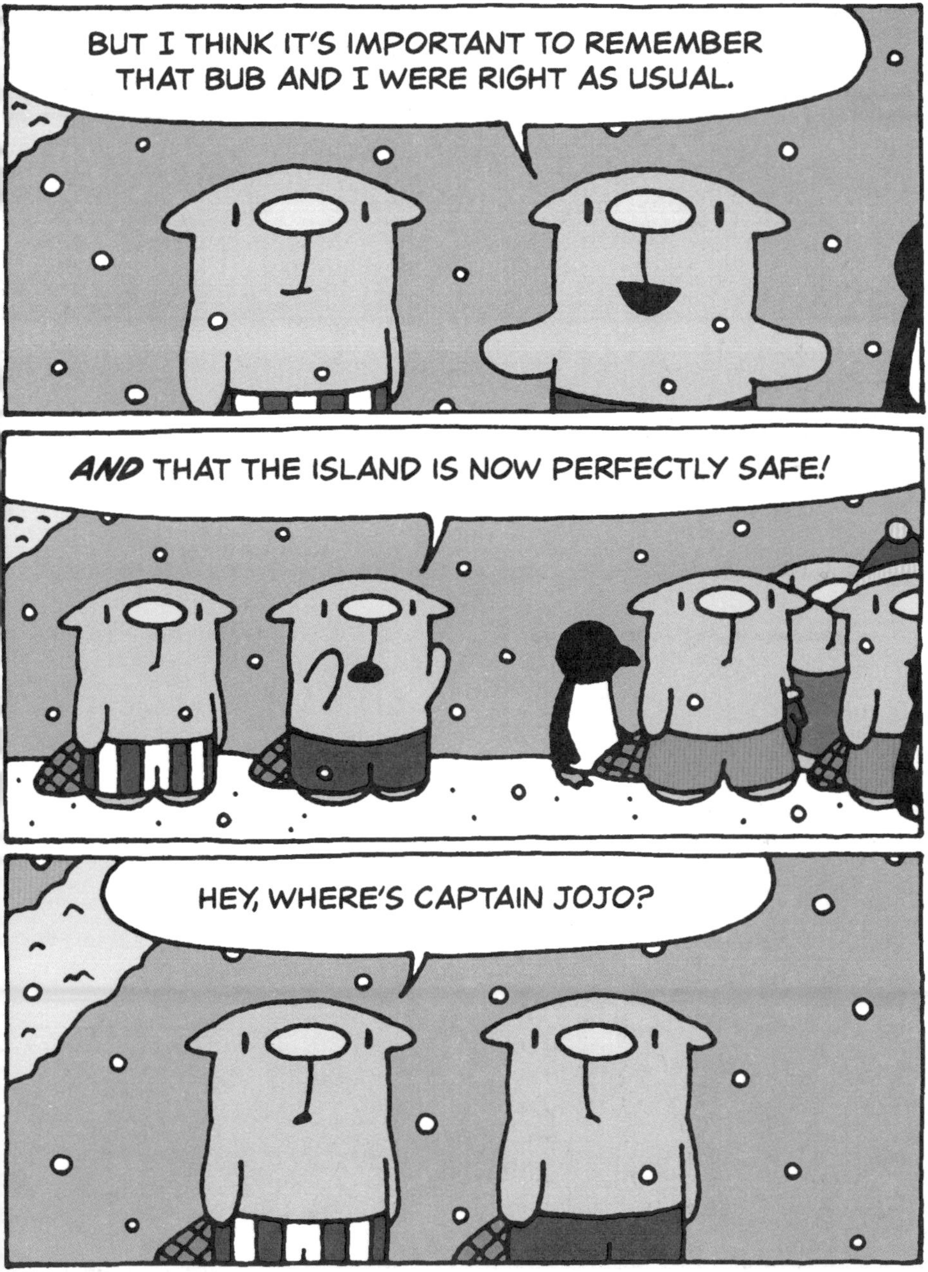
BUT I THINK IT'S IMPORTANT TO REMEMBER THAT BUB AND I WERE RIGHT AS USUAL.
AND THAT THE ISLAND IS NOW PERFECTLY SAFE!
HEY, WHERE'S CAPTAIN JOJO?

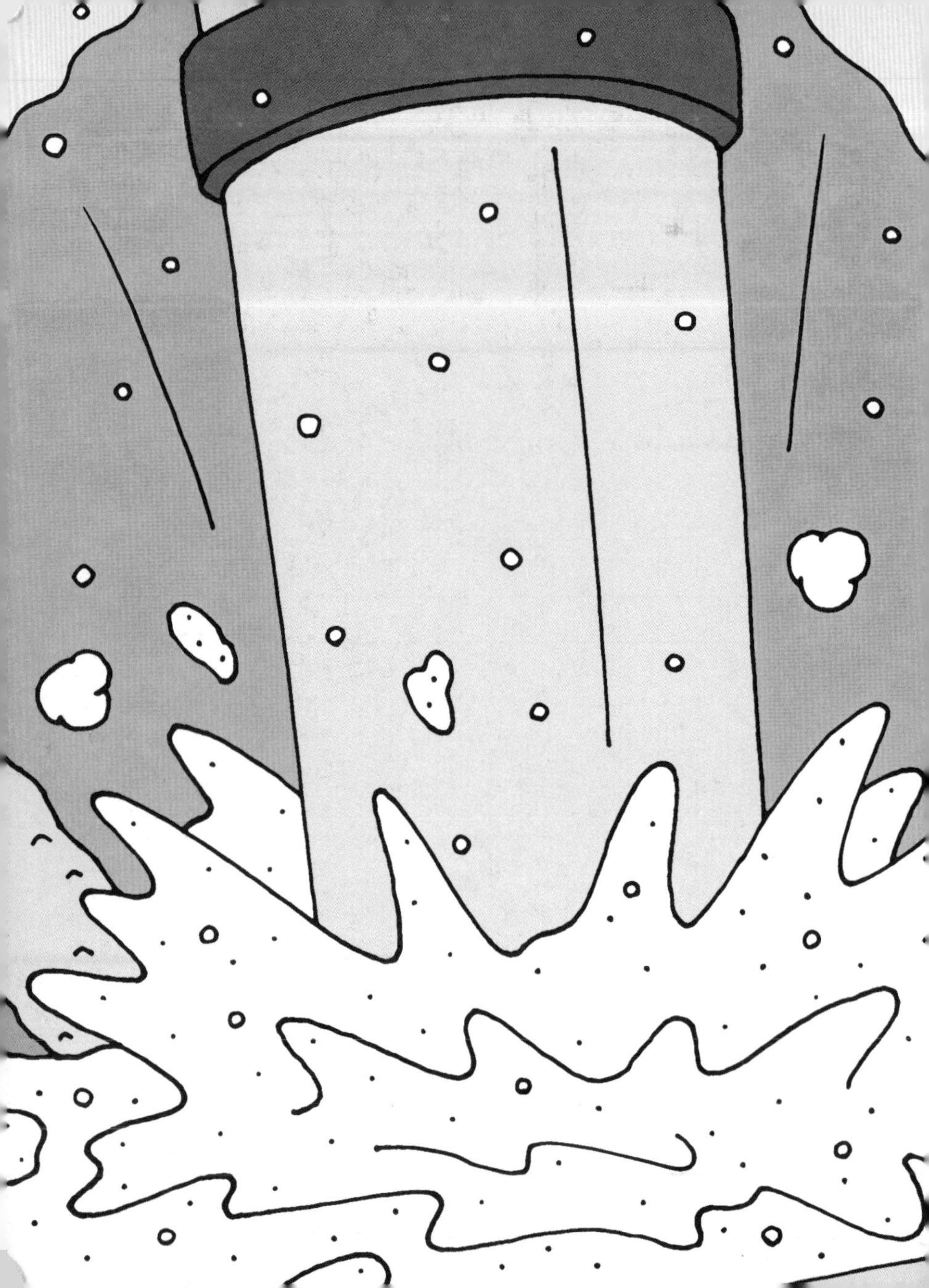

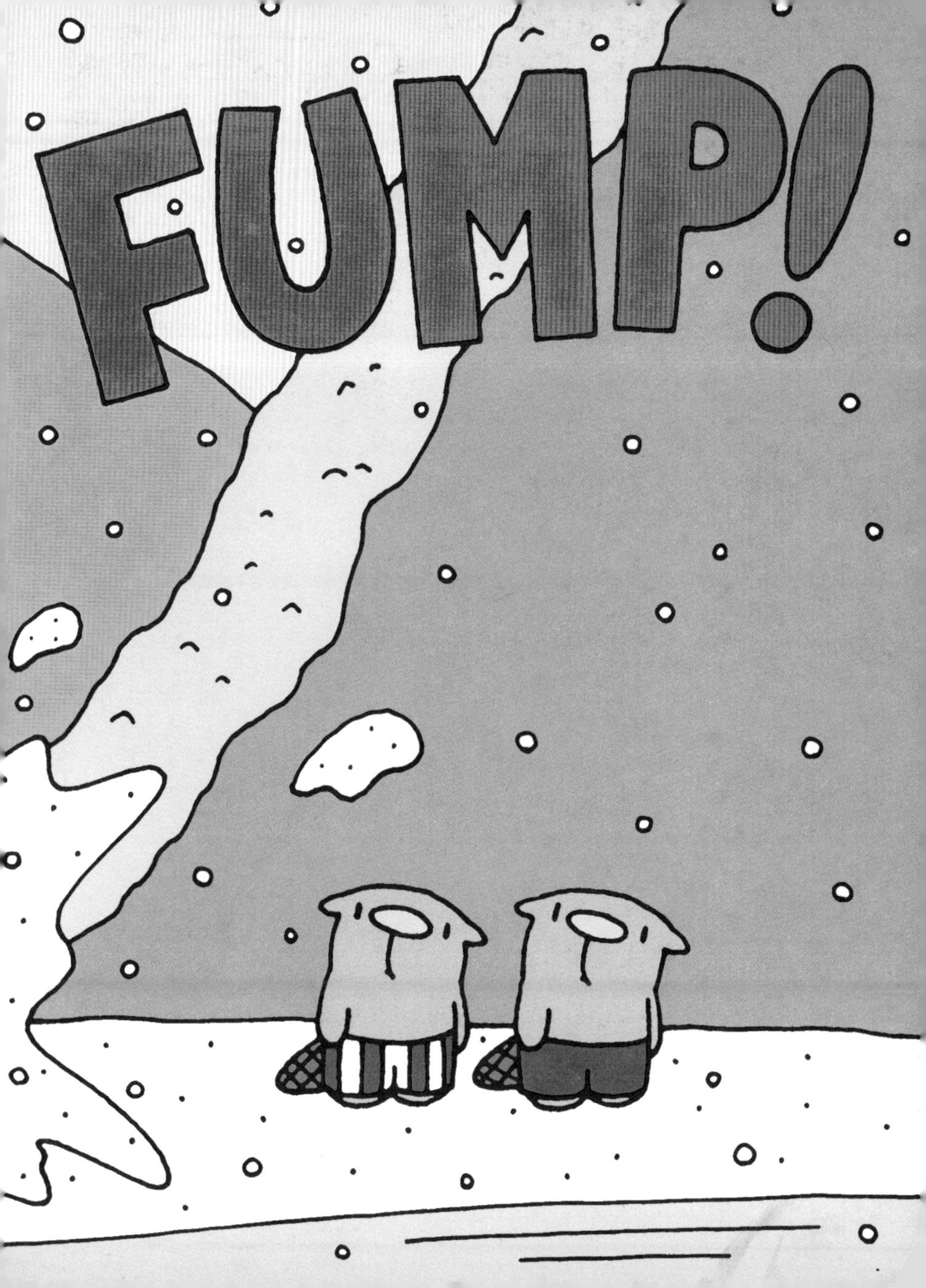
FUMP!

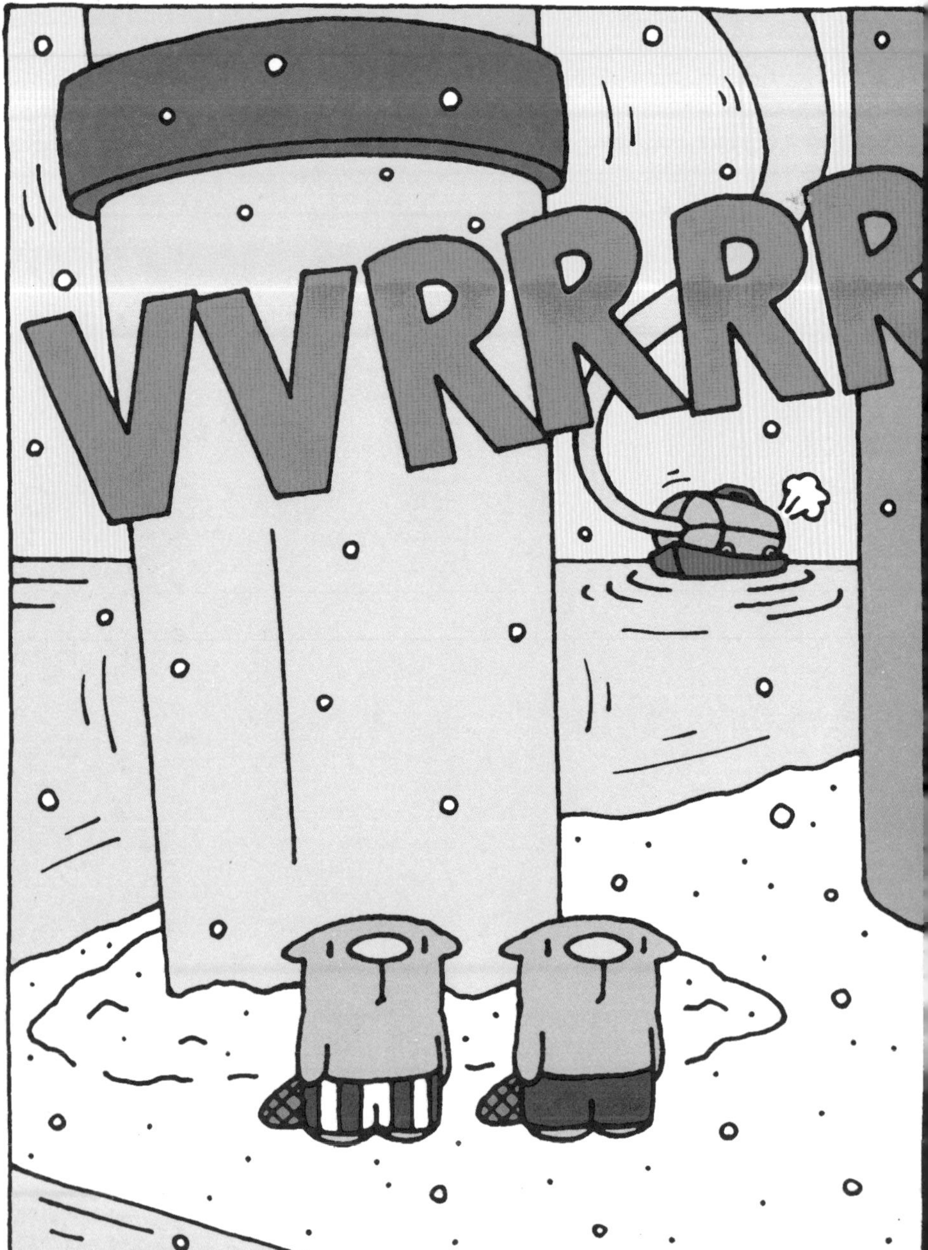
VVRRRRR